M000087788

Mahatma Gandhi
in a Cadillac

Mahatma Gandhi in a Cadillac

A Novel by

Gerald Rosen

Frog, Ltd.
Berkeley, California

Mahatma Gandhi in a Cadillac

Copyright © 1995 by Gerald Rosen. All rights reserved. No portion of this book, except for brief review, may be reproduced in any form without written permission of the publisher. For information contact Frog, Ltd. c/o North Atlantic Books.

Published by Frog, Ltd.

Frog, Ltd. books are distributed by
North Atlantic Books
P.O. Box 12327
Berkeley, CA 94712

Cover art by Spain Rodriguez
Cover and book design by Paula Morrison
Typeset by Catherine Campaigne

Printed in the United States of America

Library of Congress Cataloging-in-Publication Data

Rosen, Gerald.
    Mahatma Gandhi in a Cadillac / Gerald Rosen.
    p.   cm.
    ISBN 1-883319-35-8 (cloth). —ISBN 1-883319-36-6 (pbk.)
    I. Title
PS3568.07765M34   1995
813'.54—dc20   95-18529
                                                                                    CIP

1   2   3   4   5   6   7   8   9 / 99   98   97   96   95

This book is dedicated to the memory of my brother
Mark Rosen (1943–1991)
and
to Marijke

It is the mark of the true novelist that in searching the meaning of his own unsought experience, he comes on the moral history of his time.

—John Peale Bishop

My life is my philosophy.

—Mahatma Gandhi

Chapter One

Robert Frost was stammering in the snow. The old poet looked cold, frail, and disoriented. The wheels of his Model-T voice were spinning round and round in the same place. I was rooting for him fervently, hoping he would find, somewhere within himself, the requisite traction to continue. The camera moved to President Eisenhower. Bundled up on the platform behind Frost. Puffing smoke like an old locomotive about to run out of fuel. Looking forward to letting go of public life and returning to the warm roundhouse of old warriors' dreams.

I was watching this on television in a nearly deserted Greek luncheonette in West Philadelphia with my mad and brilliant cousin Herbie. The blizzard that had raised havoc at President Kennedy's inauguration had buried us as well. Robert Frost was having trouble reading his lines because the low sun was ricocheting off the white ice and blinding him.

"The land was ours before we were the land's."

A poet! At the inauguration! This signaled something different and somehow dangerous. John F. Kennedy was threatening the walls I had erected around the isolated city of my Self.

My cousin Herbie and I were at the counter eating ham and eggs, which I had bought for us with my father's money. Herbie was also eating the residue of someone's pancakes, which he had "salvaged" as soon as the previous owner had left. That was the way Herbie survived during the two or three months he stayed with me in my little cell-like room at Penn, back in the days before I went to the West Coast and met up with Leslie Schmidt.

The University of Pennsylvania was an old and respected Ivy League School founded by Benjamin Franklin in 1769. My father had only completed the ninth grade. He had never read a single book in his life. To be going to an Ivy League School signified to me that I was achieving something in America. It did not have any effect upon my loneliness and my feeling of being lost, which seemed to continue no matter how well I did in my studies and how many friends I had.

I was enrolled at Penn on a partial scholarship in the Wharton Graduate School. I was in the first year of the M.B.A. program, at the top of my class, studying furiously to try to earn a full scholarship so I would no longer be obliged to depend on my father's generosity.

My father, Sid Schwartz, and I were getting along better as we both matured and mellowed. He had not attacked me physically in several years. Not since that night when, after three years of severe acne, I had finally been invited to a real party, my first, with real girls, at the age of sixteen, and the evening had left me so exhilarated that I remained outside on the street with Herbie, conducting a post mortem on the happenings and the girls until three a.m. When I had ventured in to my family's apartment, my father had leaped out of his bed, half-asleep and crazed, and had begun chasing me around in his gray, washed-out Fruit of the Looms, grunting and howling and beating me with a shoe until I ran into my room and slammed the door. My object had been simply to get him off me, but unfortunately I caught his head in the door instead.

Nowadays my father was behaving better in general. Once or twice a year, my mother would get a call from the police that he had attacked someone outside his liquor store in Harlem, or that he had attempted to run someone over with his car, but these incidents were becoming increasingly rare and less damaging to himself and others.

"Hey, whatdya think?" I said to Herbie. "I mean about Kennedy's having Robert Frost at the inauguration!"

"Kennedy's a war hero, man. I'm telling ya. He's great."

Herbie had actually been a Marine, himself. We'd attended DeWitt Clinton High School together, in The Bronx. He was a year older than I, a brilliant but erratic student. He'd graduated at sixteen but he'd soon flunked out of City College, opting for the more oblique lessons offered by the night life of Manhattan. It was Herbie who had introduced me to the world of jazz clubs and coffeehouses—the Greenwich Village-Times Square-Harlem axis which was to prove so important a dark balance to my straight-A, good-boy life. Then surprisingly, after having seen *From Here to Eternity* twelve times, he'd joined the Marines.

Now the major question in his life, over which the U.S. government and his mother, my father's sister Fanny, were at loggerheads, was whether he had been crazy before he entered the Marines, or whether he had only become crazy after he had left the Marines.

We all knew his life had really turned a corner back when he was fourteen, when his father, my favorite uncle, Lenny, a local cub scout leader, had been given a life sentence for leading a gang of men from Harlem with Tommy guns in a series of daring and famous holdups of nightclubs in the Washington, D.C. area, and then had killed himself in the penitentiary in Maryland.

Now my aunt was battling with the Marines, trying to get Herbie a mental pension for service-connected disability. So far the Marines appeared to be losing. I knew they would finally be no match for her, with her Bronx Jake LaMotta tenacity, her terrible ability to take punishment. She would show up at their door each morning like a daily mud slide. She would mount a campaign of such bewildering complexity, such lack of self-regard, that she would have them longing for the old single-wing simplicities of Iwo Jima before she was through. No Protestants could deal with the ordnance of her desire.

Herbie himself had no wish for a pension. He seemed to be happy enough living on what he could mooch or steal, and he fascinated me so in his manner of living and thinking that I never noticed that, like my father, the archipelago of his life was thinning out.

"Hey, you think you're funny, huh?" It was Gus, advancing toward Herbie, a wide, unstoppable, steamboat certitude in his stride.

"Gus, please," Herbie said. "The new President is speaking."

He nodded toward the old black and white Philco TV which Gus had set up on a shelf behind the counter just for the ceremonies of the day. Gus was distracted momentarily. My friend Richie

Hotchkiss walked in the door wearing a tan topcoat and a soft beige scarf, his breath still visible as he entered. He sat down next to Herbie at the counter.

"He's gonna be a great man. You just watch," Herbie said.

"You know he's gonna be a great man," Gus said.

"And what a wife!" Herbie said. "What a dish!"

"Hey, you no talk about her like that," Gus said. "That's the President's wife."

Gus reached behind him to get Hotchkiss his usual, a cheese danish and coffee.

"OK, OK," Herbie said, backing off. Smiling. "I was just saying it's gonna be nice to have some life back in the White House again at night, man."

"'Life' is a euphemism for what you're talking about," Hotchkiss said.

Herbie smiled. Gus glanced toward me for a translation of "euphemism" but decided not to pursue it.

"The torch has passed to a new generation," the young President said, his breath visible in the same cold air that was freezing us in Philly.

"You hear that? That's us," Herbie said. "A new generation. We're gonna turn this old country around."

"Yeah," Gus said. "Look at you. Eating off other people's plates. You think I don't see? You think Gus is a fool?"

"Gus is no fool," Herbie said, imitating Gus's voice. He turned to Hotchkiss. "Gus is the only guy in the world who's seen *From Here To Eternity* more times than me."

Gus puffed up his chest. "I seen it fifteen times."

"You see?" Herbie said. "I've only seen it twelve times. What a performance! Montgomery Clift as Robert E. Lee Prewitt, boxer and bugler." Herbie clenched his eyes shut, made an imaginary bugle out of his fist, and began to play taps through it, completely absorbed in the mad verisimilitude of his imitation.

"It was about the *Army*," Hotchkiss said. "Not the Marines. Can't you even get *that* straight?"

"He's right," I said. "It was about the Army."

"What Montgomery Clift?" Gus said to Herbie. "What are you

talking about, Montgomery Clift? That was Frankie's picture. Mr. Sinatra. He stole the whole movie, goddamn it. That was his goddamn comeback. Don't tell me no Montgomery Clift. No Burt Lancaster. No Ernie Borgnine."

"Ernie?" Richie said, raising his eyebrows. "Not 'Ernest'?"

"He knows him," I said, trying to join in the fun. "Ernie's his goddamn brother-in-law."

"No Miss Deborah Kerr," Gus continued, completely serious, ignoring us.

"What about Donna Reed?" I said, teasing. "Now there's a sultry wench."

"We're gonna have to get some co-ed like that for Danny," Herbie said. "We're gonna have to get this guy laid before he goes crazy on us."

"Don't talk to me about no Donna Reed," Gus said heatedly. "It was Frankie's movie. He stole the whole goddamn show. The whole shebangle."

"The whole shebangle?" Hotchkiss said, laughing. Richie Hotchkiss had been to prep schools and Ivy League schools since as far back as he could remember, but I knew he liked to hang around with me. He had never really known anyone with a background like mine. I seemed to fascinate him.

In a way, I guess I was Richie's 'Herbie.' Perhaps each of us needs a "Herbie" in our lives. Someone way over to our left, who expresses what we can only dream of; someone who is always out there, swimming on the horizon, so that when we venture into waters over our head and we feel the chill of doubt and think about turning back, we can look out toward the horizon and see our "Herbie," way out beyond us, swimming along awkwardly but still afloat, somehow giving us the confidence to continue, to dare to reach beyond where we feel secure.

As long as we avoid thinking about that day when we look up and see that "Herbie" himself has drowned, and suddenly there is no one further beyond us, and we're on our own.

"Wait. There he is!" Herbie suddenly shouted, pointing to the TV over Gus's head. Gus whirled around so fast, he seemed to have been shot by a sniper. We all knew by "he" Herbie meant Frank Sinatra.

"I don't see him," Gus said. "Where? Where is he?" Gus was so excited, his head was almost up against the small glass screen. Any minute, I expected him to be *inside* the set, still in his apron, seated there along with Peter Lawford and the others, looking out at us.

Herbie winked toward Hotchkiss and me. Gus spun back around. "You kiddin me?"

"No. No," Herbie said, affecting great sincerity. "Would I kid about Mr. Sinatra? I swear, I thought I saw him on the screen. He's bound to be there, right?"

"Of course he's there," Gus said, excitedly. "The whole rat pack's gonna be there. Why the hell you think I brought the goddamn TV to my place here for? My health, goddamn it?"

"Hey, take it easy, Gus," Richie said, laughing.

"Hey, Gus, tell Richie about Frank Sinatra's airplane," I said.

"What?" Gus said, hesitantly. He knew what I meant, but he looked toward Richie to see whether we were kidding him or not. Gus liked Richie, and I did too. I had graduated from Rensselaer Polytechnic Institute an electrical engineer, but here at Wharton I was just a beginner, competing for scholarships with students who had majored in business and economics at Harvard and Yale. Richie, a grad assistant in economics, had given me some invaluable lessons at the start.

"What's this about this airplane?" Richie said to Gus.

Gus looked over toward Herbie and me. When he found no traces of amusement on our faces, he turned to Richie. "Well, I was telling Danny here the other day that Frank Sinatra, he got his own airplane, you know?"

"Yeah I know," Herbie interjected. "He got it for being a minor star behind Montgomery Clift in *From Here to Eternity.*"

This time Gus ignored Herbie. He spoke quietly, almost touchingly. "Well, you know, like I was telling Danny, that plane, he use it to fly from one appearance to another. With all the rat pack. Dean Martin. Sammy Davis. Joey Bishop. Peter Lawford. The whole crew. They fly from show to show. You know what I mean? So I was saying to Danny, man, would I like to go on that plane! Just once. You know what I mean? When they fly from one city to another. You think they don't have a stage on that plane?" Here he began to glow with a strange, delirious light. "And you think when they're flyin' around up there in the air, you think they don't get up there on the stage and entertain each other?"

None of us could say a word. Gus looked so vulnerable in the blimp of his crazy immigrant dreams that none of us had the heart to shoot him down out of the sky.

"They fly around," Gus said, seeing it all in his own mind, "and Frankie gets up and he sings a couple songs, and then the bartender, he serves a little champagne, only the best you know, and then Dean, he gets up on the stage and he sings a couple numbers at the piano, and then Frankie, he sings with him, and then they have some caviar or something, and then Sammy gets up there and he tap-dances with Shirley MacLaine, and then the President and Mrs. Kennedy stand up, that's Peter Lawford's brother-in-law you know, and they make a toast to the whole bunch of entertainers, and the President, he says a few words about the future of mankind and all that kinda stuff, and that's the way they travel around up there, over the whole country, and none of us down here get to see it, you know what I mean?" He turned to Herbie. "Someday, I'd like to be up there with them, up in the sky, with the whole rat pack. That's where the real show is." He was nodding his head as he spoke with a kind of sincerity that kept any of us from responding and left us sitting there in silence, gazing back toward the TV as the young president said, "Ask not what your country can do for you. Ask what you can do for your country."

"I did for *my* country," Herbie said. "I did for my country in spades. Three great years. The United States Marines."

Finally this all became too much for Hotchkiss. His face reddened and he said excitedly, "What the hell's the matter with all of you? You all think you're so shrewd and on top of things, but you don't understand anything. Not one thing."

"What're you talkin' about, man?" Herbie said uneasily.

"Don't you see? Gus is right. It is all a show. It's all a farce."

"Hey, I don't say that," Gus said, with a worried frown on his face.

"Look, my father deals with these guys all the time," Hotchkiss said. "He's one of them. He's an advisor to the Treasury. And my uncle. He works for the goddamn State Department. He's there right now." He nodded toward the TV. "He and my father. Don't you see? That's how I got to go to prep schools and all. They use people like you."

"Hey, wait a minute here, . . ." Herbie said, his hackles rising.

"It's true," Richie said. "They use you."

"You're exaggerating, Richie," I said.

"No," Richie said, "can't you see? It's all a big opera. They wave the flag and guys like Herbie run off to join up because they saw some stupid movie with Donna Reed or something, and they get themselves killed so my old man can join another country club. It's all a TV production, the whole thing. . . ."

Herbie stood up and glared at Hotchkiss with a determined look on his face. I rose quickly alongside him. Hotchkiss blanched and suddenly quieted.

"Hey, take it easy," I said, grabbing Herbie around his chest from behind, pinning his arms at this side. He swung his arms up quickly, throwing me off him, but I saw his face relax, the sudden spell dissipating.

"You think it's all a show, huh?" he said to Hotchkiss.

"Siddown," Gus said to Herbie. "Siddown!"

Herbie sat down, still staring at Hotchkiss, his eyes shining like fiery pearls against his rugged olive skin. "Let Richie talk," I said to Herbie. "I want to hear what he says."

Herbie grumpily assented in silence.

Richie continued in a quieter voice, "All I'm saying is that everything you see is planned to get you to react in certain ways. Like look up there. You see Kennedy? In his morning coat? And his vest? No overcoat. His breath standing out in the air like that? And you see Ike over there, in his heavy top coat and his muffler? Compared to Kennedy, he looks like he's freezing to death. That's all planned. Don't you see? Kennedy's people want to make a virtue of his youth, so they've got him up there without a coat on this cold day. He's probably got on three pairs of thermal underwear, for Chrissakes, but you don't see that, so when he says the torch has passed to a new generation, the image will show it even better than the words. Vigor is what they want to project. 'Vigaah,'" he repeated, in a mocking Boston accent.

"I don't buy it, man," Herbie said.

"I don't either," I said. "Sure they have to do some PR. Anyone does. But there is a difference between Kennedy and the others."

"There sure is," Gus said. "You don't see no Frank Sinatra, no Peter Lawford in the White House with Eisenhower."

"That's what I'm saying," Richie said. "It's all show business. Jesus H. Christ, can't you see?"

"I suppose Hitler was a show, too," Herbie said.

"You think you're such a cynic, Richie," I said, trying to put my two cents in without getting into a discussion of the facts, about which I knew little. "It's just a pose."

"*You're* the one who should enlighten Richie on that," Herbie said to Gus. "Your people have been dealing with cynics for years. They invented the goddamn philosophy of cynicism."

Gus looked like he wanted to disappear into a hole in the floor.

"Hitler was no TV show, college boy," Herbie said to Richie. "It all boils down to someone's gotta defend democracy. Even Gus can tell you that. His people invented democracy. Right, Gus?" Gus looked away, embarrassed that he was expected to speak, that Herbie had, in effect, put the microphone of our attention into his face and turned on the TV lights.

"Yeah," Hotchkiss said, sarcastically, "democracy."

I was feeling miserable while this went on. How was it that Herbie, who was seen by everyone in our family as a mental case, could get in there and duke it out with Hotchkiss, while I, who had been spending the days and long nights of my youth studying technical subjects at fine universities, could say nothing to defend the young President who had so stirred my heart by having a poet at his inauguration and by making such a rousing speech about giving to your country?

How had it come about that after five years of college I understood more about the behavior of an electron than about my own behavior, while my crazy cousin Herbie seemed to know more about the subjective, personal side of life, about questions of life and death and meaning and value, than I did?

"I told you Richie, you're just being a cynic," I finally commented again to Hotchkiss, just to have something to say.

"Yeah," Herbie chimed in, "you're just feeling guilty because you've been privileged, so you put it all down and you get cynical about everything." He turned to Gus. "I told you, you should speak to him on this matter."

Gus looked cornered now. But Herbie continued admonishing him, "Speak up, man. Your people practically invented philosophical discourse. Socrates and all that." Gus looked down, and it seemed to me that he felt that Herbie was beating him up in a way, and I felt his pain as if Herbie's blows were directed at me.

"You have a right to speak just like anyone else," Herbie continued. "You don't have to be one of these hotshot college boys to know something. Don't be so diffident. You can be voluble, man. Even loquacious."

"Voluble? Loquacious?" I thought. "What the hell is he talking about?"

Gus turned and skulked away. We could see him through the serving window in the back as he busied himself in his preparations for the dinner rush—the spanakopita, the pastitsio, the mostaccioli that he made so well.

Suddenly silence swept over us. The energy of the argument had passed like a sudden storm. We looked at the TV for a while. Then I turned to Herbie. "How could you do that? You totally embarrassed him. Don't you see?"

"What're you talking about, man?"

"You shamed him, right in front of all of us. And you talk about democracy and defending the common man."

"I did nothing of the kind, man...."

"Oh, come on, Herbie,"

"Why don't we just let it go," Richie said.

"OK," I said to Herbie. "Let's just forget about it."

"Sure," Herbie said, relaxing and giving us a weak smile. He turned to Hotchkiss. "I tell ya, man, if I teach Danny any more lessons today, I'm gonna have to charge his father tuition."

Chapter Two

On Forty-Ninth Street in West Philadelphia, Chubby Checker's psychiatrist was closing her office for the day. A few blocks closer, at about Forty-Fifth Street, Dick Clark was concluding the live telecast of another edition of American Bandstand. I was at Thirty-Fourth Street, trudging dreamily through the dirty snow in the morgue-like February evening air, heading toward the Horn and Hardart Automat. (Back in The Bronx, the Automat was the one restaurant my family had gone to when we wanted to "eat out.")

The snow on Chestnut street, wan and crusted with dirt, felt like an old Salvation Army mattress under my feet. The entire east coast was suffering through one of the coldest winters in memory. We'd already had five major snowstorms. The buildings of Philadelphia resembled partially buried, forgotten mausoleums. Sharp icicles clung overhead like meaninglessness, ready to plunge down on us at the slightest tremor. I approached the corner of Chestnut and Thirty-Sixth, where, a few months before, I had run into the Vice-President. Richard Milhous Nixon. With his shirt-alligator smile. His Bob Hope shoulders. His varicose personality.

I had just spent several hours in the library, immersed in magazines for a paper I was writing on G.E.'s current marketing campaigns. I had been intrigued by the fact that the two spokesmen they had chosen to appear in their ads were Ronald Reagan and the near-sighted Mr. Magoo.

On my way to dinner, I had looked up and found myself staring into the eyes of Richard Nixon. He and Pat were sitting in the rear seat of a Cadillac convertible, at the focus of a motorcade heading into Center City. For some reason, traffic had stopped a few blocks ahead, leaving the Nixons stranded, along with everyone else on the street.

11

Nixon noticed my books, and we began a labored, somewhat inane, conversation about the excellence of Wharton, the difficulties of studying, dinner, traffic, any innocuous topic we could come up with for what seemed like hours.

What struck me about this little encounter was the vulnerability of the presidential candidates. Surely there were dangerous people out there, some "anti-Gus" so to speak, with paranoid rather than generous fantasies that they projected onto the figures they saw on the television screen, and yet, although there were some Secret Servicemen around, I had simply walked along, sleepily looked up, and found myself so close to Richard Nixon that we had both felt obligated to make casual conversation.

I had expected Nixon to be somewhat like my father in a way—streetwise, an alley fighter, a man who seemed hungry and perpetually cornered. But Nixon exuded an aura of success. Slightly chubby from all those good dinners, his jacket carefully tailored, his hair beautifully cut, he looked like a man who was accustomed to being pampered, a man whose dreams were coming true.

While Nixon had moved up in class through politics, Jack Kennedy and I had chosen to attend Ivy League universities. For, from a certain oblique angle, I was going to Penn for the same reason Jack Kennedy had gone to Harvard—to move up in status, to be accepted by the cool Protestants, to rise above the liquor money of our fathers.

"Hi, Danny."

I looked up, shaking off my reverie. There, in a beautiful beige ski jacket and exquisite hand-made, soft leather boots, stood Mandy Whitson, with her cute, rabbit-like smile, her soft orange hair, her lively ale-colored eyes.

Mandy was a junior English Major from Hotchkiss's hometown in Connecticut, and he was crazy about her. Unfortunately, she was engaged to a jock up at Dartmouth, and would only grant Hotchkiss the status of "platonic friend," as the more sensitive girls of the time would put it when they needed to give someone they liked a gentle brush-off. I myself had enough "platonic friends" to form a Greek academy.

Mandy asked me if I had a couple of minutes to talk. She appeared to have something serious on her mind, and I was afraid I knew what it was. Smokey Joe's was a long, narrow, comfortable pub, usually filled with Wharton Grad guys. The dark wood yielded a rich aroma of bourbon, beer, disinfectant and the ink used to print the Wall Street Journal.

I exchanged greetings with some of my classmates at the bar, and then led Mandy to a dark booth at the rear. She ordered a Pepsi. I took a Schmidt's of Philadelphia. Mandy was nervously making circles with her finger in the condensed moisture on her glass.

"Something on your mind?" I said.

"Yes, . . . there is. . . . You know I like you, Danny. . . ."

She hesitated. I nodded yes. I did know she liked me. Or at least I hoped she did, because I liked her.

"Well, then you know it's nothing personal, but I'm not going to be fixing you up with my friends anymore."

"No?" I was not completely surprised. "Is this because of that table at Heather's place? We can pay for that. . . ."

"It's not the table, Danny. I mean, it *is* the table, but it's more than that. . . ."

"Herbie?" I said, quietly, after taking a long draft of beer.

"Yes, Herbie. And yourself."

"Myself?"

"Yes. I mean you weren't nice at all to Heather. We were at her house, we were her guests, and you got so terribly drunk. . . ."

"But what did I *do?*" I said quickly. I was trying to defend myself but I knew the matter was already closed and, further, that she was right. She had been nice enough to fix me up with several of her friends at different times, and all were nice girls, but nothing had ever worked out. Nonetheless I continued, "All Herbie did was jump up on that bridge table and make a little drunken speech about Nietzsche or something. . . ."

"Danny, you know, that ticks me off. I mean, you didn't have to be a genius to see that that table couldn't hold him. It didn't stand a chance of holding him."

"Well, look, OK, OK. I mean, you're right, of course. I admit it, Herbie's difficult to deal with. . . ."

13

I gulped down the rest of my beer, caught the waitress's eye, and ordered another Schmidt's and a ham-and-swiss on rye. "He's a sensitive person. He's been under a lot of stress since he got out of the Marines."

"But that was months ago. . . ."

"I know . . . but he's . . . well, he's lost. . . . You know what I mean? He doesn't fit in anywhere. . . ."

"Oh, Danny. . . ." Her tone was sympathetic now. "You're such a romantic. . . ." She shook her head from side to side. "Look, I don't want to hurt your feelings, but well . . . there are a thousand guys like Herbie around. . . . And . . ."

"No. No there aren't. There aren't a thousand guys like Herbie. . . ."

". . . And they won't contribute anything to society. . . . They're takers. Don't you see? My father always says there are givers and there are takers. And Herbie is a taker, Danny. . . ."

Mary, the Irish waitress, came by and set my sandwich and the second Schmidt's on the table.

"Now, wait," I said, pouring the beer into my glass. "Wait a minute. Herbie does give a lot."

"To whom?"

"To me, for example. It was Herbie who turned me on to Martin Luther King. And King . . . well, he's a great man, for God's sakes. And Herbie turned me on to jazz . . . and Camus . . . and Jean Shepherd on the radio, and Bob and Ray . . . to lots of things. Things that are the most precious parts of my life. . . ."

"So now you support him, and let him use you. And, look at how you've changed since Herbie's been here." Suddenly she stopped. She saw that she had made her point and that I was agreeing with her in spite of myself. "Oh, I don't mean to get down on you. It's not that big a . . ."

"No. You're right. You're absolutely right. You fix me up with these nice girls, and I blow it."

"Maybe you shouldn't drink so much. I mean, drinking's OK, but you get really *bombed*." She couldn't suppress a little smile. "I mean, Ritchie told me that you drink at Winter's, that crazy hellhole in that basement down the street. How can you go to a dive like that? No one from the university goes there."

"I don't know," I said. "I mean, it's fascinating in a way. . . . Ritchie calls it 'Danny's Inferno.' " On her face there shone an expression of interest in spite of herself. "I mean, I've probably spent the whole day in the Wharton library studying corporate finance or something, being the responsible good boy that I always try to be, and then suddenly there I am, drinking with all these down-and-out maniacs, and I think to myself, Jesus, I'm in a place that's so low, when they 86 a guy, they throw him *up* the goddamn stairs, for Chrissakes!"

I stared into her eyes. She was looking at me as if I were some kind of madman, but not necessarily a madman she disliked.

"Look, Mandy, I'm sorry. I don't blame you for not wanting to fix me up any more."

"Oh, I don't . . ."

"No. No. You're right." I reached down for my beer but decided not to sip at it. I had a cost-accounting exam on Friday, and I wanted to ace it, to break the curve, to beat the older Wharton students, the ones who had returned from Wall Street and were mature, and wore suits and ties and seemed at peace with themselves and their lives. I wanted to continue to beat them badly.

I took a bite of my sandwich. Turned back to Mandy. "I mean like that time with Jennifer. She was always talking about Martin Luther King and all, so I thought she'd like it being the only white people at that Negro amateur night out at that little movie house on Baltimore Ave. I mean, I always enjoyed going there. All those local rhythm-and-blues groups. They're *good* if you give them a chance."

"It's OK, Danny," she said quietly.

"And then that night with Heather. I did try to talk to her. I mean this was before Herbie wrecked her table. I wanted to have a real conversation with her, but she wouldn't listen. . . . I was trying to tell her what I really felt about everything, because to tell you the truth, I really felt lousy. I kept thinking about my grandfather. About his death."

She blanched. "Oh . . . I'm sorry. I didn't know your grandfather had died. Was it very recently?"

"Well, not *recently*. It was back when I was in the second grade."

She gave me a quizzical "psychiatric" look.

"But I've been *thinking* about it recently. I don't know why. I mean, there was no warning. One morning I woke up and he was dead. And then my grandmother collapsed, and my Aunt Rose, the one I told you about who told the jokes, she started to decline, and then, *she died....*"

I looked into Mandy's eyes. "I don't know ... I guess, sometimes, I just wonder how can we all just study accounting and finance and all, when we can die at any minute and we don't even know the first thing about it...."

"Die any minute?" she said.

"I mean, how can it be that on the outside I seem to be making such a big success, but on the inside I feel so confused and empty? How can it be that all these hopes and work and ... and the whole universe, how can it all just end in nothingness and death?"

I reached down and picked up my sandwich and took a big bite out of it, just to slow down for a second, but I had to force myself to swallow. I could see suffering in Mandy's eyes, and I felt I had gone too far, even if it was just the reflection of my own suffering.

"I don't know," I said. "I guess it's just that now that I'm getting somewhere, I'm beginning to wonder where it all leads. I mean, sometimes I feel like, What am I doing here?"

"Here?"

"Here. At Wharton. On the Earth. I mean, sometimes I feel this is all a big joke or something. You know what I mean? Like nothing makes any sense at all."

She looked surprised and troubled. Somewhat fearful for me. "No. I mean, I know you're being honest with me, Danny, and I ... I feel an obligation to be honest with you in return. So I'll tell you truthfully, I don't really know what you're saying. I mean, sure, sometimes I feel low-down and depressed. Some days I feel really crappy, if you want to know the truth. Everybody does. But look how far you've come. And look how lucky we both are, to be in a great university with the freedom to learn and think and have discussions like this in a free country and all, and I mean, look at yourself, with a degree in engineering and getting an M.B.A. from Wharton.... You can do anything."

She looked at me, but I didn't respond. I merely ate my sandwich in silence.

"I hope I haven't hurt your feelings," she said, finally. "I was just trying to be honest...."

"Oh, no.... I appreciate your honesty. I know you're my friend. You want to help me...."

"That's true. I still consider myself your friend. That never even came into it."

"I know." I reached across the table, took her hand in mine and squeezed it for a second. She *was* my friend. She had tried to help me.

"I ... I better run," she said. "I've got an exam from Horst tomorrow. The Romantic poets. It's going to be a rough one."

I remained at the table by myself, finishing up my sandwich, listening on my own private mental jukebox to Miles Davis sadly playing.

Chapter Three

On Friday afternoon I aced the Cost Accounting exam, and walked home to meet Herbie. I'd promised him I'd spring for a night of jazz. We were planning to see Shirley Scott on organ, with tenor Stanley Turrentine at the Showboat Lounge in South Philly.

Home for us was a single room at the rear of a funky three-story building two blocks from the University. Herbie was lying on his cot reading Yogananda's *Autobiography of a Yogi,* while listening to my record of Johnny Hodges playing, "Don't Get Around Much Anymore."

"Hey, dig," he said, swinging himself up to sitting. "Listen to this, first-best friend." He pulled out a wrinkled piece of yellow paper, and began to read a fable he had written that afternoon. It was called "Salami and the Seven Veals." Somehow he had combined the stories of Salome and Snow White, and he had done it in three pages stuffed with puns on various meats—wurst, steak, chop, beef—it seemed like dozens of them, the words flying rapidly by like rackety subway cars as he read it almost in one breath.

I praised him profusely as I pulled a can of Schmidt's from the little refrigerator. Drank about half of it in one gulp. "Let's go to Kelly and Cohen's. I'm hot for corned beef. We'll gorge on beef in honor of your meaty opus."

Herbie opened into a sweet smile, being naturally vulnerable, to a degree, when he presented you with something he had created. "My man," was all he said, happily, as he rose to put on another record. "My main man!"

After my shower, I stood at the bathroom mirror in my underwear, shaving with my Sunbeam electric razor, when the telephone rang.

"Will you pick that up?" I shouted, turning my concentration back to the razor, which hummed like a little metal beehive against my face.

"It's for you!" Herbie cried. "Some guy who says he's in Seattle."

At the time I did not yet understand the strange paradox that the most important junctures in one's personal history often appear to one unannounced and unprepared for, just suddenly rising on the horizon like Captain Cook, showing up unbidden in the Hawaiian Islands of a life.

Chapter Four

I took a quick swig from my can of Schmidt's, and picked up the telephone. "Hello."

"Daniel Schwartz?"

"Yes. This is he."

"Mr. Schwartz, this is Fred Warner."

"Mr. Warner?"

"Yes. From Brannan Aviation. In Seattle. I interviewed you about a month ago. . . ."

"Oh, yes. Mr. Warner. Of course."

"I hope I haven't interrupted your dinner. We're three hours earlier out here. . . ."

No. No problem, sir. . . ."

"Well, Mr. Schwartz, I have some good news for you. You've been selected to be a part of our Brannan Executives of the Future Program. . . ."

"I . . . I have? . . . ."

"Yes. That's right. You're one of the select few."

"Oh. . . . Well. . . . That's great. . . . I mean, thank you. Thank you very much, sir."

"No need to thank me. You've earned it with all your good grades and your hard work. We'll write to you with all the details but, to be brief, as you know, this is a summer job. It will begin as soon as you can get here in June, and will end just before Labor Day. We'll send you the price of a cross-country airplane ticket in advance, and we'll pay you one hundred forty dollars a week. Will that be sufficient, Mr. Schwartz?"

"A hundred and fourteen dollars a week? Yes, sir, that'll be fine."

Warner laughed. "No. One hundred *forty* dollars a week."

"Oh. Well, that'll be fine, too," I said, laughing along with him now.

"Then I take it you'll accept our offer? You won't find a better program or a higher paying summer job, believe me."

"Oh, I know, sir. That program is well known here at Wharton.... And yes, I accept. I'd be glad to be a part of it."

"Fine. I'm sure you'll have no regrets. Now, before I sign off, do you have any questions?"

"Well yes.... Can you give me an idea of the kind of work I'll be doing?"

"You'll be getting an introductory orientation to all aspects of Brannan Aviation. You'll go to lectures and demonstrations of our latest projects and scientific advances. There'll be social events with our top executives and such. And in your daily work ... let's see ... it looks like you'll be slated to work on a program for computerizing the purchasing of parts for our Readiman missile."

"The Readiman missile! I was just reading about that in Time Magazine!"

"Yes," he said, with pride. "It's America's best."

"Gee.... You know, sir, ... they give a course here, every six weeks, on computer programming. Maybe I should sign up for it in March...."

"Sounds like an excellent idea, Daniel."

"Oh, sir, may I ask just one more question?"

"Certainly."

"Well, sir, I was thinking ... it might be a good idea to know which other students here at Wharton you chose for the program. It might be nice to get in touch with them beforehand, maybe travel together, or ..."

"Didn't I tell you, Daniel? There are no other students at Wharton in the program. Of the dozens we interviewed there, you're the only one we picked. This is an elite program. We only chose a handful of people across the whole United States.... Anything else?"

"No, sir."

"Good. Then we'll call it a handshake and consider that you've accepted our offer."

I put the phone down and stood there for a second, as if I had been struck by lightning and was waiting to see whether I would topple over. Then suddenly I gave out a wild war-whoop "YEEOOOOW!!"

I ran to the cupboard, took a shot of Four Roses, cracked open another can of Schmidt's, and began to march around the room like a drum major, singing a crazy, wordless version of "Strike Up the Band."

Herbie was sitting in front of my old black and white Admiral TV with the improvised wire-hanger antenna, watching me with an amorphous expression on his face. "Hey, what's the story, Morning Glory?" he finally said, when I calmed down a bit.

"What's the story?" I related the details of Warner's offer. "Do you know what this means? This is the top program in the country. I'm gonna work on the Readiman missile for Chrissakes. I'll be going to parties with the President of Brannan Aviation. They're going to be grooming me to be one of the guys who runs the goddamn company.... I can't believe this.... This is *it*, Herbie. This is what I've worked for since I was five years old."

I finished the can of beer and tossed it over my shoulder against the wall.

"And I thought I totally screwed up that interview. I mean it was the worst interview I ever gave. That's why I didn't even recognize Warner on the phone!" I sat down on the arm of Herbie's chair. "I mean, you know what happened? I'd just finished reading *The Dharma Bums*. You know how I love Kerouac. Well this book, it just knocked me out. I'd been reading it all night before the interview, see. So when I went in there, I was totally out of my mind. And Brannan is out in Seattle. Right where the book is set. So I'm at the interview, and this guy Warner, he asks me why I might want to settle in the Northwest. Well, you know me, I've never been west of Philadelphia, for Chrissakes, but I was still high on the damn book, so I started ranting, 'Are you kidding! The great Pacific Northwest! With the Cascade mountains, and the fire stations so beautiful up there in their magnificent lonely isolation in the soft fog, and the Olympic Rainforest, and Mount Rainier, with year-round snow at the top, and you climb up there in the spring above the city and make chocolate pudding in the snow like Japanese Zen monks....' I wasn't just bullshitting, either. This was how I saw it all in my imagination, for Chrissakes.... Jesus, I can't believe this. I wrote this whole job off. I thought I had gone nuts there in the interview...."

I began to walk excitedly around the room again. "And somehow I got the goddamn job … the best job offered here. The one everyone wanted." I laughed wildly. But then, I couldn't help but notice that Herbie looked distant and subdued, not sharing in my joy at all.

"Hey, man," I said, warily, "is something wrong?"

"Look, Danny, if you wanna know, yeah, something's wrong. I mean, look at yourself. Turning somersaults over a goddamned job with some big corporation, for Chrissakes. And you should have heard yourself on the phone. 'Oh, yes, sir. This is he. Oh, thank you so much, sir. That's very kind of you to say so, sir.' I mean, shit, man, you were practically groveling at the guy's feet."

"Wait a minute. I can't believe this. This guy just gave me the break of my life, and you're going on about some bullshit because I was polite to the guy.…"

"Danny, look … it's just that you lower yourself, man, when you do that groveling shit.… I mean, what you're really looking for in life, it's *inside* yourself, man. Can't you see that? No one can give it to you and no one can take it away. So I just hate to see someone I respect giving up his God-given birthright for a mess of porridge.…"

"A mess of porridge? Herbie … I just got this great job, and you're going on about … I mean, yes, what we really want is inside ourselves, I agree … but still … don't you see? This is the trip of my dreams. I don't have to go on a plane. I can take the fucking money and drive across. I can go everywhere I've always read about. L.A., Frisco, the desert.… I can see America, man. From coast to coast.…"

"Yeah, man," Herbie said, rising. He put on his coat. "If you're happy, I'm happy, dig?" he said without enthusiasm. "I'm just saying, remember what the Buddha said. It's all temporary. Here today, gone tomorrow. So keep your eye on what's real, you know what I mean?" He opened the door. "I'm gonna get me some air and a pack of smokes. I'll be back in about a half-hour.…"

He walked out, leaving me sitting there on the floor in my underwear, astonished.

"Thanks a lot," I said, sarcastically. But then I began to think, maybe he was right. Maybe I had diminished myself by my response to Warner. I mean, why should I look for my happiness from some corporation? But when I took another shot of Four Roses my spirit returned, and I began thinking joyfully again of traveling across the country to the American West, and of the opportunity I had been given, and the way in which my hard work had paid off.

I decided to call my mother at home in the Bronx to share the good news. She was one person who wouldn't quote scripture and verse against grabbing a little rare happiness when it came your way every once in a while on this sad and lonely little planet.

Chapter Five

"**H**i, Danny. I'm glad you called. Your father's here, and he's gonna want to say something to you. We're having a flood."

"A flood, Ma?"

"Yeah. Upstairs. In Krepner's. 4B. It's a real mess. Your father had to leave the store, but it's gonna be all right now. They finally got the plumber, and he got the water off."

I wondered what my father wanted to talk to me about. I knew that, after the flood, he wouldn't be in a good mood, but at least there hadn't been a fight. If there'd been a fight, if Krepner had pushed my father down a flight of stairs as he had done two years before, my mother would have been wailing about it on the phone right from the start.

"Listen, Ma, I've got some good news. I got this call this afternoon. From a Mr. Warner. At Brannon Aviation. In Seattle. In the state of Washington. On the West Coast...." I related the entire conversation, tasting the words that described my triumph like a good burgundy. "So what do think, Mom? Great, huh? And I really have you to thank. You believed in me from the start. You made it possible for me to get an education."

"Danny, wait a minute. This Mr. Warren?"

"Warner."

"OK, Warner. How do you know who he is?"

"What? What do you mean?"

"Did he ask you to send him any money?"

"Money?" I laughed uneasily. "What do you mean, 'money'?"

"You know ... Like a fee for his services or something...."

"Mom! What're you talking about? He's giving *me* money! That's the whole point. That's why I'm so happy. Didn't you hear what I said? I got this great job...."

"But has he given you any money already? An advance, or a contract or something?"

"Of course not. . . ."

"So you see. Who knows who he is, this Mr. Warren or whatever his name is. . . ."

"But Mom! I just got this great job offer. . . ."

"Listen, Danny. I'm a little older than you are. So let me tell you something. Everybody isn't who they say they are in this world. You're a good boy. You're too good. You're like me. People take advantage of people like us. I've learned that from long experience. . . ."

"But, Mom, I can't believe this! I mean I was the only one in the whole Wharton School to get this job. . . ."

"You see. Does that make sense? That you're the only one? Listen, Danny, I think he's taking advantage of you in some way. I'm sorry to say this, but I've got to look out for you. I'm still your mother, even though you're grown up now and in graduate school."

"But Ma, he just called me from Seattle."

"Did the operator get on and say you have a call from Seattle?"

"Err . . . No. . . . He must've called station-to-station. . . ."

"You see what I mean? He could've been in Philadelphia and who would've been the wiser? Danny, listen, I don't mean to be a grump, and if this is legitimate, I wish you all the best in the world, but I think you've got to be certain of what you're dealing with here. I think we should get a lawyer."

"A *what?*"

"Maybe your father's lawyer for the buildings. Mr. Schoen. He could write to Brannan and find out if they ever heard of this Mr. Warren."

"Mom! Please! I'm trying to tell you something. Something great has happened in my life. And you . . ."

"I know. I don't mean to stifle you. But let's face it. You haven't gotten any contract, any money, you don't know this man from a hole in the wall, and suddenly he offers you this pie in the sky. . . ."

"But, Mom, it *does* make sense. Don't you see? I earned this. Me. I won this job. I *deserve* it. This isn't Manny the Butcher. This is Brannan Aviation."

"I know. A big company. I know all about them."

"They make the airplanes. The Brannan 606. At La Guardia and Idlewild. I can't send them a letter from a lawyer, for God's sakes. Why can't you believe they would actually want me to work for them? That they would find me valuable...."

"*Believe?* Who believes in you more than me? Who? You're a genius as far as I'm concerned. You're gonna make a million dollars. You watch and see if I'm right. But we're not talking about belief here. We're talking about facts. Listen, Mrs. Morganstein across the street, her son Sheldon who lives in New Jersey, he's got a Ph.D. Maybe we can call him up and have him look into this."

"Look into this? Sheldon Morganstein? Mom! What're you talking about?...."

"I just don't want anyone to take advantage of you, Danny. You're a good boy. Listen, here comes your father. Let me put him on. He's gotta run back to the store. Don't tell him about this Warren thing. Don't upset him."

"*Upset* him?"

"He's got enough on his mind, with this flood and his store and all. I'll explain it all to him at midnight when he gets back from work...."

I waited with trepidation for my father to pick up his phone. Was I going crazy, or did everyone suddenly have dyslexia of the ears? "Hi, Danny? It's me, Dad. Listen, I've only got a minute. I had to come home from the store. On a Friday. That sonofabitch Krepner couldn't have a flood on Sunday, when I'm off, no.... But listen, Danny. I wanna ask you something, and then I'm gonna run back to my place.... Danny, is your cousin Herbie staying with you? ... In Philadelphia?"

"Herbie?"

"Yeah, Herbie."

"Well ... I mean, yes, he's been visiting me ... for a while...."

"Danny, don't try to bullshit me. My sister told me. He's living with you in your room. Well listen, I want him out of there. You hear me? I want him out of there this minute."

"But, Dad...."

"Don't 'But, Dad' me, Danny. You heard what I said. I want him out of there today. You hear me?"

"But Dad, where will he go? I mean, he has no place to go."

"Danny, listen to me. Do you think I don't like Herbie? Well you're wrong. Even when he tells me I should move to Greenwich village and all that crap. I know he's had a hard time since his father died. But Danny, let me tell you something—if he wants to act crazy and live like a bum, that's his problem. He's got no business dragging you down with him."

"He's not gonna *stay* here or anything...."

"Danny. No. N ... O ... No. You hear what I'm saying? He's gotta be outta there, tonight. That's the sum and substance of it. No ifs, ands or buts. Listen, I gotta run. I only hope I don't meet Krepner in the street on my way out, because if I do, I'm gonna let that sonofabitch have it. Here's your mother."

"Dad, don't get into it with Krepner," I shouted, but he was already gone.

"Hello, Danny, it's me again. Mom. Listen, did I say the wrong thing before?"

"Well...."

"Listen, Danny, I'm sorry if I hurt your feelings. I know, I always say the wrong thing. But what can I do? I'm a mother. I've got to look out for my children...."

When Herbie returned, he seemed lit up from the inside by a brittle glow, as if illuminated by the neon energy of incipient disease, or the unstable alchemy of random drugs bought from strangers on the street. But as we ate our dinner and drank a few Rolling Rock beers, he gradually slid back into his more "normal" self.

We were eating at Kelly and Cohen's, a large, crowded, delicatessen-style restaurant owned by a Jew. There was no Kelly at the restaurant, and there never had been. As Herbie chewed on his *latkes* and corned beef, he fell into his avuncular mode. "Deacon Dan, my man, do you realize you're gonna be on The Coast, man, the land of divorcees and loose living. You can do anything, and who's gonna be the wiser? You dig what I'm saying, Dan? Mr. Herbie is telling you, you can run wild out there. You can drop the nice Jewish chicks who'll please your parents, and find a beautiful *shiksa* maiden. You can promise her anything and then just take a powder. You're going far away, my man. You can take a vacation from your fucking morals."

"And be more like you?" I said, smiling, but gently, because I knew Herbie was just surfing along on the waves of his own rhetoric.

After dinner, I bought us two Robert Burns Panatellas. As we sat there smoking them I told Herbie that my father had said he had to leave. Herbie straightened up in his chair as if he had heard a gunshot.

"He really said that? That I have to go?"

I could see he was hurt by my father's lack of confidence in him. I nodded yes. "I don't really know what to say. I mean, you don't have to go right now, of course."

"He really said I have to go?"

"Shit, man, we can still go to see Shirley Scott. I mean, hell, we've planned it all week. In fact, fuck it, let's spend a great weekend together. You can go whenever it's convenient for you. Come on, I'll drive you out to Bryn Mawr tomorrow...."

"Hell, man, I don't want to go to Bryn Mawr.... What do I want out at Bryn Mawr? ... All the girls out there are named Buffy, or Tucky, or Muffy...."

His tone of voice embodied his wounded feelings. I didn't bother to defend Bryn Mawr, as I knew that wasn't what we were really talking about. He fell mute and sullen. Toked abstractedly on his cigar for a few moments. Then he said, abruptly, "Hell, I'll go tonight, if that's the way he feels."

"You don't have to go *tonight*, man."

"No. Listen, you just drive me down to the fucking Greyhound station. It won't take but a second to pack. I don't possess things, you know. I'm not one of these fucking Wharton guys, these materialists with all their 'luggage' and shit. Hell, man, I travel light. Like the Zen masters say, I move through, and when I'm gone, I haven't even left a trace...."

"But where will you go?"

"Me? I'll go to New Orleans."

"New Orleans? But ... But, what'll you live on?"

"I'll get by."

I looked him solemnly in the eye, suddenly struck by how little he had in life, and in this regard he did seem admirable in a way;

29

but I also had an image of him trundling through the snow in his old coat, carrying his ancient little suitcase, the one that closed with two belts that looked like they had come from the pants of Eastern European immigrants from Ellis Island, and suddenly I found his condition to be unutterably sad.

It didn't take Herbie long to pack up his few belongings, and before I knew it I had given him fifty bucks and was downtown, letting him out of my car into the cold air and the trampled snow across the street from the Greyhound station. "I'm sorry," I said, quietly. "I really didn't . . ."

"Hey, my man, don't apologize. You've been real nice to me. I mean it, man. I understand. We had some good times and now it's time to move along."

He pulled his suitcase out of the rear seat. I reached across and shook his hand.

"Well, good luck, my man," I said.

"Yeah, I'm ready for some of those Southern women," he said. "Philly was chilly, Daddy. Yes, in that regard, Mr. Herbie has to admit, Philly was definitely chilly. . . ."

He smiled and walked off by himself without turning back. I watched him cross the street in the ice pick air, the obstreperous wind tangling torn newspapers against his legs like seaweed.

The Showboat was a relatively small venue for a major jazz club. An oval bar in the basement of the Negro Douglas Hotel, it had the feel of a plush and sophisticated jive submarine that sailed easily beneath the great stone city each night, unnoticed by the solid citizens above.

The bar was fairly empty when I arrived. I ordered a shot of Seagram's Seven and a beer. Shirley Scott was playing a ballad. She looked over at me and our eyes met, and she smiled for some reason and I smiled back. As I sat there by myself, looking at the young black men dressed up with their dates, beginning a weekend together, and the groups of well-dressed older black men drinking their beers, I began to feel a certain healing quality in the music and in my isolation. Solitude had become a familiar position for me over the years. I had almost come to like the sad perfumes and the bittersweet consolations of loneliness.

Then, over in the walkway at the end of the room, I spotted Harold, the old black man who tended the men's room. I ordered a Bud, his favorite beer, and brought it over to him.

"Hey, Harold, how's things?"

"Not bad," he smiled. "It be a whole lot betta than it was here last week."

"Last week?"

"Yeah," he laughed. "They had that damn Ornette Coleman here. If he never plays here again, it'll be too soon for my tastes."

"Harold," I said, "Ornette's good. And he's a nice guy. I mean, I know he's a little 'out there' in his music, and all. . . ."

"Oh, it ain't his music," Harold interrupted, "and he may be a nice guy and all that shit, I don't be denyin' that, but goddamn it, man, when he comes here we're lucky if we see ten people all week, and those that do come, they don't tip shit, man, I'll tell you true, so don't be tellin' me nothin' about no Ornette Coleman. His fans man, they don't tip shit. . . ."

He was saying this in an angry tone, but he was laughing at the same time, and I joined in, and then someone went past him into the men's room and he had to run, to get back to work. He shouted, "Hey, thanks for the beer, Danny," as he ran off.

It was late when I rolled into my room that night. I'd had too much to drink and it had taken me a half-hour to find my car. As I prepared to go to bed, I thought of Herbie, on a dark bus somewhere, journeying by himself through the frozen Hades of windy, snow-collared, night-time turnpikes. I picked up the empty box of Sunshine Krispy crackers he had left under his cot, and threw it into the garbage. I decided, however, not to remove the three photos that he had torn from magazines at the Public Library and affixed to the wall over my little Kelvinator refrigerator: One of the actress Jennifer Jones in a tight sweater; one of Carl Furillo, the former right fielder for the Brooklyn Dodgers; and one of the Dalai Lama.

Chapter Six

Portland, Oregon
June 19, 1961

Dear Herbie,
Hope you got my card from North Platte. If I'm struck by lightning, it won't be unexpected. Something has to happen to balance all the good times I've had. In Denver, I went to Larimer Street to look for Neal Cassady's father, then had a drunken conversation with Anita O'Day at this club she was appearing at out on the strip, and then, somehow, I wound up back down on skid row at this Negro club with a fabulous rhythm-and-blues band, with a great organ and two singers and everyone twisting wildly, and when I was coming back from the men's room a bunch of people came running madly by me in the other direction. The police were raiding the damn club, a whole task force of cops grabbing people left and right. Everyone near me was scrambling out the back windows, so I jumped out a window and took off with them, running like hell from the cops, down some weird Denver back streets with all these drunken people, and I don't even know why! Man! What an evening!

Next day, Mesa Verde, the most beautiful and mysterious place! And then I met these great Navajo guys, and then the Grand Canyon! I slept out, woke at 4:30, and watched the canyon shift in colors for two hours as the sun rose and I jumped up and down with a blanket on my head to keep warm and I chanted my own "Navajo" chants just to keep my feet on the Earth in the holiness of it all. Then to Las Vegas, where I immediately hit a jackpot on the slots and began to buy drinks for everybody until I wound up ten hours later at a downtown casino, having a drunken conversation about mathematics, if you can believe it, with a bartender who's a grad student in math at the University of Nevada!

Then, look out! On to L.A., where I found these terrific bookstores, met *two great guys from Sweden and Australia, both on the road together, going from Mexico City to Alaska, and we found this jam session in Hollywood with some of the best sounds ever (Shelly Manne, Barney Kessel, etc.). Wow!*

Went to Frisco! Began my binge in Chinatown. Then City Lights, North Beach! Met dozens of people. I got so excited I took a drunken ride on a cable car, yelling out to the great city as I hung outside, off the back of the car, while the passengers gasped! They finally stopped the car, and the conductor threw me off in the middle of nowhere.

Then, somehow, I met this beat-looking guy carrying broken bongos. There's too much to tell here, but we stayed overnight at U.C. Berkeley, and then I drove him 600 miles to Portland. Who would believe that Portland, Oregon would provide the wildest time of my whole life? It turned out that my new buddy lives in a house with ten other people. It's called "The Monastery," and it's a kind of beat coed-fraternity, with voluntary rent, no rules, and many guests. The absolute craziest place I've ever seen. One guy is living in a closet! The average person there had been awake for three or four straight days. I stayed up all weekend and wound up playing jazz kazoo (!) in a jam session with 14 Negro guys at this crazy club.

Anyhow, I do have a life to get back to, so I'm off to Seattle tomorrow morning. This trip has been all I've ever dreamed it could be, and more. The coast is glorious, and I want to take in as much as I can before I settle down and convert my degrees into daily work, respectability, and success—in short, the golden cage I have so richly earned by my hard work in school.

Stay loose,

The Big Bopper

I drove to Seattle on Route 99, in my scarred and pocked green 1955 Dodge. I had to get my feet back on the ground before I went to work at Brannan the next day, but the clean, fresh beauty of the Pacific Northwest made it difficult to come down. I'd expected the Grand Canyon and the desert to be impressive, but I had not been prepared for the cool, lush greens of Oregon—mint, lime, pool table—which had made me want to shout out of my car window in joy at the sheer comeliness of the world.

In Washington, the tall pines, and the huge snow-capped mountains kept me floating and off-balance. Nonetheless, I had to reach Seattle that day, to set up at the downtown YMCA until I could find an apartment of my own in the unfamiliar city, which was not yet tied to the rest of the country by cheap jet flights, the Interstate Highway System, and major league sports but seemed, rather, a far-away unspoiled place—distant, romantic, open to the mytholo-gizing imagination.

When I passed the huge Brannan plant itself, I suddenly missed the stiff flak-jacket of my normal Wharton identity. (For what is identity after all, but a certain kind of armor?)

In truth, I did not expect to come back to Brannan for a career after I graduated with my M.B.A. Back East was my home, my fam-ily, the neighbors and relatives who would be looking out of their apartment house windows someday when I pulled up in my new, brightly-colored, Ford Thunderbird convertible with the tennis rackets in the back, and I'd be wearing exactly the right blazer, and I'd open the door for my wife, just the right kind of Ivy League-type Jewish girl who spoke French and had summered at South Hampton since she was a child—classy, beautiful, tastefully under-stated in her manner, and simply but expensively dressed.

My parents would rush out to greet us, sparkling with pride, and although I was extremely successful, of course I'd be modest, car-rying myself with the kind of quiet grace I'd learned from Joe Dimag-gio, who'd played down the street at Yankee Stadium. Nonetheless, everyone in the neighborhood would know that I had really made it in America, and thus I would know it, too.

Brannan was massive and impressive. I slowed down and gazed at the acres of parking lots, the factories, the private airport with the large 606 jets scattered around the tarmac, bearing insignias from nations around the globe. Suddenly I was on the front lines, among the successful, the movers and shakers, the people who did not have aunts who, when a woman on the street called one of them a "fish market lady," would punch the other woman in the jaw with a quick right cross reminiscent of Archie Moore.

As I approached the city center, I noticed the absence of huge glass and steel skyscrapers. Majestic Mount Rainier was so much closer, so much grander than I had anticipated. I took in the clean wooden homes, the smells of pine and fir and the sea, the fresh *new* feel of it all—the youthful city, the West.

I entered the downtown area on the elevated Alaskan Way. I parked across the street from the Y. A rush of excitement pulsed through my body as I thought of my cousin Herbie's prophecies of wild *shiksas*. I *was* literally thousands of miles from anyone I knew. Anonymous and free at last, with a chance to find out who I was in my deepest soul, beneath the veneer of expectations and rituals built up by a lifetime of personal history and its precipitate, my so-called "character."

I hopped out of the car, setting my feet solidly on the new Western ground. I turned toward the Y, and broke into an exuberant trot across the nearly empty street. Then I heard a surprised man's voice shouting out from somewhere behind me, "DANNY SCHWARTZ! Holy shit! I don't believe this! Danny fucking Schwartz!"

Chapter Seven

I spun around, puzzled. A man about my own age, perhaps a couple of years older, was approaching with his hand out.

"Danny. What the hell are you doing here?"

I shook his hand. I recognized him, but for a second I couldn't set his face against the lattice of my past and come up with his name.

"Hal. Hal Marcus," he said. "Man, I haven't seen you since I graduated from R.P.I.! Shit, that's already three years ago."

We moved back toward the sidewalk together. Now I remembered Hal. We hadn't been close friends. He had been in another fraternity, one more traditionally Jewish than mine, and he'd been a junior when I was a freshman, which made him seem, at that time, like a member of another generation. I'd met him during the fraternity rushing, but I hadn't seen that much of him afterwards. He seemed to know me better than I knew him.

"Hal! Boy, am I amazed to see you. I mean I just this minute got here, driving out from the East. I'm working for Brannan."

"You're working for Brannan? That's who I work for."

"You work for Brannan?"

"Yeah." We stepped up on the curb. "Since school. I do materials development work. For the missiles."

"Wow, I can't believe this." Hal began to laugh and to pat me on the back. His hair had thinned slightly; he wore it swept back on the sides, and sported a small neat mustache. I was surprised at his joy at seeing me, because I remembered him as having been somewhat aloof at college—cynical and a bit snobby.

"When do you start work?"

"Tomorrow. I'm in this Executives of the Future program. It's just for the summer."

"But what are you doing down here? Downtown?"

"I'm going over to the Y to get a room for the night."

"The Y?"

"Yeah."

"Listen, Danny, you remember Vic Feuer?"

"Vic? From your fraternity?"

"Yeah. From your class." He kept nodding. I was amazed that he was so delighted to see me. "Well, listen, Danny, Vic is here. He works for Brannan, too. And he and I, we just sublet this beautiful place for the summer. In West Seattle. Around the bend of the bay from downtown. It's a fabulous house. We call it The Palace. And we were just going to start looking for a roommate."

"A roommate?"

"Yeah. The house is big and we want someone to live downstairs. It's set on a slope so the basement becomes the ground floor in the back and opens out into a view of the whole city skyline across the water. Listen, why don't you move in with us? Shit, it'll be great!"

"You mean, you want me to be your roommate? You and Vic?"

Hal's eyebrows lifted, and he said with relish, "Could you make thirty five bucks a month?"

"What? ... You're serious?"

"We sub-let it from some bigwig at Brannan. You'll have a suite of your own. Furnished. Fireplace. Bathroom. So why bother to check into the ridiculous Y at all? Why not just come home with me right now?"

"Well.... shit.... It sounds great."

"All right, it's a deal," Hal said. And then, amazingly, he asked me to play shortstop on his softball team.

I found that the more that Hal revealed his affection and respect for me, the more intelligent and winning he seemed. "This is too much," Hal said. "What a day!"

"Boy, I'll say."

"Vic is gonna go wild when he sees you. He's gonna be so happy I bumped into you. Wait til you see the parties we're gonna have. There's *shiksas* galore around here."

"Will we see him tonight?" I said.

"Who?"

"Vic. Will he be there when we get home?"

"Oh, no, man. Not tonight."

"Is he working late or something?"

"Vic?" Hal said, casually. "Vic never works late if he can help it. But he won't be back at all tonight."

"How come?"

"Vic's in jail," he said.

Chapter Eight

The Brannan Orientation was set in a classroom that held about thirty people. The session appeared to be a general meeting of all the people who were to begin working for Brannan on that particular day.

I was wearing one of my two suits and one of my four ties. I had always been careless about my clothes. The orientation had been scheduled to begin at eight o'clock. It was now eight-thirty. I looked to my left and was surprised to see a pretty young woman sitting next to me. My attention had been folded into my *Post-Intelligencer,* reading the usual bad news of the day: Khrushchev threatening to go into Berlin, and so on.

"God," I said, "I wish they'd get started. I hate these kinds of things."

"Yeah, I know what you mean." She smiled. A beautiful smile, her large, perfect teeth sparkling like fresh milk. Her hair, which hung down to her shoulders, was the same color and texture as mine. Brown and somewhat unruly. She was wearing a white, sleeveless dress, the kind Jackie Kennedy had brought into style, with a square neckline and buttons down the front. She seemed somewhat overdressed for the occasion, but you got the idea it was because she probably didn't have that many "official" dresses in her wardrobe.

The manner in which she had said, "I know what you mean" caught my attention. Unaffected, her large gray-green eyes looking directly into mine. It struck me immediately that she wasn't merely being polite. She did seem to know what I meant.

"Yeah," I smiled. "Hey, can you believe the size of the parking lots here? I left my car way at the end somewhere.... I think it's in Tacoma."

"At least you *have* a car," she said, enjoying the banter. "I had to come here on the bus."

"I parked so far away, I had to take a goddamn bus to get here from my car."

Her face relaxed into laughter again. She appeared to like me. Perhaps this was one advantage of my having traveled so far. I was now in a place where I could be considered exotic.

She was a tall, thin girl, with long legs and a nice figure. There was a western grace to her, a kind of rare gawky natural beauty, as if she did not belong in the world of large corporations.

"Are you two ready to join us?" a loud, snide voice said sharply. I looked up. The man in charge of the orientation had arrived, and was placing the blame for his lateness upon us.

"Whenever *you* are," I said.

He gave me a nasty look. He was about thirty years old, with the slightly dilapidated appearance of a lower-level bureaucrat. He looked like the human equivalent of the kind of house they advertise as a "fixer-upper." I was preparing my next wise-guy rejoinder in case he struck at us again, but he backed off and began to talk about Brannan.

Right now he was explaining that we would all have to punch in at the clock every morning. All! Without exception. I felt my spirit begin to Hindenberg down, wounded and burning, into a barren New Jersey field.

He explained that if we were anywhere from one second to six minutes late, we would lose one-tenth of an hour's pay. If we were six minutes and one second late, we would lose two-tenths of an hour. I turned to my left, caught the attention of the girl, and rolled my eyes in despair. She smiled again. She was getting a great kick out of me. And she didn't seem bothered by the announcement about punching in. It was as if she had written this whole job off before she came, and there was nothing they could say that would violate her expectations, as she had none to begin with. She suddenly seemed a lot older than I although, in actuality, she appeared to be slightly younger.

We spent the morning filling out personnel forms and learning the usual details and procedures for working in a large corporation.

Then our "teacher," the dork who was diminishing us, led us to the cafeteria for lunch.

I sat next to the girl in white at an otherwise empty table.

"Boy, some morning!" I said, caustically. "My name is Danny. Danny Schwartz. I just arrived here yesterday from back East."

"My name is Leslie. Leslie Schmidt. I'm just working here as a secretary for a while."

"Are you from Seattle?"

"I've lived here most of the last two or three years, but I'm from Idaho."

"Idaho! Whew! I've never been to Idaho. Must be very beautiful there."

She nodded.

"You from Boise?"

"Oh, no," she smiled. "That's in the south. That's a lot different. Down there by Utah and Nevada. I'm from the north. Jefferson. On the Snake River." Then she turned bashful again, and she said, merely, "Where are you from?" I saw that she was more comfortable when I was speaking than when she was required to.

"New York." I said. "The Bronx. You ever been to New York?"

She shook her head no. "My family drove back East to Denver once, when my brother graduated high school."

Back East? To Denver?

"You come from a large family?"

"Just my brother and me. He's a year older. Went to the University up at Moscow, in math. Graduated Phi Beta Kappa. He's in the Navy now. Writing a book on space navigation. He might be an astronaut someday.... But how about you?" she added quickly, embarrassed at talking about herself so much. I didn't need much encouragement to take the floor and tell her about Rensselaer and Wharton and the Executives of the Future program. And then I told her about my trip across country, and meeting Hal on the street, and I described the "real American" house we were living in, so different from my family's little four-room apartment in The Bronx. "It's got a complete view of downtown Seattle. God, the whole city just sparkles at night, with Mount Rainier in the background and all. I mean, I don't know, maybe Mount Rainier is ordinary to you out here...."

41

"No, it's not ordinary," she said, in a throaty voice that carried the sincere feeling of a good jazz singer. "It never becomes ordinary."

I stopped for a second, startled by her sudden depth of emotion. Then, I told her about R.P.I. How it was on a par with M.I.T. for undergraduates, and I had been admitted to both schools but had chosen R.P.I. because it fielded a football team and I had dreams of becoming a star quarterback, although my experience had been limited to playing touch football on the cobblestone streets.

"How'd it work out," she said, wryly.

"Not too well. I tried to run up the middle when I was a freshman, and the entire defense tackled my arm. I couldn't move it for weeks. That was the end of my football career. Although I did wind up quarterbacking the winners in the fraternity touch football league. I like touch football better. It doesn't hurt as much."

She laughed good-naturedly at my blarney.

"I liked it at Rensselaer. That's where I met the guys I'm rooming with now." I filled her in on Hal Marcus. "And Vic. He's my other roommate. He's just getting out of jail today. He got arrested for throwing a beer bottle at a cop or something."

For a second I thought I might have gone too far for this quiet girl, but she grinned. (It was not until a memorable Saturday, about two weeks later, that I would find out just how far wrong I was in my initial estimate of her.)

The two new guides, a young man and a woman, appeared at the door of the cafeteria and summoned us all back together. They were going to lead us on a quick orientation tour of the plant, and in the process show us each the location of our new jobs. As we walked down a long corridor, Leslie and I continued to jabber away. She was talking more now, and I was fascinated by her easy, cowgirl kind of charm.

I said, "There's this theater in town that's putting on *Death of a Salesman* Friday night. I saw it advertised in the newspaper. Do you think you might be interested in going with me?"

"Sure. I'd like to." She quickly gave me her address.

We continued to walk along, paying attention only to each other. When we looked up the two guides were no longer in front of us, although the entire class was still behind us. We stopped walking and turned back to the other people.

"What's happening?" I said to them.

They looked puzzled. "I mean, where are the orientation guides?" I said.

"The orientation guides?" a man about my own age said.

"Yeah. The people who are leading this tour?"

After a couple seconds of silence, a tall woman said strangely, "But . . . we thought you were the people who were leading the tour. We've all been following you."

Leslie and I looked into each other's eyes and we began to laugh together, both of us now shaking our heads from side to side, and she said, blushing as she laughed and actually slapping her thigh, "Oh, my *Lord!*" in that lovely way she had that no Easterner—and certainly no Jew from The Bronx like myself—could ever quite imitate.

Chapter Nine

Back at The Palace, I read some Bertrand Russell and a book on Mahatma Gandhi. Gandhi's ideas of nonviolence and civil disobedience were mostly new to me, but I found them intriguing. I was also interested and somewhat frightened by his notion that your philosophy was simply the sum of your actions in your everyday life. I was on the verge of beginning my own real life. I wondered uneasily what my "philosophy" would prove to be.

Hal was out on a dinner date, and Vic wouldn't be released from jail until the next day. I finished my unpacking, and then peered out of the picture window, trying to make myself believe that this was all actually happening to me—Danny Schwartz, of Nelson Avenue in The Bronx. That somehow *I* now had a lawn and the kind of skyline view people acquired in the movies as a sign of their success.

The next morning I arrived at the parking lot at 7:15. I had thought that would be early enough, since I wasn't due at work until 7:30, but the entrances to the lots were jammed with nervous, hurrying drivers. Once again I was forced to park in "Tacoma." The lots were coded into several distinct grades—with each step you moved up in the company, you received a benediction and access to the next closer lot. Since the distance that I had to hike from my car to the plant was so huge that I practically had to carry a canteen, my rank in the feudal hierarchy seemed abundantly clear. I was a white-collar serf. A peasant with a tie.

I passed through the gate of the plant, wearing my new security badge that displayed my photo so the guard could see that I wasn't a commie. Although my watch showed about three minutes left before I had to punch in, I noticed that some of the people around me were beginning to walk more quickly. Others subtly joined them.

Soon, everyone was trotting. I began to trot along with them. Then, almost before anyone willed it, we were all running, knocking against each other as we pushed our way up the wide metal staircase, then trying to reach over each other's shoulders to insert our cards into the clock, which read 7:30.

For a second I was not able to locate my card. By the time I was finally able to punch in, it was 7:31. For the next five minutes, I would be working for Brannan for free.

I walked over to the room in which I was to spend my summer. Large, rectangular, almost like an airplane hangar in size but with a low, translucent ceiling, which emitted a diffuse white light that reminded me of the plastic cream they gave you in tiny thimble-like cups on airplanes.

There were no panels or breaks of any kind to divide the room up into more intimate or private compartments. Simply rows of institutional-gray steel desks, with aisles along the two edges. I walked past row after row of people on their telephones, until I reached a large office with a secretary in an anteroom. She led me in to see my boss, James Stilson, the Purchasing Manager. He had forgotten who I was or why I was there, but he covered this up as best he could after the secretary refreshed his memory.

"Yes, well, I'm pleased to meet you, Dan. This the first time you've ever been out to our neck of the woods?"

We made small talk about the less controversial aspects of my trip across country. Mr. Stilson seemed friendly enough. He was a thin man, about my father's age. In fact, he bore an amazing resemblance to my father, except for the fact that he lacked my father's burning intensity. You couldn't picture him trying to run someone over with his car during a disagreement over a parking place, or having his auto antenna taken and then going out at night and stealing a radio antenna from a similar kind of car and saying, in his own defense, "Well, they took mine, didn't they?"

"I've got to run," Mr. Stilson said. "Do you know what you're supposed to be doing here on a day-to-day basis?"

"Well, sir, Mr. Warner, the man who hired me, he said that I was going to work on the Readiman missile. That I would help put the purchasing system on a computer. I took an extra class in computer programming this spring to prepare myself for it, and I'm pretty good at . . ."

"Gee, Dan, I'm afraid we've already done that."

"You've . . . done that?"

"Why, yes." Mr. Stilson seemed troubled. "We finished that up about two weeks ago."

We sat in silence. Finally he spoke. "I'm really sorry about that. I mean, I'm sure the course'll come in handy anyhow someday. But the question remains, I guess, what are we going to have you do for the summer?"

The phone rang. He listened to someone who was obviously higher up than he was. I could tell by the expression on his face and the deference in his voice. I felt terribly disappointed about the Readiman project. I had worked hard in the class to prepare myself thoroughly for my job, and now the work had evaporated. Stilson himself seemed a nice enough guy. It wasn't his fault. In fact, it probably wasn't actually any specific person's fault. That was the trouble with the bureaucratic railroad. The trains would run over people from time to time, and you couldn't really find any-body to blame it on.

"OK, Mr. Saunders. I'll be right over." Mr. Stilson hung up the phone. He was already rising from his chair when he noticed me sitting there.

"Oh, Dan . . . Listen, why don't you go out and see one of my assistants in the offices just down the hall. See Bill Hancomb." Stilson hitched up his tie and smoothed his hair with his hand. "You'll be working in his section of the floor outside. His office is right next door. "Hey, listen," he began to walk toward the door, "you know electronics, don't you?"

"Yes, sir. I'm an electrical engineer. Before I went to Wharton, I mean. . . ."

"Yes, good. Well, listen, why don't you investigate the possibil-ity of using Japanese transistors in the Readiman?"

"Japanese transistors? Aren't they supposed to be unreliable?"

"That's what they say. But look into it." He hurried out the door.

Chapter Ten

Bill Hancomb was a friendly man in his thirties. Somewhat short, with a freckled, round face, he could have played a neighbor's kid named "Biff" on the "Ozzie and Harriet Show." He was closer to my age than Jim Stilson, and less formal. "Japanese transistors for the Readiman?" He smiled and shrugged.

I smiled and shrugged as well.

"Well, the engineers over at Design'll have to approve anything you decide on anyhow. But I can get you going over here at Purchasing."

"That'd be fine."

He led me back to the main room, and handed me over to a man named Ralph Nettles. Ralph kept nodding and smiling and saying "certainly," until Bill left. Most of the other buyers in the immediate area turned toward us as they finished their telephone conversations.

"Here, let's just get you situated," Ralph said. He took me around to the preceding row of desks. "You'll be here at John Crombie's desk."

"John Crombie's desk?"

"Yeah." He looked at me. "Something wrong?"

"Well ... I just wondered, I mean, won't John be wanting to use his desk?"

"Oh, that's right. You wouldn't know."

"Know?"

"About John. You see, John's dead."

"Dead?"

"Yes. I'm afraid we had a real tragedy here. Over the Memorial Day weekend. John was giving a barbeque for our section here in the office and, well, I don't know exactly what brought it about, but he was grilling hamburgers for us behind his new house, and suddenly he just went and poured the starter fluid all over himself and struck a match and set himself on fire."

I looked at him with shock.

He shook his head. "It all happened so fast, we could hardly believe it. He went up like a Roman candle...."

"Oh ... I'm ... I'm very sorry...."

Ralph shrugged. "Life has to go on. That's the way the cookie crumbles, I guess. But John was a sweet guy.... It was a real tragedy.... Here, let's get you settled."

Fortunately, John had left his desk filled with office supplies, so we didn't have to requisition any.

Ralph searched for a while, and finally came up with a few ragged electronic catalogues from Japanese manufacturers. "You know," Ralph said, "this isn't going to be a snap. We don't normally buy from them. You're going to be starting from scratch in an international situation with a highly classified missile system."

"I know," I said quietly. I had been thinking the very same thoughts since Mr. Stilson had suggested this project.

I saw that Ralph was eager to get back to making his own calls, so I thanked him for his help and reached out to shake his hand. At that moment a high-pitched "beep" sounded over the loudspeakers. Everyone rose at once and began to run around the room like hot molecules in Brownian motion. Ralph blanched, yanked back his hand, and sprinted around to his desk. He grabbed a cup with some powder in it from a drawer, and raced over toward the wall on the left where other frantic people had already formed a line at the sink. I watched this strange hectic behavior with amazement and some foreboding. I was almost afraid to ask Ralph to explain it to me. In some deep marrow within me, a place you wouldn't want to get sick in because no doctor could reach it, I already knew what was happening.

Ralph rushed back to the desk, swallowing coffee as he darted along behind the row of chairs.

"What's going on?"

He held up his finger for me to wait a second, as he forced himself to swallow slugs of his coffee. People up and down the floor were doing the same thing. Just as Ralph replaced the cup in his desk, another high-pitched 'beep" sounded on the loudspeakers. Those who had not yet finished, quickly raised their coffee cups and drained them in one gulp.

"Nine twenty-four," Ralph said. "That's when our coffee break begins. We have to be finished by nine twenty-nine. But there's always such a long line at the sink for the hot water.... That's why we're lucky in a way. We're closer to the sink here than a lot of people."

I stood there silently for a few seconds, while he looked into my face as if he were expecting something.

"Well, thanks," I said. "Thanks for everything. I really appreciate it. I mean it."

"Anytime." He turned away and began to dial a number on his phone with the eraser end of a yellow pencil.

I went back to my desk and sat there, feeling ignored, humiliated and useless, a catalogue open in front of me, my eyes unfocused. I kept thinking that at any minute the loudspeakers might beep and everyone would leap up and begin to run around the office again for some reason I couldn't fathom. I felt like the guy who cleans up the thousands of dead flowers on the day after the Rose Bowl Parade.

But as the hours passed, I began to put all this in perspective. After all, I wasn't hired to spend my life making telephone calls to buy parts for airplanes. I was an Executive of the Future. That's why I had gone to school and worked my butt off. Right now I was just a loose pebble, exactly the kind that gets ground up in the gears of the huge machine, but in the future I would be in control of the machine.

I just had to remember that what was happening this summer did not have any permanent relation to the rest of my life.

Chapter Eleven

Vic Feuer was seated at the kitchen table drinking from a stubby bottle of beer and smoking a cigar when I returned home that evening. I took a bottle of Oly and joined him. Vic was quite pleased to see me. "Hal told me you moved in with us. Great, man!"

Vic seemed so completely content and at ease, like a retired millionaire on the deck of his yacht, that you never would have suspected he'd just been in jail for a week. He hadn't even lost his tan.

"Heard you got into a little tiff with the law."

He nodded with pleasure. "It's these new stubby beer bottles. You can't help but throw them after you've had a few."

At about five-foot-nine he was shorter than I was, but wiry and strong for his size. I'd known Vic at college, but at a distance. Although he'd appear now and then at the edge of some wild times I was having, he was capable of pushing them into tunnels of self-destructiveness beyond where I was willing to follow. Yet his wildness could be attractive if you were in the right mood. Once, drunk myself at a party at a snobbish fraternity that was particularly vehement in not admitting Jews as members, I'd heard a loud,crazy laugh coming out of a clothes closet. When I pulled open the door, I came upon Vic pissing on the brothers' clothing.

"I hear you work at Brannan," I said.

"He won't be there long, if he doesn't get his ass back in gear." It was Hal, coming into the room behind me. "I know, I know. Mother Brannan will be pissed!" Vic said. "I covered for you all week with Petersen," Hal said. "I kept telling him your grandmother was hanging on and you couldn't leave her bedside."

Hal looked at Vic with big eyes. Vic did have that kind of fascination for people. Like a car wreck.

"My own 'dying grandmother' got me through some tough

moments in college," I laughed.

"Hey," Hal said, "I really did stretch it there with Petersen. Just be sure to be there on time tomorrow."

Hal poured himself some Cutty Sark on ice and joined us at the table. He turned to Vic and said, "You should have seen this guy at work," meaning me.

I gave him a puzzled look. He punched my arm lightly, and said, "Three hours he's there and he walks through my department and already he's picked up this little *tchotchkeleh*. This *shiksa tchotchkeleh*," he teased. "Look! He's blushing!" He turned red himself in his excitement.

"I saw you," he continued in a sing-song, smarmy voice. "I saw you with that dish with the long legs. Oooo, they may be skinny, but they'll do when they're wrapped around you...."

"Hey, knock it off man," I said.

"Oooo, he likes her!" he said, in that same nasal, teasing voice. "What's Mommy and Daddy gonna say? Little Yankel has fallen for a *shiksa* with long legs...."

A woman about our age came into the room. She had short blonde hair and was wearing white shorts and a white tennis shirt. From the way she was stretching and rubbing her eyes, she had probably been in Vic's bed.

"Brenner, this is Danny. The guy I was telling you about," Vic said.

Brenner took the fourth seat at the table. She crossed one barefoot leg over the other. "Oh, er ... listen, good buddy," Vic said to Hal, "I'm not gonna be able to make it in to work tomorrow. Brenner and I are going skiing for a few days."

"*What?*" Hal said. "What about Petersen?"

"Screw Petersen," Vic said, casually.

Hal didn't know how to respond. "Want a beer?" Vic said to Brenner. She nodded nonchalantly, engrossed in the process of biting her toe nails.

When we finished all the beer, we adjourned to Vic's room and began to drink straight scotch out of a bottle of J&B. After we had finished off the scotch, Vic put on his favorite record at the time, John Coltrane's *Giant Steps*. He picked up a little recorder and began to blow it with amazing speed and dexterity, struggling to keep up with Coltrane, adding harmonies and embellishments in just the right places, always on the beat, never missing a note, and we joined him on some of the musical instruments that lay scattered about the room—bongos and a conga and tambourines, laughing and shouting and drinking and hopping around, and then, for some reason, I leaped up and began to jump up and down on Vic's bed, and Brenner was cracking up at me and yelling, "Go, Go, Go!" and I jumped higher and higher on the bed, making wilder and wilder gesticulations like some trampoline artist finally gone out of his mind, until I leaped up so high my head hit the ceiling and I lost my foothold on the bed and stumbled off, tumbling down onto the rug on my back.

I was stunned for a second, but when I rolled over and righted myself on the floor I looked up and I saw that they were all laughing even harder now, so hard there were tears in their eyes as they struggled to catch their breath, and then I saw a crazy excitement kindle in Vic's eyes and he moved towards a huge old TV he had set on his dresser. He struggled to lift it, and waddled across the room with it and then he somehow heaved the ungainly TV right through the closed bedroom window.

Chapter Twelve

The next day at work my hangover served to protect me from feelings and thoughts that I was not yet ready to face. The vast, unpartitioned, fluorescent-lit space in which I found myself seemed like a kind of aquarium of corporate behavior for which I had never been given the proper gills.

I spent the day leafing through catalogues, comparing the charts and graphs of specifications for Japanese transistors with the performance characteristics Brannan required for the manufacture of the Readiman Missiles. I was surprised to find that several of the Japanese transistors satisfied our standards. They were not yet as good as the American items, but they were adequate. When I compared the catalogues with some older ones I located, I noted that the Japanese were improving rapidly.

That evening, I had an early dinner at The Palace with Hal and his "future fiancee," Valerie—a sweet, quiet girl who was in love with him and whose family, he had told me, were among the oldest and wealthiest of the Jewish families in Seattle. Hal saw her most Friday and Saturday nights, usually saving his drunken carousing with his "wild *shiksas*" for weeknights and Sundays. Then I drove over to pick up Leslie Schmidt on the southern end of Broadway, between downtown and the black section, in a neighborhood composed of unfashionable houses and low-rent businesses like auto-body shops and plumbing-supply stores. Leslie lived in an older three-story building with two apartments on each floor. Her windows faced the street on the second story. She answered the door wearing a thin, light-green print dress, cinched around her waist by a soft white-leather belt.

"Good to see you. I'm glad you could make it," she said.

We didn't shake hands. Just stood there treading water, exchanging friendly smiles. "It all happened so fast at work, I wasn't sure we'd really connect up."

"I've been looking forward to it."

"I'll just get my purse." She ran into the front room. It appeared that her apartment had two rooms, the kitchen in which I was standing and a large bedroom. The kitchen was somewhat bare, as if she had only recently moved in, but it was appealing in an economical, spare kind of way. A colorful, worn, round carpet lay on the floor beneath four old, mismatched chairs set around a weathered mahogany table.

There were a few plants scattered about, and unframed paintings on the walls, an original abstract blue and yellow watercolor signed Sam Dawn, and several prints—a Renoir, a beautiful Degas nude done in pastels, and a Pre-Raphaelite woman who, it struck me, looked somewhat like Leslie.

On the wall across the room, above an old bicycle, there was a painting of the Virgin Mary that had been clipped from a magazine. Beside her was tacked a beaded chain from which a small cross hung.

When we left the building, a wino came up to us, and I gave him some change because he reminded me of my father somehow. He patted me on the back and said, "You're all right, pardner." I liked that, when winos or bums told me that I was all right.

The theater was just a short drive from Leslie's apartment. I was surprised at the quality of the production, which left me in tears at the end, when the brother-in-law makes that speech about Willy's nobility, and a smile and a shoeshine and all that.

"See, we're not really living in caves out here after all," Leslie said.

"So I'm learning. Hey, would you like to go someplace where we can talk a bit?"

"Sure." She slipped into her dark-green cardigan sweater. "But I have to make it an early night. I've got to get up at six o'clock. I have a friend who's leaving the country, and we're going up north to spend the day together in the woods."

We took a cushioned booth at a clean all-night coffeeshop and cafe on Broadway, between the theater and Leslie's house. I ordered a Rainier Ale. Leslie a pot of tea. I wanted to learn more about this quiet girl. To get her to start talking about herself.

"Tea doesn't keep you awake at night?" I said.

"Oh, no. I sleep like a horse."

"Standing up?" I joked.

She laughed. "Standing up! What do you know about horses? You've probably never seen a real horse up close in your life."

"Whaddya mean? We had a horse in our neighborhood in The Bronx. He used to pull the wagon for the used-clothes guy when I was a kid. The guy that would sing out, 'High-cash clothes!' as he passed in the street."

"New York," she said. "What an amazing place!"

"Not as strange as Idaho is to me."

"You probably had more people on your street than we had in our town."

"Did you have horses where you grew up? I mean, can you ride one?"

"Sure," she said, almost like "Pshaww!" "I grew up on a farm, with animals all around me. Criminey, we didn't move into town till I was about ten.... I guess you'd consider us a little backward.... You know, they still float logs down the river to the mill?"

"You're serious? Like in the movies?"

"That's it," she said, with pride. "You'd like it. I think it's about the last place in the U.S. where they still run the logs like that. It's real nice to watch. My mom works at the mill."

"Oh, yeah. She a logger?"

"No, I'm afraid she's in the office," Leslie laughed.

"Man, horses, loggers, farms ... I don't know *anything* about that stuff. I've always lived in these little apartments. I mean, we didn't even have a tree on our block. If you wanted to see a tree you had to join the Boy Scouts. They'd take you on a hike across the George Washington Bridge, to Fort Lee, New Jersey, and they'd say, 'Boys, remember this. This is a tree.'"

She said something like "Oh, Pshaw," and she looked at me with a lively interest in her eyes that made me feel warm and fine inside.

"Does your father still farm?" I said.

"He rents land at the bottom of the Jefferson Hill."

55

"What's the crop? Wheat?"

"Barley. It's on the edge of the Palouse country. In Eastern Washington."

"Is that good farming land?"

"GOOD? It's some of the best in the world. But that's up on top of the hill. My father farms *on* the hill. You should see him plowing on that steep slope. It's amazing the tractor doesn't turn over on him."

"Is that dangerous?"

"UUUUH!" she said, in a way no Eastern girl would ever say it, as if she had been punched in the stomach and all the wind had burst out of her. "Is it DANGEROUS? Criminey! Do you know how much a tractor WEIGHS?"

"Of course I do," I said. "I know all about tractors. How do you think I cut the hay on the north forty behind our house in The Bronx?"

"No, look," she said, excitedly, *taking my hand* in hers on the table for a second, with her long fingers, as if to say in some Western Gabby Hayes way, "Hold on there a minute, Pardner," and she said, "It's dangerous, alright. A tractor falling on you is one of the WORST things that can happen. Believe me. My Lord, you don't want to get stuck under a falling TRACTOR!" Then she heard the way her voice had risen in volume, and she blushed slightly, ashamed at the lovely way she had of putting her whole self into everything she said, of getting lost in the emotion of the moment.

"Well, I'll certainly remember that," I said, "next time I see a farmer on TV." Then I added, teasing, "You do have TV in Idaho?"

"One channel," she said, with mock pride.

"You're serious? Really? Only one channel?"

She nodded yes.

The waitress brought us our tea and ale. Leslie put sugar and cream into her cup. I sipped at the sweet golden-brown ale.

"Hey, this is good stuff," I said. "I've never had it before."

She nodded. "Well, don't like it TOO much. GOLL-LEE, I mean some people out here like Rainier Ale SO well, they pretty much have it for breakfast, lunch, and dinner."

"Hey, wasn't that some play tonight?"

"Yeah," she said. "That's one thing we sure don't have in Idaho."

"Good theater?"

"Any theater."

"Well, New York is the place for theater all right. But talking to you, I don't think you'd like what's on Broadway right now. Plays like *The Sound of Music* or *Fiorello* or *Bye, Bye Birdie*. But man, tonight was great!"

She nodded.

"I'd never seen it performed live before," I said. "I mean, I saw the movie, with Frederick March. God, I cried when I saw that film.... I guess Willy Loman reminded me of my father or something.... How he works so hard and he doesn't really get anywhere, and he and his son want to talk to each other, but they really can't...." I stopped, choking up with emotion, fearing I was getting sentimental, but Leslie looked at me sympathetically.

"Your father must work very hard for you."

"Yeah. I'll say. You know, even now, my father and my aunts and all, they STILL seem like they're afraid they might actually starve or something."

"I know what you mean," Leslie said, quietly, without her familiar smile now. "You know, when my mother was a kid she was ashamed to go to school because she didn't have SHOES. Can you believe it? Her family had nothing. They used to cook a pot of beans at the beginning of winter and just keep putting things into it as the winter went on."

"Did they beat you up a lot?" I said.

"Beat me up?"

"Yeah.... You know...."

"You mean physically?"

"Yeah," I said, wondering how I had gotten onto this path.

"Well, no ... not actually beat me...." She studied my face carefully. "Did your parents beat you?"

"Well, yeah, actually.... Sometimes ... when I did something that bothered my mother, sometimes, she would sic my father on me, and he would go completely nuts and beat me with his belt and they'd have to pull him off me...."

She nodded slowly, still looking at me.

"Once," I continued, "my old man bought my mother a cat-o'-nine-tails, to whip me with. Can you believe it?" I couldn't help but smile. "I guess I was too big by then, because when she tried to work me over with it I was able to wrestle it out of her hands...."

We sat there quietly. Leslie was looking down now, at her cup of tea.

"But my mother," I said, "she's really a lot like Linda in the play. I mean the way Linda stands behind Willy, and behind their boys, too. You know, a lot of my friends at college, they were from a different class of people than us, but they liked to stay at our house. They said it was filled with life." I sipped at my ale. "I mean how many of these wealthy guys have people like my cousin Louie the Mook hanging around?"

"Louie the Moose?"

"Mook," I said, smiling. "It's a fine distinction. I'll explain it to you someday. Although it isn't easy...."

"To define a mouk?" she said, sparkling with amusement, throwing off dancing light in all directions, like water plashing down over rocks.

"Listen, hey, can you believe this?" I said. "My grandfather, he owned three apartment houses in The Bronx, and neither he or my grandmother could read or write. Not in any language. And my father, he's never read a single book in his whole life."

"You should see MY father," Leslie said fondly. "Coming into town with his old overalls and all. You know, they used to call him 'Hog Pete.' That's his name. Pete."

"Hog Pete," I said lightly, trying to picture him.

"Yeah, he once had the biggest hog in the state. Something like seven hundred pounds or something."

"Can I get you folks anything else?" the waitress said. I hadn't seen her approach. I had been completely engaged by my talk with Leslie.

Leslie glanced up at the clock on the wall. I noticed she was not wearing a watch. "Criminey! It's after midnight! We'd better run."

When we came back to the car, I opened the door for Leslie, and as she got in I put my hand lightly against her back, just enough to guide her slightly, to make contact.

As we drove back to her house, she sat quietly and then she said, as if to herself, "Danny Schwartz." She turned to me. "Is that a German name? Schwartz?"

I glanced over at her to see if she was kidding. "No," I said, a little uneasily. "It's Jewish."

She seemed surprised for a just a second, then said, laughing lightly, "I can just picture my father if ever you met him. I know exactly what he'd say." She deepened her voice and imitated her father's twangy western locution: "Jewish, hey? We got a Jew in our town. Not a bad guy. Handsome fellow. Looks like that there Jeff Chandler, the movie actor." Then she added, "You mark my words, if you ever meet my father, that's exactly what he'll say. And then he'll look at you to see if you look like Jeff Chandler."

She smiled easily, and I felt relieved. It didn't really seem to matter to her that I was Jewish.

I stopped for a red light. "I don't really follow the religious part of it that much.... It's funny, but the only time I really felt Jewish was when I went to engineering school and they wouldn't let me in the fraternity I wanted to join."

"They wouldn't?" She seemed shocked.

"I couldn't believe it.... I mean sure, in The Bronx, once in a while when I was a kid, some morons from Sacred Heart School would call me a Christ-killer, and torture me in an empty lot, but here, at a top engineering school...."

We rode in silence for a while. Then she said, quietly, "Well, I'm Catholic, myself."

I swallowed. "Do you practice it?"

She nodded. "It's very important to me." She sat without speaking for a moment. Then she added, "I come from a German background. My mother's got a bit of Irish in her, but I'm pretty much German. German Catholic."

She turned toward the windshield. I wasn't sure what to say. I almost said, "Well, that's nice," but that didn't sound appropriate.

I parked directly in front of Leslie's house. She turned to me quickly and said, "Hey, thanks, Danny. I'll just run upstairs. It's pretty late." She looked me in the eyes and took my hand and gave it a squeeze. "I've had a really nice evening."

"So did I." She let go of my hand.

"I hope I can see you again sometime," I said.

"I'd like that, too."

"Maybe next week? We could go to hear some jazz or something. My roommate Hal says there's these great jam sessions on Saturday afternoons at a place called 'Dave's Fifth Avenue'...." When she didn't respond, I said, "Or we could do something else if you like...."

"I'm sorry, but I'm going home next weekend. I've got a ride with a guy I know...."

"Oh.... Well.... Maybe we can do it the week after...."

"I don't know." She looked up and noticed my pained surprise. "It isn't anything to do with you. I've really had a fine time. And I'd like to see you again sometime...."

"But...."

She looked up at me, guiltily. "But I'll be taking classes this summer. Every Tuesday and Thursday night. I'm going to have to ace them so I can get a loan or a scholarship."

"What about your parents? Won't they help?"

"They really can't afford it."

"They can't?"

She shrugged sadly. "They really sacrificed to send my brother up to Moscow.... It wasn't easy for them...."

"But what about you? That's not fair."

She shrugged again. "They expect me to get married, I guess. I've been seeing this local guy off and on for years. He's in law school up at Moscow. My family really respects his family. They're upstanding citizens, and they belong to the country club and all."

"And you? Do you want to get married?"

"I don't know what I want exactly. I do know, though, that I'm really going to try to do well at Seattle U." She looked into my eyes with some distress. "Gee, maybe I shouldn't have gone out with you tonight."

"I had a good time," I said. "I just thought, well, I'd like to see you again."

"I had a good time, too," she smiled. "Don't look so glum. I won't get married over the weekend. Maybe we *can* see each other, once I get myself grounded at school."

"I'd like that. Remember, I'm only here for ten weeks or so."
She nodded. "Well, let's see what happens."
The dark, unfamiliar streets were almost deserted as I made my way back to West Seattle. I switched on my windshield wipers when it began to rain lightly. I could smell the sharp, fecund perfume of wet fir trees.

Had I said something wrong? Did I talk too much? Was it because I was Jewish? Or was she merely confused as I was and telling me the truth? In any case, it didn't look as if I'd be seeing much of Leslie in my short summer at Brannan.

I felt sorely disappointed. Suddenly my old loneliness returned. I had come to Seattle with a vague dream of meeting one of my cousin Herbie's "wild *shiksas*." I was going to have a prestigious job, cash in my pocket for virtually the first time in my life, and I could be temporarily like one of those plastic, unfeeling guys in the cigarette ads. I would meet this wild girl and have this anonymous, crazy passionate affair that would have no consequences in my real life.

But instead I had met this quiet, bright, innocent country girl, whom I had really liked.

And then she had dropped me.

Chapter Thirteen

The next afternoon I drove downtown and bought two books: Dante's *Inferno* and a general survey of Catholicism. Actually, I had grown up amid thousands of Irish Catholics in my neighborhood in The Bronx. It was Protestants I'd never met. In fact, one of the primary reasons I had wanted to attend an "out-of-town college" was to meet Protestants and to learn how to emulate their style and manners and speech, and to function in their world. A world, to my mind, of country estates and horse shows, and top positions in corporate America. A world of clean lines and less friction, in which people ate foods I'd never tasted, like squash, and named their daughters Holly and Jennifer and Cynthia.

But the Catholics were a different story completely. They were all around us in The Bronx when I was growing up, with their priests named Father Xavier and Father Joseph, and their Mother Superiors and their nuns in ancient black habits with their faces peering out of the white cardboard wimples like the whipped cream in a Charlotte Russe, gliding silently along the street like Muslim women, altogether strange and mysterious.

I had known nothing of the historical or doctrinal differences between the branches of Christianity, but somehow, to an ignorant little Jewish boy like myself, compared to the Catholics, the Protestants had not seemed truly Christian (i.e., dangerous). "Protestants" called to mind a man like President Roosevelt and other avuncular figures on the radio and in the magazines, people we never met and therefore could think the best of. But the Catholics!

Most of the Catholic kids didn't go to the public schools but to Sacred Heart instead, behind the spiked iron fence on the church grounds. Sacred Heart! With its evocation of tattoos of a bleeding heart in thorns. Primitive as a dank, inhabited cave. Where strange medieval rituals could take place and no one would think twice about it. Dark events, prior to the age of reason.

The only Catholic kids we had much contact with were those unfortunates who did go to the public schools (which were 95 percent Jewish), the kids who somehow couldn't *afford* to go to Sacred Heart. The kids with broken teeth, from chipped families. The kids who fought with each other during lunch hour, bashing each other's heads open on the sidewalk. Maniacs who came to school with scum bags, and put them on their fingers and moved them up and down while they looked at you and made weird, demented faces whose significance even they themselves could not comprehend.

And then there were the majority of Catholic kids, those who went to Sacred Heart itself! The terrifying Kevins and Seans and Terrys, who would cut their girlfriends' initials in their own arms with pocket knives, all those quiet Marys and pretty Kathleens and those brazen Theresas, and then drink from pints of liquor and do God knows what to the girls in the alleys at night after all the nice priests went home to pray, or whatever it was priests did at night, if they even *had* homes, for none of us knew where the priests actually slept, our main concern about priests being simply that they somehow continue to keep their parishioners in check with talk of hellfire and any other terrifying ideas they could come up with so there wouldn't be any pogroms in the neighborhood for a few years until we could get to the suburbs with the Protestants, where it was safe.

Later that afternoon I found myself sitting at home sipping a beer with just Vic and Hal. A quiet rest stop on the Jersey Turnpike of time before we were to drive over to a huge party on the north side of town.

"How're the girls treating you so far?" Vic said to me.

"Not bad."

"Danny's stuck on a girl he met at work," Hal said.

"Oh, yeah?" Vic said.

"I'm not STUCK on her. I just liked her is all. Anyhow she's practically engaged."

"Look at his face," Hal said. "He's stuck on her. I'm telling you. A Catholic farmgirl with no money and no prospects from Nowhere,

Idaho, and Danny's stuck on her...."

"What's it to you?" I said, sharply. "You're the one who keeps going on about it."

Hal just raised his eyebrows in a kind of despair.

"What's her name?" Vic said.

"Leslie."

"Leslie...." Vic said. He thought for a few seconds. "I know a chic named Leslie. Tall and slim and pretty?"

I nodded yes.

"And she's really wild? Hangs out on the jazz scene. Plays trombone. Always drunk...."

"No, wrong Leslie," I said. "This one's a devout Catholic."

"A devout Catholic," Hal said sadly, nodding his head like an old man.

Chapter Fourteen

I trudged across the parking lot on Monday morning, my head swollen with an angry hangover. The party on the north side had lasted for thirty-two hours. At one point a large mirror behind the bar in the basement had been smashed. As we were leaving, several people said that I had done it. Apparently I had tripped while doing a crazy manic dance with myself and my high ball glass had sailed through the mirror. I couldn't remember any of it very clearly, but the host was a nice guy so I agreed to pay for it.

A huge Brannan Aerocruiser 606 came in low, right over me, landing at Brannan Field. The Air India logos were clearly visible. The big engines felt like they were trying to throb my brain to pieces, but nonetheless I could not help being impressed.

Brannan made the finest, best-designed passenger airplanes in the world. They had made the bombers that struck back at Hitler during the war. And now Brannan was making the missiles that would protect our way of life, still democratic in spite of its faults. And the fact that the Russians respected our ability to hit back kept them from hitting us in the first place, didn't it? That was what everybody said.

Yet, what did all this have to do with the ache at the center of my heart? With my friends and me pickling our brains each night in tanks of alcohol. With Leslie trashing all her vibrant potential in order to try to fit in with the country club set in some little town somewhere.

I spent most of the morning typing up a letter to Mitsubishi, the "General Motors of Japan," informing them we were investigating the possibility of buying transistors from them, asking them to send the latest manuals and specifications. Since our order would ulti-mately be paid for by the Defense Department, I told them them that, as a formality, they needed to send us a letter of credit from their bank.

In the afternoon, I began to type a similar letter to Matsushita. I would then follow with letters to several other large Japanese companies. As there were no word processors, I would have to type each letter individually. That done, I would face my next, and more difficult, task: Inventing a way to fill my time for the next three weeks until the answers to the letters arrived.

But I felt a tapping on my back.

"Leslie!"

She laughed.

"How'd you find me?"

"It wasn't hard. I'm in Personnel, remember? I know all about you." She took on a coy voice, and tried to keep from laughing as she intoned, "Subject is interested in the outdoors, wants to camp out on the Olympic Peninsula, seems like an excellent prospect for permanent residence in the area, strongly recommend hire."

"My job interview!"

"I told you, I know ALL about you," she said, with glee.

"Only my hairdresser knows for sure.... Hey, should you be here? I mean, won't you get into trouble?"

"Nah. I'm a great typist. They can't afford to lose me. The whole company'll close down."

"I believe it!"

"Actually, I'm on lunch break. I'm on a schedule a half hour earlier than you are."

"You DO know all about me."

"I told you so."

"Then listen, tell me, what's wrong with my life?" I joked. "Really, Leslie, what should I do with my life?"

"Find a way to serve humanity," she said, lightly. "Hey, listen, I've really got to run, but I had to stop by and see you. I work just around the corner up there." She pointed. "Just before you get to the airplane hangar."

"The airplane hangar?"

"Haven't you seen it? It's where they rebuild the planes. If you've got time on your hands, you can go down there and hide in an airplane for a while. That's what I do. Read magazines. Hey, I've got to go to lunch. But I didn't want things to stay where I left them the other night. I don't start school til tomorrow, and I was wondering if you'd like to go to dinner tonight? Dutch treat. I could wait for you after work."

Leslie directed me along some unfamiliar streets, toward Lake Washington. When we passed the Rainier Brewery I inhaled deeply, feeling heady from that incorrigibly rich odor of roasting barley malt.

We made our way down to Lake Washington Drive, bought ourselves two cans of ale, and drove over to a small, deserted lakeside park. I removed my jacket and tie, and snatched an old newspaper from the back seat, which we set on the grass and sat on together, down at the end of the land.

The sky was overcast, hinting of rain, but the warmth of the day was holding, keeping off the chill that would lead to precipitation.

We were facing a long sailboat dock. Over to our left a ramp stretched out, perpendicular to the land until it reached four rows of sailboats moored to docks that ran parallel to the shore. All the colors, even the sounds, seemed downy and yielding in the tender dusk of early evening that had enfolded us along with the great Northwest evergreens and the placid water and forgiving sky.

I leaned slightly up against Leslie beside me, and I could feel her setting some of her weight back against me in return. I could feel her body through her thin blouse in the quiet, heavy, air, this lovely girl, leaning on me, breathing.

Neither of us said a word. We looked out together at the large, still lake, its far shores covered with evergreen and pine. The sky and the water were both the same shade of whitened gray and it was difficult to distinguish between them, as if they each had been rubbed with a soft, blue-gray gummy eraser.

We watched the many geese and ducks floating between the edge of the land and the first row of the dock, the geese sometimes emitting little honks like tiny foghorns that sounded over the water. Our breaths gradually lined up and we breathed together, neither wishing to break the spell by speaking, as little wavelets lapped at the grass below our feet.

Then a car pulled up, an old clunker, and two black women emerged with a little girl. They approached the lake over on our left. When they reached the grass that the lake had licked and wet, one woman went to her purse and handed the girl some broken bread pieces in a paper bag.

The geese seemed to recognize the women. They waddled their way up onto the grass, honking off the smaller ducks who tried to follow. The young girl began to throw pieces of the bread to the geese, a little nervously because the geese were larger on the land than they had seemed when floating on the placid lake, almost as tall as herself.

"The Negro neighborhood is not far from here," Leslie said, quietly, in a breathy, intimate voice. "The poor people here don't have all that much, but at least they have the lake." Then she added, "I don't live too far from that neighborhood myself."

I could feel her body move against my side as she spoke.

"It's really beautiful here," I said, almost in a whisper. I was feeling myself melt into the soft loveliness of the scene and of the breathing girl next to me.

Leslie nodded. "I come down here on my bike," she said, also in a kind of whisper, as if we were in a library or a cathedral. "It puts a bottom on my sadness."

We watched the geese again, black with long necks and a single patch of white that ran from their cheeks to down under the jaw. We looked up at the rows of graceful sailboats in washed-out blues and grays and eggshell whites. Their holds were covered with canvases of dark green, or cobalt blue or mustard.

"It's so easy to become abstract here," Leslie said, gently. "That's why I like the cowbells." Her voice seemed to dissipate almost before it reached me in the warm, moist air.

For the first time I noticed that some of the boats bore cowbells, which sounded their mournful tones at unpredictable intervals as the boats rocked easily in their slips.

"Abstract?" I said.

"Yeah. I find it's so easy to get lost in my own postcards. My mental-slide show, you know? And then I start to miss what's really happening. But the cowbells always bring me back. They remind you

that all the boats are in motion. Always moving. Everything bobbing up and down. You see what I mean?"

We sat there watching the boats rock up and down under the
wand of our attention. Leslie had been right. In focusing on the
quiet and powerful serenity of the scene, I hadn't been noticing
the little movements of the lake and the boats upon it.

"They remind you to look closely," Leslie said. "And then you
see there's this incredible dance going on. Nothing's in synch with
anything else, yet overall ... it's all perfect in a way. ..." She nodded reticently toward the gray lake and cobbled sky, and the faded
blue-and-gray and off-white boats. Somewhere in the distance I
could hear a foghorn sound as if through cotton-wool.

The black women and the child drove off, leaving us alone once
more. I noticed now that the boats were bouncing slightly, and
slowly rocking together. You could see the masts moving like paint-
brushes against the motile sky, doing their little minuet along with
the ducks and the geese, who had returned to the water now and
seemed a part of it too, bobbing down there on the always-shifting
water, everything subtly moving together, just slightly, not in uni-
son, but still somehow together, in some kind of overall blue-and-
gray Matisse sway, but only if you watched closely and looked for
the harmony, just as Leslie had said.

And I could hear the sounds as part of it now, too, the duck
quacks and geese honks joining in some crazy, joyous Thelonius
Monk chords, along with the diffuse call of the deep, muffled cowbells and the squashing sounds the choppy waters of the lake made
as they slid under the larger boats that slapped into the water repeatedly, up and down.

Finally, I turned to Leslie and said softly, "You like that, don't
you? ... The idea that it's all a perfect dance somehow."

She nodded shyly, seeming timid in the face of what she had
revealed about her heart. I put my arm around her as the air cooled,
and we sat there as darkness fell around us, I don't know for how
long. We could see the Mercer Island Bridge floating on the dark-
ening water to our right, and the trees turning black on the shore
across from us.

After a long silence, as the last of the day's light left us, we turned toward each other, and she seemed to me sorrowful and open at the same time, like a sad dahlia, and I kissed her and she didn't resist, but turned and moved toward me, and then we sat together on the edge of the dark lake, side-by-side in the rich-leather warmth of the summer evening, and we held each other closely, and I could feel the warmth of her body through her thin clothing, both of us slowly breathing the fresh, tangy, ozone- and pine-scented, green-sea air.

Chapter Fifteen

Although Seattle's small Chinatown was up on the edge of the hill over Pioneer Square, I could smell the raunchy odor of the salt sea as Leslie led me into The Jade Cat, a small restaurant on King Street.

"Ah, Leslie," an older Chinese man said with a smile as he seated us.

"Hi, Herbert. How's Francine?"

"She fine," Herbert said, pleased that Leslie had asked. "She doing much better at the Sanatorium."

"Say hello to her and Doris for me. Tell her we want her back here at the Jade."

"She be glad to hear from you."

He sat us in one of the plain, wooden, high-backed booths. "That's his daughter. Francine. She's got TB."

"TB? I thought that was conquered years ago."

"Some people still get it."

We opened the menus. The prices were incredibly cheap. "Not bad, huh? I bet none of your Eastern girls would eat in a joint like this.... It's clean, though. And the food's good."

"You come here often?"

"Can't afford to. But when I do give myself a treat, this is where I usually go."

When Herbert returned, she ordered almond chicken and I asked for mu-shu pork.

"I didn't know Jewish people could eat pork," she said.

"I don't really follow the religion that closely. Actually though, there is one thing I won't eat. In fact, no Jewish person will eat it, whether they're religious or not."

"What's that?"

"Beef jerky," I said. "No Jew is going to pay good money to chew on someone's saddle."

Her face registered her delight at this kind of banter, which seemed unfamiliar to her. "Seriously," she said. "Do you have any ties to your religion?"

"Not many. After my grandparents died, my parents eased up on it.... "

Leslie seemed surprised. "But do you have any feelings about God? On your own? ... If you don't mind talking about it."

"I don't know, really.... I mean, I guess if I do have any feelings, its anger mostly. I mean, since my aunt Rose died."

I told her about my aunt Rose, my mother's younger sister. How, after her parents died, she seemed to give up. "She had no job, no training for a career or anything. She was supposed to get married, and she didn't. So she wound up nowhere. Guys took advantage of her, I guess. I don't know. She was great, though. She had this terrific sense of humor. I wish you could've met her. You'd have liked her. She did these imitations. Eleanor Roosevelt and all. She was the one I could always talk to. But then *she* died, too. One of those diseases where you just deteriorate...."

I stopped, because I was getting choked up. Herbert brought us two Olys. I drank a full glass of the beer, right down.

"Multiple sclerosis?" Leslie said.

I nodded. "I guess I've been pretty angry about things ever since."

"You know the definition of an atheist?" Leslie said. "A person who doesn't believe in God and hates him."

"A joke! I don't believe it. A German Catholic girl throwing out one-liners."

Leslie glowed with pleasure.

"That's amazing," I continued. "Did you know they were once going to publish a book, 'The History of a Thousand Years of German Humor'?"

"Oh, yeah?" Leslie said.

"Yeah. But they had to give it up. The manuscript was too short."

"Agggh!" She punched me in the arm and I took her hand and squeezed it for a second, and just that quick touch reminded me of when I had held her on the grass at the lake, and my breath dropped away.

I was having a wonderful time. It was so easy to talk to Leslie. I wasn't afraid of sounding out of fashion, or of saying "the wrong thing." "How about you? Do you take your religion seriously?"

"Yeah," Leslie said, looking down, bashfully. "I mean, it's kind of a family thing with me, I guess...."

"A family thing?"

"Well, you see, my mother and father, they're divorced."

"Divorced? I thought Catholics couldn't get divorced."

"Well, no, I mean, they CAN get divorced, but the church, it won't recognize it.... See, my father, he was married.... He was a musician...."

"I thought he was a farmer."

"He also played the accordion in his spare time, and he had a little band, you know, cornball stuff, but it was lovely in a way. In fact, he's the head of the local musicians' union. God, don't talk to me about country musicians. They're always coming up to the house to threaten him with guns. Criminey, all he's asking is for them to pay their dues or the whole union'll go under, but here they come, up to the door with their damn guns...."

She shook her head from side to side. "Anyhow, Pa got divorced from his first wife, and he married my Mom, and they had my brother and then me, eleven months later...."

Her voice trailed off. Herbert came up to the table with the steaming dishes of chicken and pork and rice, and set them in front of us.

"So then ... You're not really legitimate."

"That's right. So far as the Church is concerned, they're living in sin!"

"How do they feel about it?"

"Horrible! But they went to Father Dibble, and he told them the best they could do would be to raise my brother and me as good Catholics and to pray to Christ for forgiveness...."

"So, in a way, your parents' salvation depends on you."

"Well, that's a way of looking at it."

We sipped at our beers and sat quietly as I took all this in.

"That seems a hell of a lot of responsibility to put on you. I mean, after all, you weren't the one who got divorced."

She shrugged, helplesly.

"Hey, we'd better get to this food before it gets cold." I reached for the pancake for the mu-shu pork. I wanted to take Leslie off the spot. She look so troubled and forlorn sitting there across from me. I could feel her pain as if it were my own.

We ate for a while in silence, only speaking to comment on the food, which was delicious.

"You seem to know something about medicine," I said, after a while, just to make conversation on another topic.

She nodded. "I was a pre-med major at the university."

"The University of Washington? Or Washington State?"

"Washington. Washington State's basically the ag college over in Pullman, near where I grew up." She laughed about something, then explained, "Out here they call Washington State 'The Cow College,' and U.W. 'The Udder U!'"

I loved when Leslie told a joke. She shone forth like a sunflower.

"You said you WERE pre-med?"

"I transferred to philosophy."

"Philosophy?"

"Yeah. I was getting good grades, that wasn't the problem, but after a while I saw that I didn't know anything about the real issues. Questions of value and metaphysics."

"Wow! I mean, that's just the way *I* feel. Like I get all these As and fancy degrees, but I don't really KNOW anything!"

She began to nod her head as if she were listening to be-bop. "Yeah, that's exactly it." She was chewing on her food and talking excitedly at the same time, just as I was myself. "I mean, I began to realize that here I was, going to try to keep people alive for as long as I could, and I didn't even have a reason for staying alive myself.

"I didn't know beans about life and death, or anything. I began to think, hey, maybe people are sick because they don't have a reason to live, or a sound philosophy or something. I mean, I liked the idea of helping people, but ... well, I guess I was kind of desperate ... if you know what I mean."

"But ... but that's just the way I feel," I said. "I don't have the slightest idea of what I'm doing, or why, for God's sake! I mean, that's just what bothers ME. Sometimes I feel desperate, too. I mean, I'm making these missiles to defend the United States, but I don't know ANYTHING really about American history. I mean, I love my country just like the next guy, but why am I drunk all the time? And why is it I'm only really happy when I'm totally smashed with Negroes at jazz clubs or dancing to rhythm-and-blues. I don't know the first thing about life...."

"I don't know anything about myself," she said, quietly.

"Exactly," I said, excitedly, my mouth full of chicken and pork and rice. I had never talked to a girl who spoke like this before. She was as lost as I was.

"But now I've transfered," she added, looking at me with almost a guilt in her eyes, as if this were unpleasant to tell me. "To Seattle U."

"Seattle U.?"

She nodded. "It's a Catholic school. I transfered last quarter. I'm taking two classes I need to make up out at the U. this summer. But I'm enrolled in Seattle U."

"But ... why would you do that?" I said, troubled, remembering that I had read somewhere that Bernard Shaw had called a Catholic University a contradiction in terms.

"I want to study theology." She looked down at her food as a way of not looking into my eyes.

"Theology?"

"It's really not so different than philosophy."

"But ... but it sounds so medieval.... I mean, one reason I studied science was to try to get to some METHOD of establishing truth. A method that everyone could AGREE on. I mean EVERYONE has their VALUES...."

"Sure, I know what you mean," she said, in a voice so low I had to strain to hear her. "Yet, when I was studying at the U., there was something missing. For one thing, you know, science will never get to a place that's above values ... I mean, the scientific method itself is the product of a value system."

I could see that she didn't want to argue with me, just as I feared to offend her.

"What is theology, actually?" I said.

"Well, I guess you could say that theology starts out by assuming what philosophy is ultimately trying to prove.... I mean it's only something I'm trying now.... I just got so excited when I read St. Thomas Aquinas. You know what he's done? He took the whole system of Aristotle and he completed it by putting it into a Christian context. I mean, I've only been studying him for a few months but, my Lord, is he brilliant!" She was looking into my eyes again. "Have you ever read him? St. Thomas?"

"All I know about St. Thomas is the great Sonny Rollins jazz tune," I said, as a way of covering my ignorance. She nodded and smiled. She knew the tune. I explained to her about Catholicism in my neighborhood. How it seemed to me to be about obedience to authority and beating up Jewish kids for "killing Christ." "You know what Lenny Bruce said when I saw him? He said, right up there on the stage, 'All right, I confess. I did it. I'm the one. I killed Christ! I killed him just like you said.'"

"You SAW Lenny Bruce? In PERSON?"

"Yeah," I said, in as nonchalant a manner as I could, glad to slide again into my man-about-town role, which I had lost somewhat when I had revealed how little I knew about anything we had been talking about during dinner. I did not repeat Lenny Bruce's comment that people were leaving the churches and going back to God.

As we got ready to leave, Leslie reached across the table and put her hand on my shoulder for a second, and looked into my eyes and said, "I've enjoyed being here with you, Danny. Really, very much."

Her touch was delicate, but it seemed to sear a tattoo of her hand onto my shoulder.

"Well, I've enjoyed being with you, too. I mean, I can really talk to you. In spite of how different our backgrounds are. Somehow you seem so ... familiar."

Chapter Sixteen

Dave's Fifth Avenue was situated in a long, narrow storefront across from where the Space Needle now stands. The Saturday jam sessions were known throughout the Northwest. Musicians would come from as far away as Portland and Vancouver and Spokane to sit in. For some reason, tenor saxes were most prevalent. It was not unusual to have four or five tenors hopping up to solo on a single song.

Checking out the patrons around us, I was happy to find other nervous and alienated people like myself, people with tics and problems and secret dread. Jazz clubs always seemed to me like friendly temples where you could shout and stomp your feet, and act like the goofy, fragile, oafish and beautiful dying mess you really were beneath the white surface of your workaday life.

Hal and Vic and I began to drink draft beer. As usual, the weather outside was perfect, seventy-five degrees and sunny. All of Seattle was heading for the water, family by family, dragging their boats behind their cars and pickups. The city was surrounded by beautiful bodies of water, and to remain indoors at a bar on such a glorious day, nodding one's head to the music of loss, was to make an unambiguous statement in the language of the blues and minor chords, a language saturated with alcohol, the sacrament of our interracial community.

"That guy played with Woody Herman!" Vic shouted. "That guy soloed with Stan Kenton." As the afternoon waned I kept thinking about Leslie. What would she think of all this?

Hal and I were sitting with Lilly now. She was one of a group of Warm Spring's Indians we had met when we heard the great local tenor man Jabo Ward at Pete's Poop Deck, down by the docks, the best jazz club in the city. Vic had gone off to meet Brenner and

Lilly had shown up by herself at some point, and the three of us were allowing the end of the drunken afternoon to slip out of our hands like a pearl necklace.

Many of the musicians had left. There were just three tenors, a trombone and a rhythm section remaining on the stage. They began to play a quiet, slow blues, with the tenors laying down the carpet and the trombone doing a floppy dance upon it, and I turned around to the street as a young woman, obviously drunk, lugging something in her right arm, came bursting in the door. I couldn't see her face as she staggered toward us with the light from the street behind her. For a second I thought she was one more friend of Hal's until she shouted out, "Danny! Am I glad to see YOU!" She lurched in my direction and I looked at her hard, but I could hardly acknowledge what my eyes were registering.

It was Leslie! She was drunk out of her mind, and careening toward me, wearing jeans and a sleeveless white blouse, dropping an ancient decrepit suitcase beside my chair and then soddenly leaning on me and hugging me and kissing my face. I saw Hal smirking as Leslie swung her body into an empty seat. She peered into my eyes as if from the bottom of the sea, and she said, "I'm so glad I CAUGHT you. I couldn't MAKE it. Do you know what I mean? Oh, Danny, I failed MISERABLY. I had to run back here on the bus to get away." Then she quieted for a second, seeming to come a little unstrung, as she added, "I tried, Oh, my Lord, did I EVER try...."

At this point she realized that the two other people at the table were with me. I introduced her to Lilly and Hal. Hal smiled at me, the equivalent of a wink, as he said, "Oh, yes, I've heard about you. The quiet Catholic girl from Idaho," and Leslie laughed wildly and said, "And don't you A-1 forget it," and I thought to myself, "Is this Leslie Schmidt?" for truly, I could not comprehend the reality of what was unfolding in front of me. It was all passing by too quickly, like a series of roller-coaster cars.

But before I could attempt to put this jigsaw puzzle of events together, I heard someone saying loudly and drunkenly, "Leslie!" and I looked up saw that the trombone player had come down off the stage, and was putting his arm around Leslie and giving her a friendly squeeze. She was laughing gaily, and several of the musicians on the stage were laughing too and waving to her, and she was waving back, and the trombone player was saying, "Here, just a slow blues," and he was *handing her the trombone,* and she was saying, "No, no. You know I can't play with you guys, Frank. You're too GOOD." But he was saying, "Come on, Leslie. We're all drunk. We'll play slow. We LIKE to play with you," and the tenor men were shouting, "Yeah, come on, Leslie. We'll follow you."

Leslie looked embarrassed and persisted in her refusal, but the smiles of the band were so friendly, almost like brotherly smiles toward this thin, drunken, awkward, pretty girl, that finally Leslie said, with resignation, "Oh, all right. But you know I don't play anymore," and she took the trombone up onto the stage and the saxes began to play a riff behind her, above the slow-driving lag-along rhythm section, all the musicians still smiling at each other, having a wonderful time, you could see it, and I was wondering, "Can this be happening? Is this a dream?" as Leslie Schmidt, my diffident Catholic scholar from Jefferson, Idaho put the trombone to her lips in front of that group of drunken men on the little stage and she began to play the blues.

She was not a great trombonist, that was not the point. The musicians slowed up even more to adjust to her rusty technique, and she played simply and in some places missed a note, but she was playing with such a naked enthusiasm, with a scope of gesture and concentration worthy of the largest endeavors, like felling a huge tree or riding an unruly elephant, and she looked so damned lovely up there, a little behind the beat, yes, and fighting to keep up, but somehow her struggle seemed fascinating and wonderful. With solely her own gawky, raw, Idaho grace, she was going to keep up with the boys, yes, keep up with them if it killed her, so her slap-happy trombone music was engaged on some deeper level in a life-and-death struggle like all great art, and it drew from the full will of a life, as her notes splatted out with the flare and boom, the syncopated unpredictability of summer fireworks.

And when she finished her solo, and she stood there glowing in her exhaustion and smiling bashfully, everyone who was left in the club started cheering and applauding, and the band flat-out stopped, the musicians all coming over and hugging her as she stood there, exhilarated and loose like a moist flower.

When she came back to the table, I took her in my arms and squeezed her, and she looked up at me and smiled and said, "I TOLD them I couldn't play," and I said, "Couldn't play? Whaddya mean, couldn't play? You were great!" And I meant it. And then she chugged the end of my beer and sat happily in her chair, her chest and shoulders heaving with deep breaths, and the club quieted and the musicians began to fold their gear and after a while I asked Leslie to come out with me for an Italian dinner.

But before we could leave, a large, slim, dark-skinned Negro, maybe six-foot-three, about twenty years old, with torn clothes and very old shoes and what had once been a conked hairdo, now tall and gone to seed, making him look a bit like the young Chuck Berry only with Little Richard's hair, came in the door and Leslie spotted him and ran over and began to hug him, and to chatter excitedly with him, as if it were a reunion of sorts, and then she floated back, leaving him waiting at the door, and said, "Oh my GOD, EVERYONE is here today. Listen, that's VIRGIL. He's the nephew of a friend of mine, my ex-history prof at U.W., Bill Thompson. God, you'll have to MEET Bill. He's a GREAT guy. But listen, his wife threw him out. Virgil, I mean. They're having a GODAWFUL time of it, and, well, LISTEN, can we buy him dinner too? Would that be OK?" and she looked directly into my eyes, her face naked and vulnerable like a pierced ear without an earring, and she said, imploring with a blunt drunken pathos, practically in tears, "Oh, Danny, he's in SO much pain. Don't you see? Virgil's got to be there too. When we sit down at the table, there's GOT to be a place for Virgil," and it was as if she were talking about the Last Supper or something, so I said, "Of course," and as we approached the exit and she smiled toward Virgil and took his arm and led him outside with us, his face softened and a large sweetness suffused it, a vulnerability and shyness which I had not noticed when he had first walked in the door.

Chapter Seventeen

By the time we finished our dinner, the late Seattle sunset had ended. On our way back to the Palace, Leslie and Virgil and I detoured to her apartment. Leslie had sobered up on a couple cups of black coffee, and was troubled by a suspicion that she had not locked her door when she had left.

"Oh, my God!" she said, as I pulled up to the curb. "My windows! They're open! Someone's been in there!" She leaped out before I had fully stopped.

"Wait! Don't!" But she dashed up the stairs. I left the car askew and ran up after her with Virgil. We found her standing in the kitchen, astonished into silence, as an older woman on her hands and knees washed the floor. The furniture had been rearranged, and an older man sat sagging on a stool in the corner, his head hidden in his hands.

Virgil and I stopped short. My jaw dropped. I turned to Leslie but she ignored me. She was staring transfixed at the strange scene, as if it spelled her doom.

Finally, she spoke. "Mom ... Mom ... What are you doing?"

The woman, beginning to gray, with clear framed glasses, dressed in baggy, Sears-type slacks and a blouse, looked up while continuing to scrub the floor, and said, tight-mouthed, "What do you think I'm doing? I can't let you live in this ... this *flophouse*. You're breaking Daddy's heart."

The father, lanky, in farmer's overalls, continued to sit motionless on his stool, his face in his hands. "But ... But ..."

"Look at this place!" Leslie's mother said. "It's a pigsty."

"It's clean. . . ." Leslie looked up for a second. I followed her glance and saw something was missing on the walls.

"My painting!" Leslie exclaimed. "Where's my painting?"

"You mean that thing by Sam Dawn?"

"What have you ..."

"You can't have that junk by Sam Dawn on your wall. Suppose Scott came by...."

"But ... it's *mine*. ... You threw it out, didn't you?" Leslie began to search for it in a manic fashion, looking in unlikely places like the cupboards. "And my Degas," she said. "Where's my Degas? Did you throw that out too?"

"No.... Daddy did."

We all looked toward her father, but he didn't respond. Her mother stood up and shook her head with an almost amused expression. "Sissy.... This is a Catholic household. You can't have a picture of Our Lady on one wall and a naked girl on the other!"

"But ... but ... I love that painting! It's beautiful!"

"Look, Sissy, we're going in a minute. We're staying the night with Aunt Edna in Snoqualmie, but I've got some good news. That's why we drove over here. You left us worried sick about you when you ran off like that...."

"Good news?" Leslie seemed to be in a daze. There was no emotion in her voice.

"I spoke to the Reinhardts. I apologized for you and they're willing to forgive and forget."

"Forgive? ... You spoke to Scott's parents?"

"And to Scott. And listen, Scott, he wants to marry you. It's obvious. And the Reinhardts, they're willing too.... It's incredible.... You can get married at the country club...."

"Marry me?"

"Yes. Don't you see, Sissy? We all want you to come home."

Leslie seemed suddenly beyond grief. Her voice was completely flat. "You spoke to the Reinhardts about me and Scott getting married? ..."

"Well, not in those exact ..."

"... and you threw out my paintings?"

"You don't have to worry about *those*. That's all part of a life you're going to leave behind you...."

Leslie stood there as if the ceiling had fallen down on her.

"I ... I think we'd better leave," I said. Virgil and I moved toward the door.

"No ... no, wait downstairs for me." Her voice was quavering. "I'll be down in a few minutes. Please...."

As I left I glanced at her father, still hunched over on his stool in the corner, his hands covering his eyes.

Vic was not at the house when we returned. Valerie sat on Hal's lap, in an easy chair in the corner of the living room. They were drunk and necking lightly. We settled in the living room as well. I played Dave Brubeck's "Jazz Goes to College," always one of my sentimental favorites, on the hi-fi. Leslie and I sank into the soft white leather couch across the room from the piano, and Virgil nodded out on the rug.

Leslie and I sipped brandy together in the dim light of three candles in Chianti bottles which Hal had set around the room. I slid closer to her on the large sofa. On our left, we could look out the picture window.

"You had a rough time of it back in Idaho," I said. I hadn't spoken to her in the car. She had seemed lost in her own thoughts.

She nodded as if she were about to retell an ancient story. "I try.... Believe me, I try so hard...."

"What happened?"

"Well, I never get along with cops, you know. I mean I try...."

"Cops?" I said, trying to keep my voice from cracking.

"Yeah. I mean, they don't like me and they can smell from a mile away that I don't like them."

"Did something happen with the cops?"

"Well ... It started as a traffic ticket.... I mean, you know me, when I have trouble with the police, I'm usually right, but this time I admit it, I was wrong. I was driving Scott's car, and I was thinking about everything that was going on in my life, and I guess I ran a stop sign, and this station wagon swerved and almost hit me, and this cop car was right there, and they know me, you know, I mean, once you're in the reformatory, you don't stand a CHANCE with the cops in a small town, they'll arrest you for JAYWALKING for God's sake. In fact, they did arrest me for jaywalking, lots of times, me and Sam Dawn, he can hardly cross a street in Jefferson without getting picked up. Criminey...."

"Reformatory?" I said.

She smiled at my apprehension. "Oh, it wasn't really a reformatory, more a Catholic home for wayward girls. My parents put me in it. I guess I was a problem child when I was a teenager. At least my parents thought so. My brother was so PERFECT, you know. Eagle Scout, always winning medals on the rifle team ... and everything I did seemed like it wasn't good enough. I mean, I WAS a little wild," she said flashing a small smile she couldn't hide, "when I ran around with this former sailor when I was fifteen...."

"You ran around with an ex-sailor when you were fifteen?"

"Almost sixteen," she said, sheepishly now. "It was foolish. I know it. His name was Tucson. At least that was what they called him. But my parents wouldn't let me do *any* of the normal things. Football games. Dances. Nothing. I mean, I wasn't one of the 'in' social girls in the school, and my family had NO social standing, and all I wanted to do was make friends and be like everyone else, but because of them I was completely *ostracized*."

"What did you do?"

"I would go to bed at nine at night, like they wanted, and then, later, I'd climb out my window and go party with Tucson and his buddies. Anyhow, I got a rep in the town, and I got arrested by the cops for any little thing I did, and ... well, it all degenerated in a big crying scene with my parents and Father Dibble, and I wound up at the reformatory up on the hill. And, my Lord, what a place THAT was! It was so cold that when we'd wake up at six in the morning, our wash-bowls would have ice on the top!"

I sipped at my brandy. "Were you in there long? In the ... home?"

"Oh, eight months maybe." She saw the look of concern on my face. "Don't worry. I went back to school. In fact, I graduated valedictorian."

"You did?"

She laughed again. "I'm not really all THAT dumb."

"I didn't mean you were dumb. . . ."

"I know," she said, in a kindly voice now. "I was just teasing you. And it wasn't one of those big schools like they have in New York or anything."

We sat there for a few seconds, listening to Paul Desmond as she caught her breath, and I tried and failed to put all this into one coherent package.

She put her arm around me and kissed me gently on the forehead. Then removed her arm and sat back and looked deeply into my eyes. "But why am I suddenly telling you all this?"

"Why didn't you tell it to me right at the start?"

She shrugged. "I was afraid of you up and walking away from me. So I didn't really own up to who I am. And now . . . now I'm spilling it all out. . . . But that's me . . . always putting my worst foot forward." She looked up at the ceiling for a second. Then exhaled deeply. "But I might as well 'fess up. We are what we are. I mean, it does have a way of coming out."

I nodded, wishing she would continue. I was especially interested in the boys of her life—Sam Dawn, and Scott, and now this Tucson—but I hesitated to ask.

"You know I really was getting As in pre-med at the university."

"I know."

She took a swallow of her brandy. "There were some cool girls in that reformatory. One of them, Robbie Parker, rode out to Seattle with me on a freight train when I came back here last spring."

"Freight train?" I felt that our conversation was becoming somewhat like riding a freight train, not knowing which track it might suddenly be switched to, or what hidden cops or dangerous tramps might appear.

"Look," she said, turning toward me as if to confront me directly, "I'm gonna tell you everything. I can't hold back. Then, if you don't like me, you don't."

"But I do like you. In fact, I like you best when you're open and honest."

"Well, I left Seattle about a year ago. When I had that kind of crisis in pre-med school and didn't know what the point of it all was. Hooking people up to machines to keep them alive and everything. And I realized I didn't know beans about anything. And I felt so bad about disappointing my parents, with my brother practically an astronaut and all and me .... Well, what I did was, I went into a convent."

She looked at me, trying to read my response. This was obviously what she had dreaded telling me, and she had been right. I swallowed hard. I had never dated a girl who had been seriously Catholic before, that was a big step for me, but this was another story entirely. A *convent!*

"It was in Kansas. I decided to become a nun. I wanted to become a BRIDE of Christ. That's what a nun is, you know. A nun MARRIES Christ."

"No, I didn't know that," I said, in the forced-ordinary tone one uses when a doctor says, you know, this disease will require me to amputate limbs.

"Yes," she said. "That's what it's about."

"And you gave it up?"

"They threw me out."

"Oh? ... Why?"

She shrugged. "For reading Sartre and Bertrand Russell. I mean, in a way they were right, of course."

"Right? How could that be right?"

"Well, they didn't INVITE me to join. I asked them. And I promised to obey them and learn discipline and all...."

"But surely ... you could at least READ what you wanted to.... I mean this was 1960, for God's sake...."

"No, that was part of the bargain. I was asking to be accepted by them on their terms. To give up my own ego and to serve Christ. But where they were wrong, I think, was after they confronted me about it. I AGREED, damn it, I agreed to give it up, but they still threw me out.... They gave me a damn bus ticket for Idaho, and they just left me there, in the center of KANSAS for God's sake, without even a cent to my name. I mean, suppose I needed to make a phone call or something.... God, it was so awful coming home.... My parents ..."

"But don't you see?" I said heatedly. "They didn't want you to read those books because they were afraid of them. They had to cut you off from all other ways of thinking. What kind of religion is that?"

"Well ... I see what you're saying, of course ... but there's a lot of power there.... I mean, it's so difficult to really get in touch with anything spiritual in any other way in this society.... I wanted to be isolated ... to make a commitment and to learn to sacrifice myself for Christ."

"But why would you want to SACRIFICE yourself?"

"To find something deeper. You see what I mean? I know you understand this ... I mean, I feel I KNOW you, already; I can see it in you.... This society ... It's too shallow.... It's too painful.... Sometimes I can't bear it...."

"Then why not DO something about it?"

"I'd like to. But to really do something, I think you have to come from a deeper place. A place of more than earthly desires, even if they're noble desires. You have to lean against something really solid if you want to push back."

"And that's how you see Christ?"

She nodded yes. "Christ to me is love. The Heart of the Universe. The mercy and forgiveness we need like water, and Christ is the clear stream right in front of us, and we can't see it because of our egos and our desires...."

"And that was an example of love? Kicking you out. Not giving you a second chance. Just deserting you there, a thousand miles away from home, without a cent? Is that what you call love?"

"Of course not," she said, without looking up. "But they were probably right, in a way. I wasn't ready to give up my self." She glanced up and saw I was about to object, so she added quickly, "But that's the world. That's what we have to work with. Our egos and the sad, fallen world. And that's why we need Jesus's love. And mercy. Or else it's just too dry and too sad to even begin...."

She stopped and turned away. She felt she had said too much.

I was confused more than ever now, careening out of control into the land of cops and reformatories and convents.... Some of what Leslie said had made sense in a way, but when I thought of what my parents and my friends like Hotchkiss would think of all this....

But then I pictured Leslie blatting away up there at Dave's, so pretty and intense, and I looked again at the basically shy girl sitting across from me on the couch, knowing she was thinking she had blown it with me for sure, and that she liked me in some way, and I felt my spirit begin to rise. After all, she was just a confused, lonely girl at heart. Just a lost, unformed American like myself, looking for something ... a reason to live...."

When she turned and looked up at me with her sad eyes, I reached toward her and took her in my arms. I held her against my chest and kissed her fragrant hair.

Until the front door opened and Brenner, the girl Vic had been with the first night I met him, stormed into the room, banging the door into the wall protector behind it with a loud CRASH. Vic trailed in after her, with a little devilish smile on his face as she shouted toward me, "This is too much! Really, wait 'til you hear what he did."

Valerie and Hal popped up out of the chair on the other side of the room, surprising me because I had forgotten they were there, present throughout my entire conversation with Leslie, and I realized that I hoped Hal hadn't heard any of what Leslie had said, but I couldn't tell as I looked at him because he was staring at Vic with a certain fascination that he couldn't hide on his slim, long face, and I thought, my God, it's so obvious, Vic is Hal's Cousin Herbie!

Brenner addressed all of us as a jury of her peers: "This time he's gone too far," glancing angrily back at Vic as he stood there wearing an insane grin.

Chapter Eighteen

Virgil, hearing Brenner's complaints, had risen to a sitting position on the floor. He relaxed once he saw Leslie smiling at him.

Vic continued to stand there beaming this strange smile. He had gotten a short crewcut, and both he and Brenner were wearing tan Bermuda shorts and white shirts.

Brenner was furious, but at the same time almost incredulous. "We went to Tacoma. To see my sister. On the way we stopped at a convenience store. There was this horrible fat guy behind the counter."

"A real jerk," Vic interjected. "You should've seen the slob."

Brenner glared at him. "He was a slob. OK. But that gave you no right. . . ." She turned back to us. "So, all right, the guy was a jerk. I admit it. . . ."

"And then he hit this little kid."

"The kid was probably his son, for Chrissakes. The little boy dropped his ice cream on the floor, and his father gave him a smack across the face."

"It was more than a smack," Vic said, not smiling now.

"Well, OK," Brenner admitted, "if it hadn't been for Vic, who stepped in and told him to cut it out, he probably would've beat the hell out of the kid."

"So what's the problem?" Hal said.

"The problem? The problem is, Vic says to me, 'Excuse me for a second, will you?' and he goes out to the car, and then he comes back carrying this . . . this huge pistol. . . ."

"My forty-five," Vic said, now openly smiling.

"And he starts to shoot it off all over the place, yelling 'Dance, mother-fucker!' at the guy who'd been beating his kid. My God, you should have heard that gun! And this big slob behind the counter, he was so terrified...."

"Yeah, too bad...." Vic said.

"Oh, my God," Valerie said.

"He started to do this crazy dance, and Vic was laughing like a madman, I mean it, like he was out of his mind...."

"I only took about four shots in all...."

"We could've been killed, Vic! Don't you see? He could've pulled out a gun from under the counter and shot you. Or you could have accidentally shot *him*.... Don't laugh. I'm serious."

"Guns!" Virgil said wearily to himself, shaking his head from side to side. "Don't ever bring nobody no good," as if guns were a dangerous life form that sought out people to use them, a metal nemesis that would be around forever and had always been around, like an incorrigible member of a family.

Hal seemed almost as shocked as Valerie. He turned to Vic and said, somberly, "Really, man. That's going too far."

Brenner turned back to Vic. "What's happening to you? I mean, really. What's going on in your mind?"

Vic seemed to come down off his manic high. "I don't know," he said. "I must be cracking up or something."

"That's easy to say. But in your voice, there's something else. Something that says, 'I don't care.'"

Vic considered this for a second. "You know, that's right," he said. "I haven't been able to put it so clearly. But that's exactly what's happening. I'm cracking up, and I don't care."

"Hey, come on, man," Hal said, moving forward and punching Vic in the arm. "You're not cracking up. You just need to straighten out your thinking. Maybe take a vacation or something."

"Yeah. Maybe my grandmother can die again," Vic said, changing the mood, laughing again. I turned to see how Brenner would take this, but she seemed ready to let the whole mess go. She moved toward the door, probably to get something from the car. Then Vic noticed Leslie.

"Hey. Leslie!"

She smiled in acknowledgement, but appeared to wish for her anonymity back.

Vic turned to me. "See, I told you. This is the Leslie I knew." He turned back to Leslie. "He thought you were some quiet Catholic scholar or something."

She smiled wanly and shrugged.

"Hey," Vic said, with renewed energy, "let's play some music. Whaddya say?" He grabbed a can of Oly from a six pack Brenner was carrying past him, on her way from the front door to the kitchen. She gave him one more dirty look, but you could see her heart was no longer in it. Vic punched a hole in the can with a gadget from his Swiss Army knife.

"I can play some bass, man," Virgil said, in a deep voice from down on the floor.

"This is Virgil, Vic," Leslie said, and Vic reached down and shook Virgil's hand. Vic seemed to be shifting into his familiar gear. "Yessirreee, Bob!" Vic shouted out, and ran off into his room followed by Hal. They returned toting all the instruments they could carry, and dropped them in a big pile on the floor. Vic picked up a recorder and began to play a little Herbie Mann Latin riff off Gershwin's "Summertime," walking around like the Pied Piper, inviting everyone to join him with his wild, alluring eyes.

Virgil stood up to his full height, stretching slowly. "You got a bass, man?" he said to Hal.

Hal shook his head no, smiled, and indicated the instruments on the floor. Hal picked up a set of bongos and gave Vic a beat.

"No, man, I play bass," Virgil said, in a friendly tone, and he suddenly bent over as if he were wrapping himself around a huge stand-up bass fiddle, and he started to play an imaginary bass, intensely humming out a bass line with a Latin beat through his nose. Leslie was digging him and laughing with this maternal look on her face.

I grabbed a harmonica and blew a rhythm-guitar riff, as Leslie moved over to the piano and began to play the proper chords for "Summertime," with a Latin inflection, and Valerie took two sticks and began to click them together, and Brenner walked in with a tray of cans of beer she had opened in the kitchen, and I called over to Leslie, "You play piano?" and she said, "Anyone can play the chords to 'Summertime!'" and Virgil began to play more frantically, taking a kind of imaginary solo, and Leslie continued to stroke the chords, but she was watching Virgil as if he were one of the seven wonders of the world, and she was laughing like crazy, and it all seemed to be falling into harmony again, just as Leslie had said it would, that evening on Lake Washington. If you looked for the harmony, you could find it, she had said, and it seemed to be there once again.

Later, I brought my forty-fives up from downstairs, a selection of old discs I had lugged across country in the back of my car, and we all danced with each other's girls to Lloyd Price's "Stagger Lee," and The Penguins's "Earth Angel" and "Hey Senorita," and Ritchie Valens's "Donna" and "La Bamba," and "Bye-Bye Love" by the Everly Brothers, and their slow "I Wonder if You Care as Much," which I danced to with Leslie, holding her sweating up against me, not wanting the moment to end.

We bopped to Buddy Holly's "Peggy Sue," and Little Richard's "Long Tall Sally," and we slow-danced to one of my all-time favorites, "In The Still Of The Night" by The Five Satins, a song I was so used to listening to alone that I could hardly believe I was dancing to it with Leslie, just the right girl who would love it as much as I did, and then I played Jackie Wilson's "Lonely Teardrops," and I told Leslie I had seen him do this number in person at the Apollo in Harlem, and her eyes opened wide and she said, "YOU saw Jackie Wilson LIVE at the APOLLO?" and she held me closely and I sang out along with the music as I held her in the drunken night, "Just say you will, say you wi-ill."

The other couples drifted off to their rooms. Virgil was sleeping behind the couch. I played one last record, Robert and Johnnie's, "You're mine, and we belong together, for-or eterrrrnity," and I did the fish with Leslie, both of us smiling at the baroque lines and curves of the exaggerated dance while sliding our bodies against each other, and then we began to kiss, not noticing that the record had ended.

I put my arm around her in the quiet living room, and we walked over to the large picture window that opened out to the bay and the skyline of the city. The sky was filled with sparkling stars, and we could dimly see great white-capped Mount Rainier, the old King, over on the right in the distance.

"God, I love the stars on nights like this," I said. "We didn't have stars like this in The Bronx. It wasn't until I went to college that things were dark enough to see the stars."

Leslie looked up into my eyes with a sleepy, pleased smile. We were both tired and happy. Neither of us wanted the evening to end.

"I love Mt. Rainier," I said.

"Yeah ... Me, too...."

"So majestic and dignified. You know, sometimes when I'm in the house by myself, I stand here and look out, and I think about how it was once spewing out all that fire and lava and everything, and now it's just silent ... silent and grand and indifferent.... Like God...."

Leslie turned to me and looked into my eyes, and she said in a troubled voice, "But ... but God isn't indifferent. God is love."

"Well ... I just ... I mean, sometimes I think of God like the sky. You know what I mean? A vast and shining indifference. Like the stars ... I mean, suppose Mt. Rainier wasn't there. What would it matter really? It isn't 'there' on cloudy days. The city's a lot less beautiful.... But ... I don't know ... Life would continue. And death, too. Our lives would still be eaten away by death, day by day, whether Mt. Rainier was there or not...."

"But don't you see?" Leslie said, with anguish, "The analogy doesn't hold. Love is stronger than death. I mean you, all you guys, you all believe death is some final fall into darkness and nothingness. And somehow you think this belief is scientific or something. But it *isn't* scientific. Don't you see? There isn't one shred of evidence for this belief. It isn't scientific at all. And it makes everyone so miserable." She dropped her shoulders and let out a deep, sad sigh. "Don't you see? It's life that's the fall. And death ... death is just a returning to God's love."

I could feel her frustration and loneliness. I knew she had opened herself dangerously to me in what she thought of as one more futile attempt to reach out to somebody, to share her deepest beliefs with another person, an endeavor which her experience had taught her would just leave her feeling more isolated than before. "I'm sorry," she said quietly. "I'm sorry for going on this way.... You know I hold Mt. Rainier in the greatest respect. I even love, it in a way. But it's just that I don't confuse it with God. I don't think IT loves ME."

I didn't answer her for a second. Then, backing off, wanting to diminish her pain, I said, "Well, I really enjoy talking to you.... And I really appreciate your openness with me.... It's just that, well, this is all very new to me.... I know I've got an awful a lot to learn...."

Leslie looked up, the camaraderie she wanted to feel for me returning to her expression. "Who doesn't?" she said, in that bluesy tone that suffused her voice when her emotions brimmed up to the surface.

I tightened my arm around her again, to bring us back to the physicality of our being there, on the ground, in a real world of time and space and flesh. I kissed her, and then we stood there silently together in the dim light. The air around her smelled of sweat and flowers and a thousand spices. The scent of brandy and smoke wafted off her hair.

We gazed out over the bay toward the city and the black, star-filled summer sky.

"The dark seltzer of the unknown," I said, and she turned to me with that look I loved, that look that said, "Where the hell is this guy coming from?"—but said it with affection.

Chapter Nineteen

Leslie and I walked downstairs to my room. We lay on top of the covers, and kissed under the voodoo sway of that most powerful aphrodisiac, the passion squeezed out of mutual desperation.

Finally I took a chance, and said, "Can you stay with me tonight?" She nodded yes. I hugged her, then began to remove her blouse. She sat up on the edge of the bed, planting her feet on the floor. "But there's one thing I do have to tell you. I won't go all the way."

"Oh ... well ... that's OK. ...."

"I mean ever. I want you to understand that. That's a highway I'm not going down. I'm trying to live a decent life. I can't get all screwed up and into chaos again. ..."

She looked at me dolefully, her shoulders hanging low.

"Don't worry about it," I said. I wasn't as disappointed as she feared I might be. After all, she had said she was going to stay the night, and here she was, in my bed, in the flesh, when just a few hours before I had wondered whether I would ever see her again. And who knew what colorful and rich side streets we might explore without traveling down the main highway which in her mind ended at Chaos Avenue?

In fact, I often was secretly relieved when my relations with women stopped at this point. For a reason I had never shared with anyone, male or female: I was afraid of sex because I was terrified of knocking up a girl I didn't want to marry.

I knew no abortionists. Even if I did find out how to send the girl to Mexico or somewhere to have an abortion, I was afraid that something would happen to the girl, as I would consider myself responsible.

And then there was the terrifying possibility that the girl might want to keep the baby. This was the most frightening scenario of all. Because I could not bear my life as it was. I needed the freedom to learn and to change. But I did not see myself as a guy who could desert the girl, if I knew the baby was mine.

I rose and dropped off my clothes. Watched Leslie slip out of her jeans. When she turned toward me and smiled for a second, looking slim and so pretty as she stood there in the soft light, I noticed that her panties and bra were washed out and frayed, and it struck me with sudden unexpected force that this girl was really poor. I had hitched rides in college, and waited tables, and refereed basketball games to make a few bucks, but this girl could not even afford underwear! She was using literally every cent she had to pay for her education, and something about this touched a tender spot in the Jewish pawnshop of my soul.

"Hey, look what the cat dragged in," Vic said, smiling.

Leslie and I joined Brenner and Hal and Valerie, who were sitting at the table sipping white wine, while Vic, wearing an apron that said "Seattle Rainiers Baseball," was deftly maneuvering two large frying pans. "You're just in time for Monsieur Vic's omelettes de maison." Vic was sipping on a Bloody Mary at the same time as he sliced the omelettes and scooped them onto six large plates, while the toast popped beside him.

"Have you seen Virgil?" Leslie said.

Everyone shook their heads no.

"Where the heck is he?" Leslie said.

"He hasn't been around since I've been up," Hal said.

Leslie scooted inside to look for herself, then left to check the backyard. Vic distributed the plates and began to eat.

"Hey, Leslie," Vic called out from the table, "your eggs are getting cold."

Leslie appeared at the back door. "Gee, I hope he's all right."

"Virgil?" Vic said. "You couldn't hurt that guy with a chainsaw. He's probably making a fortune playing imaginary bass at some rich guy's party over in town."

Leslie smiled, but her face still registered her concern as she joined us. We ate for a while in silence. Then Brenner said, "You know, I hate to be a spoilsport, but I just can't get that scene from yesterday out of my mind." She turned to Vic. "I'm sorry. I know I shouldn't bring it up. But I thought about it all night. I guess I've never seen a gun fired like that . . . I mean, indoors. Near a person and all. . . ."

"That's OK," Vic said. "You'll come to see it wasn't such a big deal." He put down his fork and reached for his Bloody Mary. "There wasn't all that much chance of anyone getting hurt." He turned to Leslie. "Danny says you've become a serious Catholic."

She nodded. "I'm trying."

"Well, listen," he said, setting down his drink and filling his mouth with food, "I just had an idea. What I did yesterday, I mean with that creep and his son, well, maybe that was a Christian thing. You know what I mean?"

"Really," Brenner said with disgust.

"Wait a minute," Vic objected. "I might have been terrifying that big geek, but I was protecting that innocent kid, right?"

"Come off it," Hal said.

"No, I mean it," Vic said.

I studied Vic carefully. It was hard to know whether he was really serious in some way, or just verbally sparring. Suddenly I found myself speaking. "Didn't Ivan Karamazov say that the one thing he couldn't forgive God for was the suffering of innocent children?" I was glad for a chance to use one of the books I had read as my ticket into a serious conversation.

"Forgive God?" Valerie said, as if it were an idea that had never entered her mind. I liked Valerie. She said little, but when she did speak she was always honest and unpretentious.

"Believe me, people don't have to worry about forgiving God," Hal said, refilling his glass with white wine. "It's forgiving the Pope that's tough. I mean, think about World War II. Pope Pius didn't say one word about the Jews."

"Forget the Pope," Vic said, now in his wise-guy voice. "We're talking about something serious: *Me.* Listen, I mean it, Leslie. Couldn't what I did, I mean, getting that bastard back for fucking over that kid, from some weird angle, couldn't that be considered a Christian act?"

Vic's face was taut and shifting. Even when he seemed relatively calm, he reminded me of dry tinder, ready to be ignited by any vagrant spark.

Leslie was wondering whether Vic was kidding her, but finally she said, "Well, I don't mean to contradict you...."

"That's OK," Vic said.

"But to tell you the truth, what you did ... it's exactly the opposite of a Christian act.... But, really, I don't pretend to judge these things."

"But wait," Vic said. "Why isn't it a Christian act?"

"Well ... and again, this isn't meant to put you down or anything, but to my mind it isn't a Christian act because it's based on revenge." Leslie sipped at her white wine. "And revenge ... well, to be honest, it seems to me that's at the heart of what's opposite to Christianity. I mean, wasn't that the whole point of Christ's life and his acts on the cross? To teach us to forgive our enemies...."

"Forgive our enemies!" Hal snapped, his mouth filled with food. "Turn the other cheek and all that horseshit! Look, man, according to that standard, the Jews are more Christian than the Christians. I mean, for God's sakes, who's been killing the Jews for all these years? Christians!"

"Hey, take it easy, Hal," I said.

"Yes," Valerie said, "Danny's right. You're getting too excited...."

"Take it easy?" Hal said. "The easiest thing in the world is to project all your troubles onto the Jews and then to kill them. That's the real sacrifice of Christianity. Not Christ. But the sacrifice of the Jews for two thousand years."

"Or look at the Inquisition," Vic interjected. "It's all the result of the same 'I'm right, you're fucked' philosophy."

I was wary of the direction in which this was heading. Mute questions about Christianity had been present with us all the time when I was with Leslie, even when we were in bed together, like the pea under the Princess's twenty mattresses.

"Yeah, the Christians!" Hal said. "What bullshit! As long as you've got faith, you can do anything in the world and it doesn't matter. You can kill a few Jews, as long as you confess and make your contributions to the Church."

"That's St. Paul," Leslie said, with a hint of sorrow in her voice. "That isn't Christ."

"Then what IS Christ?" Vic said, the kindling suddenly ignited and dangerous. "That's what I want to know. What the hell is Christ, man?" He swallowed the end of his Bloody Mary. "I mean, look at the priests! They go to live with the lepers on some South Seas island or something, but what they don't understand is that Catholicism itself is a leprosy loose in the world. They think they're bringing something valuable to the natives, but the natives are actually CATCHING IT, like a disease."

"And they talk about humility," Hal jumped in. "But it's SCIENTISTS who have the humility, man. We put forth what we think, but as HYPOTHESES, and we try to test them. All the Christians have are CONVICTIONS. They never have to test them. They have 'theology,' " he added sarcastically.

"Maybe theology is a kind of science, too. A science of the Supreme Cause," Leslie said, teasing him.

"Science!" Hal said. "Come off it!"

I wanted to say something myself, perhaps my favorite comment about the means not being able to justify the ends because the means have a tendency to become the ends, but I couldn't figure out a way to make it relevant to what was being said.

"Scientists want to control the world, not live in harmony with it," I said finally, fitfully struggling to be a part of what was happening. I swallowed a large mouthful of food, and then added, to Hal, "You're just saying that Truth is God," and he replied, "No, that's not what I'm saying! What I'm saying has nothing to do with 'God' at all."

"Truth!" Leslie exclaimed. "How can you talk about Truth when science excludes everything that's important in life? Our deepest feelings. Beauty. The love that we know in our hearts to be real and eternal...."

"What?" Hal shot forth. "Science does nothing of the...." but here he began to choke on his food, and Valerie hopped up to pound him on the back. When he stopped coughing, he just sat there, red-faced but OK, trying to catch his breath. Then Brenner said, "Jesus, I just wanted to talk about how Vic flipped out and shot up a goddamn grocery store, and now we've gotten to beauty is truth and all that happy horseshit."

Just at that moment we heard this kind of jazz bass solo from over by the entrance to the kitchen. It was Virgil. He was smiling, bent over and playing his imaginary bass, but this time sober, and in fact performing a kind of good-natured satire on himself. He held out his hand and approached the table, and we all slapped him five, and he laughed and said, "I hope you left some of those eggs for a jazz bass man," and Vic, his face opening into a childlike smile, jumped up and spooned out the remainder of the eggs from the pans onto an empty plate.

We were all glad to see Virgil. He was a sweet guy, and the funny thing about him was that his bass playing was good in a way. He knew and loved jazz—that was clear to anyone who really listened to his crazy solos. He always played interesting notes, and he played them passionately, even if it was only through his nose.

Leslie and I were strolling toward the water on the beach at Alki Avenue down below my house in West Seattle. "Alki"—it seemed the right name for where we were all headed.

I was in the process of taking Leslie home and then to the University of Washington, where I would leave her to study at the library. Virgil had gone with Hal and Vic and their girls to Green Lake for a picnic. Virgil would be staying with us for a few days until his wife Flora's anger cooled and he could return home. Leslie had a great deal of respect for Flora, who was a devotee of Martin Luther King and was studying to be a teacher. She said their problems stemmed from the fact that Flora had found her direction while Virgil was still seeking his.

The Alki Avenue beach was almost deserted. Leslie and I ambled across the sand, up to the low ridge that caught the sticks of driftwood and soggy itinerant logs that had washed up. We looked over toward the city across Elliott Bay.

"That was great," I said. "I mean, that discussion at breakfast."

"Yeah," she said, easily. "I love to talk about ideas."

"Me too, . . . only I wish I had a better background. Somehow, nothing I've studied ever comes up. Semi-conductor theory and Keynesian economics and that sort of thing."

"Oh, you do better in an argument than you think you do. All you East Coast engineer guys. . . ." A kindly crinkle appeared around her eyes. "You can all hold your own, even if you don't really know what you're talking about."

I reached down and picked up a stone and tossed it, happily, into the water.

"How'd you get into electrical engineering anyhow?" she said.

"Oh, I don't know. . . . I had to have a professional goal or my father never would've sent me to college." I picked up a couple more stones. "But I was really afraid to study something like liberal arts, where the rich kids had an advantage. . . . In engineering, you could start equal with everyone else. . . ."

We walked toward the edge of the water.

"I always was interested in television," I said. "I still remember the first time I saw a TV back in the The Bronx. It must've been 1946. They had this little set in the window of a store. I was fascinated by it. I was dying to understand how this amazing thing worked."

"Did they teach you at R.P.I.?"

"Yeah. But now, I'll tell you the truth, I sometimes wonder what all this has to do with the rest of my life. . . ."

"Well . . . At least you know how a TV works. . . . Not everyone can say that. . . ."

We walked up to the edge of the beach, where the sand was damp and covered with millions of little stones. We stood there, not talking. I began to skim the stones, one by one, over the surface of the water. The air smelled ripe with ozone and salt spray, and the sharp tang of fish. The sun shone overhead, but the sky had become somewhat hazy now.

Far out on the bay, several ferries made their way. In the distance you could see the silhouettes of large ships, heading somewhere. Everyone heading somewhere. Toward some destination.

"I had a really good time last night," Leslie said, looking out toward the water.

"I did, too," I said, suddenly wary at her tone and at the way she was not looking at me.

"I'm glad I came back," she said. "I feel bad for my parents, but I don't know. . . ."

101

Her face registered her unease. I watched her carefully. She seemed almost ready to burst into tears for some reason. The sun glinted off of the gold cross on her chest.

"Oh, Danny, I'm so confused."

I took her in my arms and held her for a second. Kissed the top of her hair. When I released her, she stood there, looking mournful, her arms folded across her chest, as if she were about to drop them and reveal the heart of sadness.

"Is something wrong?" I said. "I mean, with us."

"Oh ... It isn't us so much. . . . It's just . . . well . . . I mean, I really want to see you. I LIKE seeing you. But do you KNOW how far behind I'm getting in my schoolwork already?"

"See me? You may not see me?" I moved a step closer to her and looked directly at her. "Are you saying that you won't see me anymore?"

"No. It's just that. . . ." She moved subtly away from me. "I mean, I will see you. . . . I told you, I like to see you. But listen, I've just GOT to get back to work. I've got to avoid seeing you for next weekend. I'm losing it at school. . . ."

I pawed the rocks with my right foot. "Well, I can understand that. We'll just go out the following weekend."

She looked away. Then turned back. "Well, that's just it. That's what I'm afraid to tell you. . . . It's Scott. . . ."

"Scott?"

"My parents told me that when I ran off he was all upset. Not so much about my getting into that hassle with the cops and all but, I mean, I've known him and his family for years. . . ."

"So?"

"So he told my parents to ask me if he could come see me in two weeks. For the weekend."

"And you agreed?"

She nodded. "And we can't go out during the week?"

She looked at me haplessly, then turned away.

We drifted slowly together down the beach. I wasn't sure what to say. It was hard to blame her, really. Everything she said made a kind of sense. But I had such a short time in Seattle. I felt like I was watching my life being eaten away by the slow lye of time.

"Danny?" she said, bringing me back to her. "Just let me get caught up in school. Just give me two weeks to deal with that and with Scott, and I promise you, I'll see you right then, two weeks from tomorrow, that Monday, you can come to my place, and I'll be there."

I shrugged. "I'd still like to see you SOMETIME during the next couple weeks."

"Please, don't PUSH me," she said, with a sudden force that jarred me. "I won't be pushed!" But then she began to look helpless in a way. And guilty.

"I'm so confused," she said. She looked to me to deny this, but I just nodded. Then, with hardly any transition, she spun around toward me, suddenly excited. "Don't you see? You, Scott, the Reinhardts, my parents, school. . . . You're driving me crazy. That's why I can't see you. I need a couple weeks to get my life back together. I'm falling apart."

"I'm driving YOU crazy? What about me? Don't you see? You're driving ME crazy!"

"Just one minute" she countered, her voice rising to a shout. "This is MY LIFE. You come out here for a summer, and fine, it's a lark, and you find this shiska or whatever you call it, and that's all great for you, but what about ME? I'm gonna have to live here. And make a life for myself. After you're gone."

"This is real for me too, you know," I said, sharply, in her face. "I'm a real person. And I have real feelings."

"Don't you understand?" she shouted at me. "Don't you hear what I'm saying? This is my HOME. I have to LIVE here. This is not 'What did you do on your fucking summer vacation?' This is my real LIFE."

Then she screamed "AGGGGGGGGGGH!" wildly, in a fit of shameless frustration, and picked up a handful of rocks and *flung* them all at the surface of the water as if she were breaking a sheet of glass. Her scream startled and even frightened me in a way. It was so strong a response, so out of proportion to what I expected. Just this crazy scream. "AGGGGGGGGGGH!" Suddenly I saw how close to the edge she really was.

"Don't you see?" she shouted fiercely, directly into my face.

"Don't you SEE?" People were looking over at us to see if she was OK. She sounded like someone being murdered.

"I CAN'T STAND IT!" she cried. "My life ... my life is falling apart!" Suddenly she seemed capable of tearing her hair out, or of throwing herself into the bay. She turned away from me, then spun back. "I can't see you anymore for two weeks. Not at work. Not afterwards. I need time to work all this out. I need to go to the library. And to straighten things out with my family. And I have to work, too, you know. On top of everything else. I CAN'T HAVE THIS BULLSHIT TEARING ME APART!" Now all of the people on the beach were staring at her, but she stopped shouting as suddenly as she had started, and she just stood there, in mute anguish.

I was pissed, but I felt a great compassion well up inside me for her at the same time. I could see that she really was afraid she was cracking up, the several Leslies threatening to run off in different directions and pull her apart.

We drifted down the nearly empty beach for a while, each lost in our own thoughts. I don't know for how long. Then Leslie said gloomily, "Maybe we should get going."

As we walked back to the car, she put her arm around me, a sad, contrite expression on her face, and in spite of myself I felt my spirits lift somewhat.

"I wouldn't be going through all this if I didn't like you," she said.

We approached the street. She took her arm down but said, with a sad little grin, "I'm not engaged or anything."

I knew she was trying to apologize. But a part of me didn't care at that moment. When she had screamed at me, in the way my father would shout at me before he beat me, I had withdrawn into the bunker under the house of my vulnerable self. The one with the emergency rations and the first-aid, kits and the rifles to keep out the neighbors if they charged.

I drove her to her house on Broadway. Neither of us spoke until we got to the Negro neighborhood around Jackson Street.

"This is where Bill Thompson lives. Virgil's uncle. He's a great guy." She reached into her purse. Took out a pack of Salems. "I'd like to take you to meet him sometime."

I nodded unenthusiastically.

"You smoke?" I said.

"Once in a while."

"Can you keep it down like that?"

She nodded yes.

I waited in her kitchen while she changed her clothes. Then I drove her out to the U-District.

As we rode along, my customary sympathy for her began to return. That was one source of our closeness. I could feel her pain so easily.

I had a good sense of direction, and I was getting to know my way around the city. I took a slightly longer route than I had to. We passed a small movie theater, The Guild, on North Forty-Fifth Street, with a little cafe-like appendage attached.

"I worked here when I first came to Seattle," she said, suing for peace. She had a hangdog look about her. "I was a beatnik waitress."

Her lips parted in the hint of a tentative smile, and I had to join her, she looked so sad sitting there, trying not to drive me away. And of course it didn't reduce her attractiveness to me, that she had been a "beatnik waitress," with the sex and the poetry, the tight black turtlenecks and the dark stockings those words brought to mind.

"You can leave me here," she said at University Way.

I pulled up to the curb. Not wanting to drive off at that moment, I said, "Maybe we can go to this Bill Thompson's house sometime. If he's a history professor, he might be able to answer a few questions for me."

"We'll have to go right after we begin seeing each other again," she said quickly. "He's leaving in a few weeks. Going to Africa. For good."

"Is he the guy you went with when I first met you?"

She looked puzzled.

"When you went off into the country for a farewell day with an old friend."

Then her face lit with recognition. "Oh, no. That wasn't Bill. That was the Swami."

"The Swami?"

"Yeah. Swami Rama Vishnu. He's an old friend of mine. I met him when I first came to Seattle. In fact, Vic knows him."

"Oh yeah? Is this guy a real Swami?"

"Absolutely. He was one of the first Westerners ever ordained as a true Hindu monk. He's a genius."

"Oh?...."

"He speaks twenty-three languages. He's from London. He went to Oxford and did graduate work in Heidelberg. He can speak four Indian languages—Bengali, Tamil, Hindi and ... and Urdu, I think. And he speaks them without an accent. The Indians think he's a native when he goes over there."

She reached for the door handle, but I added quickly, "Is that where he was going? Was he on his way to India?"

She nodded. "But he was going to Hollywood first."

"Hollywood? What's a Swami who's celibate and all doing hanging out in Hollywood?" I said, half kidding.

"Oh, he's not celibate. He's into something called Tantra. You ever hear of that? It's a kind of seeking of God through highly ritualized sexual ceremonies between a man and a woman."

I found myself unable to speak. I fidgeted with the rear-view mirror. Then I said, "And that's why he went to Hollywood?"

"No. He went to see a friend."

"A girlfriend?"

"Not really. He was just stopping off to see Marilyn Monroe. They're old pals. From when he first came to the U.S. Before he showed up here in Seattle. They were...."

"He went to see Marilyn Monroe?"

She nodded yes, smiling, as if it were just one more colorful thread that fitted perfectly into the weave of her crazy life.

As I drove home, I felt a cool fury settling over me. What was all this bullshit about the problems of chaos in her life and of not "going all the way"? First there was this Houston or Phoenix or Salt Lake City or whatever the hell the ex-sailor's name was, and then this Scott, the Idaho Jimmy Stewart, who had also known her before she had become a virgin and thus was probably still claiming squatter's rights or something, having arrived at the territory before the law, and then there were all the jazz musicians and beat guys she had been running around with before she went into the convent, and now I had learned that she had also most likely been performing weird sex rituals with some crazy Swami.

The cold bitter Saturn zone of my personality came around on the revolving stage. True, there was something not inconsiderable, something world-class, about dating a girl with a Swami for my rival, a Swami who spoke twenty-three languages and was probably banging Marilyn Monroe right this very minute in Hollywood as part of some primitive pagan ritual I could hardly imagine, with slow insistent drums and phials of colored elixirs, and ancient methods of keeping yourself from coming for days.

But this edge of fascination wasn't enough. This was not what I had really wanted. I felt as though I were being tossed back and forth by the bait-and-switch tactics of the fates.

As I drove across the Spokane Street Bridge, low-floating clouds were gathering overhead like a Rorschach Test I did not want to interpret.

Chapter Twenty

That evening, Vic, Hal and I were seated at the kitchen table eating chocolate ice-cream. Virgil was talking to Flora on the phone in the hall.

I had spent the early evening reading a book on mysticism. Before I met Leslie, I had often worried about death and nothingness, which I saw looming up ahead of me like a dark, unavoidable tollbooth, yet mystical or theological concerns had seemed merely like an unwanted inheritance my grandparents had carried over with them from the old country along with storefront synagogues and men with beards and curled sideburns.

I told my friends about my tribulations with Leslie. "So what's the problem?" Vic said. "She's a smart, passionate girl. Just have fun with her when she's available, and when she's not, have a ball with someone else."

"But he's saying he LIKES her," Hal said. I couldn't help but notice a sour tone in his voice that surprised me.

"Yeah," I said, somewhat reluctantly. "I mean, I like her."

"So much the better," Vic said. "She's a nice chick. But she's got a life to live after you go. I mean, let's face it, you're not exactly going to bring this wild *shiksa* home to meet Mom and Dad." He walked out of the room.

"We need to have a talk," Hal said somberly. The way he said it made me wary. I had the feeling this was going to be one of those talks in which someone feels he has to "hurt you for your own good."

Hal rose and fetched a bottle of Christian Brothers brandy out of the cupboard. He grabbed two glasses and poured brandy into each. He sat across from me at the table and drank his shot in one gulp. He poured himself a large refill. I did the same.

"What's on your mind?" I said, watching him carefully.

"Well, to be honest, it's you. You and Leslie. I'm a little older than you...."

"Is this going to be fatherly advice?" I said, impatiently.

"No, it's not going to be 'fatherly advice,'" he snapped back. "Just some words to the wise from someone who's a little more experienced than you."

My chin stuck out stubbornly. "Is there something bothering you, man?"

"If you want to know the truth, yeah, there's something bothering me. And it concerns you. You and Leslie."

"Is that your business?" I found myself getting sad rather than angry. I always became sad in situations like this, when I knew the world was going to be a little uglier and more stupid in a little while.

"Yes, it's my business. Because I'm your friend. And I don't like to see you throwing your life away."

"Throwing my life away. With Leslie. I ... man, I've dated the girl about two times."

"But you're serious about her. I can see it. Already. And if it isn't her, it's going to be someone else like her. I know you. You're not kidding around."

"I can't believe this. I see the girl two times...."

"I know what you're going to say, Danny, that it's nothing. But you're fooling yourself. That's why Vic was telling you to just a have a good time with her. He sees it too. You don't know enough about life yet. This isn't the kind of girl for a guy like you to get involved with. I mean, sure, get your rocks off...."

"Wait a minute. What're you saying? Is this because she's not Jewish? I see you with Lilly and other girls...."

"Yeah, sure. I have a good time. Why not? And so should you. But you don't seem to know the difference between girls you have a good time with and girls you get serious with."

"I dated her *two* times!" Something pugnacious was arising in me. "But so what? Suppose I do like her?"

"So what? Didn't you hear what Vic said? Is this the kind of girl you bring home to your parents? They'd have a shit fit!"

"Just because she's a *shiksa*?"

"No. Not just because of that. But even that. Don't you care about our people? Just because you, Hymie Schmuck, were lucky enough to be born over here in the States, is that a reason to let go of everything our people have sacrificed for over two thousand years? Just because you want to get your rocks off with some wild *shiksa* who isn't even in your own league in any regard except that she has a nice ass."

I gave him an angry look and he backed off a bit.

"OK, OK, I won't go on about her looks, you're right, but think about what you're doing. Don't you see, man? If you were to marry a *shiksa*—any *shiksa,* not just Leslie—then you're giving in to Hitler."

"Oh, come off...."

"No. No, I mean it. You're a member of the first generation after the Holocaust, and what do you do? You turn to the first *shiksa* who comes along, and to a German one to boot. Don't you see, man? You'll kill your parents."

"That's bullshit. You don't even know my parents. It's *your* values that I'm threatening. Your little cozy adjustment to your missiles, and your plans to marry a rich girl and have two-and-a-half Jewish kids and...."

"You don't even care *what* happens to the Jews, do you? You wouldn't have cared if Hitler killed every Jewish kid in the world, as long as you could have your booze and your *shiksa* ...."

"Wait a minute! What is this bullshit? I don't see you going to temple every day...."

"I belong to the temple. The same temple as Valerie's family. And I'm going to marry Valerie in a year or two. Believe me...."

"Yeah. Temple. You probably go twice a year on the high holidays like all the other ..."

"So what? So what if I only go twice a year? I give my money, and I keep the tradition alive so the millions didn't die in vain."

"Die in vain!" I said, mocking him.

"And when I have a son, he's going to take Hebrew lessons and be *Bar Mitzvahed,* and he'll do the same to his son...."

"Forever and 'ere and aye," I said sarcastically

"That's right. And I'm not ashamed of it."

"Is that why you called me on the carpet here, Dad? You're afraid I'm gonna marry a *shiksa?*"

"No. If you want to know the truth, it's more than that. It's Leslie herself."

"Now wait a minute. . . ."

"No, I'm going to have my say here. You're my friend and I'm going to say what I feel, and then if you don't like it, we can shake hands and forget it, but Danny, . . . I have to say this. I heard what you and Leslie were talking about last night."

"Last night?"

"In the living room. When I was on the chair with Valerie. I couldn't help but hear it." He looked me in the eyes, and his voice turned imploring. "Danny, please, don't you see? I'm worried about you. This girl, Leslie, she's a nice girl in certain ways, and she's not a dope. . . ."

"But . . ."

"But you've got to let her go."

"What're you talking about?"

"I'm not even thinking about what can happen down the road. I'm talking now. Danny, don't you see? Your whole career is on the line. Everything you've worked for for all these years. She works at Brannan. She's unstable. Didn't you hear her? Reformatories, convents, freight trains, crazy sailors, playing trombone drunk in bars, sleeping with everyone since she was fourteen. . . . Danny, at work, they're watching you. They've chosen you, they spent money on you to bring you out here, they have big things in mind for you, but you can't be with this kind of girl, especially if she *works* for them. They'll find out. . . ."

"Well, they can kiss my ass if they think they can tell me who to date. . . ."

"Danny, wake up. If you're going to get anywhere in this company, you're going to have to have the highest security clearance. Top Secret. Danny, they know her. She's unstable. They won't trust you. Your whole career . . . that's what I'm trying to tell you. . . ."

"No. That's what you think you're trying to tell me. But in reality, you're just jealous because I just show up here and this pretty girl likes me. . . ."

"Jealous. You think I'm jealous. Don't I have pretty girls? And don't I have my own girl, too, Valerie?"

"I like Valerie. But you treat her like shit...."

"No I don't. I'm just sowing my wild oats before I get married and settle down. Do you think I don't know what I have there? Danny, Valerie descends from two of the oldest and wealthiest Jewish families in Seattle. They're in the highest circles of society. Scoop Jackson, the senator, he practically lives at their house when he's in town.... I've met him already...."

"So that's your beef. That Leslie is poor and her family has no influence. That's how you evaluate people, on their ..."

"Danny, I'll be blunt. You find Leslie fascinating because you've always been a good kid and she hasn't. She's been a kind of delinquent, and she's done all the *goyish* things you only dream of, and she has some street knowledge and a smattering of philosophy that impresses you because you've been studying practical subjects for ten years. But I want to tell you something about Leslie."

He threw down a large shot of the brandy, then continued.

"Listen, Danny, Leslie is not like you. In fact, she's the exact *opposite* of you. That's what attracts you to her. You're on the verge of a great success. A success you've worked for since the day you began kindergarten, a success that your parents have struggled to set up for you, paying for your tuition and all, and you deserve it. You worked your ass off and you sacrificed your sex life and a lot of other things so you could get this far, and now you've made it. Meanwhile, Leslie, she's sacrificed nothing. While you were indoors studying for your regent's exams in high school on all those nice days in June, she was out in the fields with guys...."

"That's not ..."

"No, let me finish. You've succeeded at everything you've ever done. You got through R.P.I...."

"Yeah, by drinking...."

"Yes, you would drink, but after you'd studied for two or three straight all-nighters, then you'd get drunk out of your mind because of the pressure. We all did. But what was Leslie doing all this time?"

"She was looking for truth...."

"She was failing again and again. At university, at the convent, in high school when they put her in the reformatory—she's never completed one single thing because she's always given in to her worst instincts, and that's why you're being groomed to run this world-class corporation and she's an entry-level secretary. She's gotten nowhere in her life, and now she's beginning to see the mess she's in, so she latches on to a guy like you because *she* never had the strength of character to make something of herself, and that's why for all her talk of Jesus and love, *you're* the one who can give something to the world...."

"Her misspent youth," I said sarcastically. "You know, you're missing the whole point of this girl."

"Everything I said was true."

"But you've missed the whole point."

"Lay off him, Hal," Vic said easily from over by the sink where he was reaching for a glass. I hadn't seen him come back into the room.

He joined us at the table and poured himself a brandy.

"Lay off him?" Hal said. "Man, Danny's driving *himself* nuts! I can't believe this guy. He wants to be a beatnik. A poor little hobo who rides the rails like in Jack Kerouac. And at the same time he wants to be first in the Wharton School and run a major corporation."

"Come off it." I said.

"No, it's true, Danny." Hal turned to Vic as if he were the judge. "I mean, look at this guy. Do you know how much ambition it takes to get the highest-paid summer job in the country? He's always looking down on everyone, but at bottom he's just like the rest of us. He wants what we all want. Some bucks, some ass, a nice car, some wild times, and then a chance to settle down and raise a family, but to hear him talk ..."

"I'll tell you what I want," I said. "I want to live a life that isn't meaningless in the face of death."

"You think my life is meaningless?" Hal snapped back. "You think a normal guy who works hard and supports a family and does a job that serves his country, you think that's meaningless?"

"If it all leads to nothingness and darkness forever, it is."

"Seize the day," Vic chimed in. "That's what I've been trying to tell you guys. Seize the day, man."

"I can't believe this guy," Hal said, appealing to Vic again. "He's torturing himself with all these ideals and shit, and it has nothing to do with his real life." He turned to me. "You know what you want?"

"No, tell me, father," I said.

"You want to be a saint and go off by yourself somewhere and meditate and talk to the flowers, as long as they film it for Hollywood and you get big bucks and get to go on TV and talk about it."

Vic laughed.

"It's true!" Hal continued. "Danny here, he wants to be rich and he wants to be poor. He wants to be powerful and he wants to be powerless. I know him. I've been talking to him, and I can't believe the shit he's been saying." He turned to me. "I'm only trying to enlighten you a little."

"Yeah, sure."

Hal turned back to Vic. "He wants to be Jewish and he wants to be Christian. And maybe even a Zen Buddhist to boot. He wants to be pure and celibate, and he wants to be an ass man with a blonde on his arm. You know what he wants to be?" he concluded. "You know what he really wants to be?"

"What?" Vic said, amused.

"Mahatma Gandhi in a Cadillac!" Hal said.

Hal and Vic burst out laughing.

"I mean it," Hal said. "That's what he wants to be. Mahatma Gandhi in a fucking Cadillac! And believe me, he's gonna drive himself nuts in air-conditioned comfort."

I couldn't help but laugh in spite of myself, like a man in a chair that is collapsing under him.

We all quieted and sipped at our brandies in silence.

And then Vic said, just as simply as if he were telling us it had begun to rain outside, "Listen, I've been meaning to tell you guys something. . . . I joined the Marines this week."

"*What?*" Hal said. We both looked toward Vic, waiting for him to tell us it was all a joke.

But somehow I knew it wasn't a joke. I knew it as soon as he said it.

Vic just sat there with this bad-boy, sphinx-like smile. "You're kidding," Hal said, but you could see that a part of him knew Vic wasn't kidding—the part that was wild and irrational and that he had to suppress each day to fit in at the office.

"I signed the papers last Wednesday. It's too late to do anything now."

Hal was shaking his head as if something had fallen on it. "You . . . joined the Marines? . . . ."

Vic nodded. "I gave my notice to Fred at work on Friday. Thirty days."

Vic drank his brandy and poured himself another one. Hal sat there stunned. He was clenching his teeth and trying to hide his feelings. Vic was his closest friend. I was shocked as well. I had looked to Vic and Hal as examples of what my future life might be when I graduated from Wharton. But here was Vic, throwing it all away, just to follow in what I saw as the footsteps of my Cousin Herbie.

"Thirty days?" I said.

"Yeah," he said. "Hey, Danny, maybe I could sell my car and drive back with you. I'll have a couple weeks before I go to Parris Island."

"Yeah, sure, Vic. We'll have a great time," I said, without enthusiasm.

Hal pulled a pack of Chesterfields out of his chinos. He was trying to be cool, but it took him three tries to strike the match. "What're you talking about?" he said. "You can't just give up everything like that."

"I couldn't stand it at work any more, man. That place . . . it eats away your soul."

"What're you talking about?" Hal said.

"Are you kidding me? They suck the life out of you, man, day by day."

Hal's face was flushed with excitement, like a person in immediate danger. "What the hell are you saying? That you want to run off and become some kind of hero or something? Sacrifice your life for your country or some crap like that. Well, I'll tell you something, man. The *real* heroes are the people who *go* to work every day."

"Yeah, sure," Vic said.

Hal looked right at him. "The real sacrifice is when you become a parent and put up with all the shit you have to do to feed your kids and send them to college."

"Come off it, man.... Do you hear what you're saying?"

"No, I won't come off it. Don't you understand? Without our technical knowhow, your Marines aren't shit! This isn't the charge up San Juan Hill anymore!"

"I'm not into all that sacrifice shit, man. You can save that for Leslie. You know who has all the power in the world? The guy with the gun. That's who. That sacrifice bullshit of Leslie's, that's fucking slave morality, man."

"But wait a minute!" I said. "This is a different time now. Haven't you heard of Martin Luther King? He's a *great* man! Can't you see that? And John Kennedy. There's a new generation taking over, man. We're gonna put all that military bullshit beyond us. Kennedy went to Harvard, man. His whole cabinet, they're all professors and Ivy Leaguers." I downed a shot of brandy. "Kennedy's a young guy like us. He's not gonna play by the old rules and oppress people, and get us into war. These are all educated guys. He's got McGeorge Bundy, the goddamn Dean of fucking Harvard University, as his National Security Advisor, for Chrissakes!"

"I don't believe this," Hal said, ignoring me and turning to Vic. "I just don't fucking believe what I'm hearing you saying."

"I just don't want to be POWERLESS," Vic shouted. "I can't stand it anymore." He cooled a bit and we all sat there in silence. Then Vic looked up at me and he added, oddly, in a somewhat weary tone, "You want peace, man. I'll get you peace. Strength is the way to peace."

Then suddenly another voice joined in. From over by the door. It was Virgil. In the heat of the argument we hadn't noticed him. I wondered how long he had been standing there. He said, slowly, "Man, there ain't no 'way' to peace. Peace IS the way."

"Another country heard from," Vic said, but he didn't pursue this. I looked at Virgil carefully, wondering what he would say next, I was so surprised and moved by his comment, but he just said, "Mind if I have some of this here ice-cream?" and he grabbed a spoon and a small bowl from beside the sink and began to help himself as if nothing had happened.

And I found myself suddenly thinking of Leslie. How she had said there had to be a place for Virgil at the table. She had seen something in Virgil that I had missed up until now. He had hidden it behind his imaginary bass playing and his satires on himself.

I thought of how, during the argument, Vic had referred to Leslie with a certain respect, even when disagreeing with her. How she had deepened the tenor of the discussion with her wild and passionate notions of service and sacrifice and love.

We sat there in the gold-tinted kitchen light, trying to figure out where we all went from here. Finally Virgil spoke. "I didn't make that up, man. What I said before. About peace being the way. That was from A.J. Muste. He's one of them peace guys. My uncle Bill told me about him. The one Leslie knows." He poured himself a little brandy. "That was before my uncle got into all this militant sassafras."

Vic popped up out of his seat. "Listen," he said, "let's go party all night at Fong's After Hours in Chinatown! Come on. Whaddya say!"

We all excused ourselves.

"Well, man, I'm gonna boogie!" Vic turned to Hal and with his knuckle gave him an affectionate "noogie" on his head. Hal couldn't help but smile, and as Vic left he said, "Listen, man, if I don't make it to work tomorrow, tell Fred I went to Ed Sullivan's wedding. Tell him that Ed Sullivan's my grandfather."

Chapter Twenty-One

Hal made an excuse for Vic at work, but it didn't matter. Vic was finished with normal nine-to-five life, and his boss knew it as well as the rest of us. At first Hal seemed to fall victim to a kind of gear-slippage, going nowhere, but then he took a few days off and joined Vic in a series of drunken rampages and crazy parties, the beginning of a month-long goodbye festival to consecrate their "divorce." The merry-go-round of our lives had slipped its governor and we all began to spin out of control.

There was little for me to do at work. I spent hours A.W.O.L., hiding in the airplanes. Sleeping or reading about mysticism. Time-study guys had now appeared and were walking up and down the aisles of our office sampling our behavior, but I knew a summer hire like me didn't figure into their calculations.

The atmosphere at work seemed different since Vic had resigned and Hal had been sucked into the maelstrom in his wake. It felt as if we were breathing the same air again and again, as if, each time it was recirculated, the compressor squeezed a little more of the life out of it.

Finally, I received my first reply from Japan. From Mitsubishi. They had made the Japanese Zeros in World War II.

Dear Mr. Daniel Schwartz:
This is in refer to your letter of June X. We stand delight to do business with you if you so see fit. Here is our catalogue for you to read. We think you see that our products are now most highest quality.

In regard to your question about bank credit. No worry about this, please. We know Brannan here in Japan. They are estimable and long establish company. We be glad to do business with you anytime. No need you to get

bank credit. We know Brannan have good credit. Just order what you wish
and we ship it to you as regular order.

Your interest we appreciate. Any questions, you just write and we answer
soon.

Sincerely,

X

This was the sum of what my weeks of work had come to. I had to
write back to Mitsubishi and tell them it was *their* credit we were
concerned about. Not *ours*. By the time I received their answer it
would almost be time for me to leave for school.

Besides, the missiles were not mass-produced. How could the
few dollars we might save come near to compensating us for the
cost of becoming entangled in the red tape surrounding the purchase? But I had known this from the start. Even my boss, Mr. Stilson, seemed to know that my investigation was on the fast track
toward the dead projects graveyard which no human being had
ever seen. One day, he added me to the team studying whether
Brannan should continue to keep its own steelyard or use local steel
wholesalers.

It was a classic business-school problem, comparing gains and
losses in terms of relative time, cost and dependability of supply.
Yet it was clear to me that I had been assigned to the team merely
to keep me occupied until I finally disappeared: I'll never forget
what's his name.

Still, it was better to visit steelyards than to sit at my desk and
watch the time study guys come by and check to see whether I was
dreaming.

Often I was dreaming. About my future. Soon I would have to
choose the direction of the rest of my life. I could not shake the
queasy feeling that I was approaching the greasy slope that led to
normality and death. But if I slipped off the track of major ambition, what other path was available to me?

So I kept returning to the continuous party that had informed
our lives since Vic had joined the Marines and set everything over
the edge.

Chapter Twenty-two

On the following Monday, my two-week banishment from the life of Leslie Schmidt officially ended, but our softball team, the Sons of Brannan, had a game that night, so I decided to forgo seeing Leslie until the next day at work. I wasn't even sure she'd want to see me after her weekend with Scott, "the Perry Mason of the Plains."

The next morning, Harriet, a nervous young woman who worked alongside Leslie in Personnel, scooted up to my desk. "It's Leslie! Come quick. She's been out all night at a Negro after-hours club. She says you stood her up. She's DRUNK! At WORK!"

I sensed a stirring in the usual fluorescent placidity around me. Leslie, in her white dress, was tottering precariously on her high heels down the long aisle.

"Oh, dear," she said, drunkenly, as she met my eyes and somehow her center of gravity shifted outside of the sweep of her slim supporting legs, and she began to teeter and then, unbelievably, she fell, with what sounded to me like a tremendous CRASH!, her whole body coming down like a tall building being demolished with dynamite.

And there she was, lying on the floor. At work!

"Oh, God! She'll be fired, for sure," Harriet said. We ran to Leslie's aid. Two of the Purchasing people reached her first, but she swatted their arms out of the way and lurched to her feet by herself.

"I can walk," she said defiantly. "I danced the whole damn night after I got stood up by this exec of the future here, so I know I can goddamn WALK on my own."

"Leslie, take it easy." I took her arm to steady her.

Everyone was watching in amazement and delight. Nothing like this had ever happened in the Purchasing Department. Leslie was acting out everyone's dream and, best of all, *she* would be punished for it, not them.

"I waited till midnight for you to show up." She slurred her words, beginning to totter again.

"Do something!" Harriet said. "She's going to get fired."

"Less go make out in the freight elevator," Leslie shouted to me. Grabbing her arm, I began to half-guide, half-drag her back down the aisle.

"I waited for you, but you stood me up," she said, plaintively now.

I whisked her along in a kind of tangled, syncopated manner until I was able to set her down in a first-class seat in a Pakistani Air 606. I sat down next to her. Her eyes were large and electric, but it was hard to tell if anyone was home.

"Oh, you stood me up," she wailed. "I bought a cake for you and I had all this homemade wine in my bedroom, and you stood me up!"

Suddenly, she seemed about to weep.

"I didn't 'stand you up.' I had a softball game. You haven't spoken to me in fifteen days. I didn't even know if you WANTED to see me anymore. I was going to come over to see you today. At your desk."

"You were coming to see me?"

"Sure. I would've come by. We found this great R-and-B bar I want to take you to."

She hesitated for a second and then she leaped across onto my lap and said, "Oh, Danny!" twining her arms around my neck, and she began to cry, the tension in her body collapsing. She hung onto me as if she were drowning, laying big, wet kisses all over my face as she said, with the skidding intonation of the drunk, "Oh, DANNY. I'm SO glad. I'm SO HAPPY. I thought I LOST you." She kissed me again. "I thought I LOST you!" and then we toppled off the seat together onto the floor and we began to neck passionately, rolling over on top of each other on the burgundy-colored rug in the empty Pakistani airliner.

Somehow, with the help of a dexxy she got from Hal at lunch, Leslie made it through the day. In fact, by late afternoon, she was in high spirits indeed. Hal had invited us to a party on a boat on Puget Sound. Leslie and I decided to drive over to pick up Flora and Virgil. I flipped on the AM radio in the car.

"Ugh. Paul Anka," I said.

Leslie nodded in agreement. I left the radio alone. We had both acceded to an unspoken pact not to sift through the remains of the past two weeks.

"Hal told me about Vic," she said. "Is Hal OK?"

I shrugged.

"You know, Hal can be a pain, but I don't really mind him," she said. "You should've seen him today at lunch. He was going on and on, trying to convince me that scientists have feelings, too. Something about an engineer who invented a portable heart pacemaker. . . ." She opened up into a warm grin as she thought of it.

I turned the car toward the Negro section. "Virgil's doing much better," I said. "He got this job his uncle turned him onto, in a record store. And we smoothed things out with Flora. I spent a couple evenings with them. Flora's great. She works like a demon."

"Yeah. Full-time at the U. and a job, too."

"She'll be a great teacher. She only wanted Virgil to get some work."

"Did you meet his uncle Bill?"

I shook my head no.

"He's moving in a week or so. How about if I could get him to see us Saturday afternoon?"

"Sure." The radio played "Let's Twist Again, Like We Did Last Summer."

"Chubby Checkers," Leslie said, this time without the derision she had expressed toward the earlier records. She wagged her head just slightly from side to side, in time with the happy music.

I nodded. "He's from Philly." I was feeling good again, better than I had in some time.

We drove to the boat with Virgil and Flora. Flora was a round-faced, pretty black woman, maybe twenty-three, with large bones and intelligent, sympathetic eyes. A history major, she had just written a paper on the Kennedy administration. Her thesis was that someday Kennedy and Martin Luther King would get together, and they would be unstoppable.

This got me going, and I began to praise the intellectuals and Ivy Leaguers on Kennedy's team. John Kenneth Galbraith and Arthur Schlesinger, and Adlai Stevenson and the rest. I knew the whole list. Then Flora added excitedly, "And what about Professor Reischauer! The Ambassador to Japan. He was *born* in Japan, for God's sakes! And his wife, she's Japanese."

I looked back in the rear-view mirror as she said this, and I could see Virgil sitting there, so proud of Flora, his arm loosely around her, looking prosperous in a long tan sport jacket and a beautiful beige shirt with a large, open collar.

The party on the boat was already in full swing when we arrived. Many of Vic and Hal's friends lived for their parties in the way that the working class fans at Fenway Park or Wrigley Field lived for their teams. It was only the parties that seemed to make the rest of their lives almost possible.

We sailed out onto Puget Sound to drink and watch the sunset. Vic had brought my forty-fives on board, and everyone was dancing energetically to Little Richard's "Long, Tall Sally," and "Miss Ann," and Jerry Lee Lewis's, "Great Balls of Fire."

Leslie and I walked over by ourselves to a deserted part of the deck. She was unforgettably pretty in the wrinkled and spotted white dress which she had been wearing since the day before, her large, bright eyes, set so far apart, reflecting the mauve and gold of the sunset. I stared at her vivid, emotion-filled face, so vulnerable and alive, and I took her in my arms and kissed her.

As we stood on the deck by ourselves, watching the last of the sunlight fade, Leslie put her arm around my shoulders. Something had changed. I didn't know what had happened to her over the past two weeks, and I didn't care. All I could think about was how worried Leslie had been when she had thought she had lost me.

She turned to me and said, "Boy, I missed you. I swear."

"I've missed you, too."

"I'm getting As in both my classes." She smiled shyly, but with pride.

"Hey, that's great! I'm proud of you."

"Can you stay with me tonight, Danny? Back at my place?"

I nodded yes.

"Listen, you know Johnny Flagon?" she said. "He works over in engineering with Hal?"

I shook my head no.

"Well, he flies a plane, and he and Hal are going up on Friday right after work. They're going to fly over the Olympic Peninsula. Oh, Danny, wouldn't you like to go? It'll be soooo beautiful...."

Chapter Twenty-three

Johnny Flagon and Hal were waiting for us beside a little green-and-white Cessna. The entire airport was not much more than a tar strip in the fields, with a few planes scattered about.

Hal introduced me to Johnny, calling me "The Mahatma," as he often did now. This kidding rankled, as I admired Mahatma Gandhi who, along with Tolstoy and Thoreau, had influenced my hero, Martin Luther King, but I said nothing so as not to encourage him. Johnny was about our age. A technician at work, he was slim, with horn-rimmed glasses. There was something a bit askew about him. Something of the nerd running wild.

Leslie and I climbed into the rear seats. Hal sat in the front. Johnny took us up quickly. I had never been in a small plane before, and I was surprised at how fragile and flimsy it felt. The entire fuselage continually flexed and gave like a healthy rib cage. When he turned it, Johnny banked the small plane almost over on its side, and you could feel every movement of its structure. We soared out over the glorious Olympic Peninsula, with its rows of snow-capped mountain peaks amid the rolling silent majesty of the dark-green and charcoal-brown Earth below.

Then, without warning, Johnny banked the plane to the right and took us into a dive. Faster and faster we accelerated as we fell, and you could feel the wind trying to tear the wings off. Hal yelled, "Yeah, Yeah," and at the last moment, when it seemed almost too late, Johnny pulled out of the dive and swung the plane between the mountains, banking left and right as he threaded his way among the peaks, so close to the land you felt you could reach out your hand and grab the snow or the rocks.

"All right!" Hal shouted, and he pulled a pint of J&B out of his jacket pocket and swallowed a large draft and then he handed it to

Johnny, who took a big swig himself and passed it back to Leslie and me and we joined them, and the bottle went around the circle once again while Johnny came closer and closer to the mountains as he pushed the little plane into smaller crevices, and Hal was yelling, "Yeah, Yeah," and Leslie said, "Wow!" after each tilt and glide into another tight passage.

But what had happened to the quiet peace? To the sense of grandeur. Why was there a need to risk our lives, when there was so much natural healing beauty around if only we would stop racing and diving and just look at it?

Johnny took the plane into a steep climb. You could feel the engine straining to lift the four of us almost straight up. I took another swig of scotch and passed it back up front, where Johnny and Hal took turns at it.

Then I felt my stomach drop as Johnny dipped the plane quickly and put it into a mad full-dive. The wings pulled back under tension, seeming paper-thin in the rushing air as we fell faster and faster, and the wind seemed ready to rip the wings off like the wings of a fly, and the entire plane sang and moaned as if it were being tortured, and it struck me with full force that my life was in the hands of some wacky guy I knew nothing about.

Hal was riding high on the liquor buzz. He had been half out of his mind through the past two weeks anyhow. Leslie was grooving on the flight the way she would flow with the ride on the back of some guy's motorcycle roaring around Jefferson. I started thinking that perhaps this is the way these planes respond—they give and shake, stretch and wail. At the last minute, Johnny tried to pull the plane out of its dive, but we had been falling so fast we kept sailing in the same direction. Finally he won the struggle, and the plane leveled off and we skated along between the peaks, never knowing what would confront us as we swung around one and toward a new set of peaks behind it.

"Hey, man, take it easy," I said, laughing to mask my concern.

"Take it easy?" Hal said, exhilarated on the adrenalin. "What's the matter, Mr. Mahatma? Come on. Aren't you Zen? You're not scared are you? Hey, the Mahatma's scared!"

I wanted to say, "Not as scared as you were in your Mae West on

Jimmy's boat," because Hal couldn't swim and hated water, but that seemed too cruel, so I merely said, "I'd just like to look at the scenery a little."

I glanced toward Leslie. She wasn't saying anything. Did she trust Johnny more than I did? Or did she simply not care that much whether she lived or died?

Or was I exaggerating the danger?

"The Mahatma's scared!" Hal said, happily, drinking more scotch.

Johnny took us up again. The engine strained and pulled. The entire plane seemed to be pushed beyond the limits of its design. Johnny was concentrating fiercely with a strange look on his face, like an ordinary guy driving in the Indianapolis 500. He seemed possessed.

"Hey, take it easy, man," I said again.

"I told you, man, Zen it out," Hal said, still smiling and enjoying his chance to rib me.

"Zen? What're you talking about, man? This is the opposite of fucking Zen." Then I added, feebly, "Remember what Alan Watts said: 'Don't just do something. Stand there!'"

But before Hal could respond, Johnny took her down again, madly, and it felt like the first dip on the roller coaster, and then it happened. BANG BANG BANG BANG BANG BANG BANG. What was going on? Why couldn't I see? Where were the mountains? Was the plane coming apart? How could we avoid the mountains if we couldn't see? We're going to die.

I glanced toward Leslie, who was looking frightened and vulnerable, but sitting silent and passive as if this were simply one more absurd event in the consistent pattern of insults and humiliations that added up to her biography.

Then I located that cool axis I had found I could rely on when linemen where charging me as I dropped back to pass. And in that center, I felt, amid the parts of myself that were in terror, that if I were going to die, Leslie was the right person for me to die with. I reached over and placed my arm around her in a manner that was almost composed.

BANG BANG BANG BANG BANG BANG BANG.

"Pull it up!" Hal shouted, terrified. "Pull it up, Johnny!" Finally,

Johnny tugged way back on the controls and the spirited little plane pulled itself skywards once more, and the front windshield suddenly cleared and the BANG BANG BANG BANG BANG stopped, and Johnny himself said, "Wow!" I could see he had been as scared as we were, and this time he took us gently up over the peaks and leveled out, and began to reduce our speed within tamer limits.

"What the hell was that?" I said.

"The hood. The hood ripped open," Johnny said. "The latch that holds it down must've gotten torn off or something. There's nothing holding the hood down."

I stretched to look over Johnny's shoulder. The airplane had a metal shield over the engine like a car hood. It lifted up from the front, and the latch had been torn off so that now the hood was free to swing up in our faces. Johnny took the plane slowly and delicately lower. The hood swung up again and began to slap against the windshield frame, BANG BANG BANG BANG, and once again we couldn't see anything at all in front of us.

"Pull it up!" Hal shouted.

Johnny leaned back and the plane rose, gently this time. Johnny was negotiating with the bird now, giving it all the respect he had denied it earlier.

"What can we do?" I asked.

Johnny said nothing. He seemed frozen, holding onto the wheel for dear life.

"It looks like it only blows up in our faces when we go down," Hal offered.

"Why don't we experiment with it?" I said. "See how gently you can take it down before it swings up at us?"

"Yeah," Hal said.

Johnny nodded. What none of us was saying was the obvious conclusion no one wanted to draw: If we couldn't see anything when we descended, how were we going to land the plane?

"Listen," I said, "why don't we head back to the airport? We can do our experimenting there, without the mountains." Johnny swung the plane around carefully. As he banked into the turn, the hood popped up again, BANG BANG BANG BANG BANG BANG.

He leveled it out, and the hood finally quieted and returned to its proper place. It seemed like an hour before we saw the airport below us.

"Here. Try it now. Take it down, gently," I said. "Simulate a gradual landing."

Johnny leaned forward on the stick and the plane responded by dipping slightly. BANG BANG BANG BANG BANG BANG BANG.

He pulled back on the stick and leveled out. "Try it again," I said.

"Yeah," Hal said. "Try to do it on a smaller incline."

Johnny pointed her slightly down again. BANG BANG BANG BANG. He righted her immediately.

"How much fuel do we have?" I said.

We all looked at the fuel gauge. A quarter tank.

"This won't work," Johnny said.

"Damn it," Hal said. "Try it one more time." Johnny turned the plane down just slightly.

BANG BANG BANG BANG BANG

"I told you man, it's no use."

We flew at a level altitude, circling the little tar strip. At times, the plane would dip a bit, flinging the hood up, and the BANG-ING would commence again until Johnny lifted the nose.

"Listen," I said, "maybe we should just go down lower, nearer to the ground, and try it there, as if we were really doing it. Who knows? Maybe the air pressure will be different or something?"

Johnny and Hal both looked at me hopelessly.

"Anyone have a better idea?" I said.

Johnny took the plane to a lower altitude.

BANG BANG BANG BANG BANG BANG BANG BANG BANG BANG BANG.

"Well, great," I said, as Johnny leveled out. "Just great! I told you not to fuck around in the mountains. You practically tore the whole fucking plane apart."

"Just cool it," Hal said, nervously.

"Yeah, that's easy for you to say," I said. "You fucking encouraged him!"

But I saw this wasn't getting us anywhere. "OK. OK," I said. "Let's just try to think of some way out of this mess."

We flew around the airport a couple times, everyone struggling to come up with some solution.

"I've got an idea," I said, finally. "Since we can't go down slow enough to keep the hood on, why don't we reverse what we're doing? Take the plane up really high, and come down like a bat out of hell and try to RIP the fucking hood off."

There was a silence for a couple seconds, and then Hal said, "What have we got to lose?"

Johnny pulled the plane up to near its maximum altitude.

"Remember, man, if it doesn't come off, leave plenty of time to pull out of it," I said to Johnny. He didn't answer.

"Ok, here we goooo," he said, and he pointed the plane into an almost completely vertical descent, and we began to fall through the sky with the hood banging louder and faster than ever, BANG-BANGBANGBANGBANGBANGBANGBANGBANG, slapping furiously at the windshield, the blasts of air buffeting the plane, tugging it in several directions at the same time, the metal keening and rattling and whining heartbreakingly as we fell faster and faster toward the terrible ground, and then, quickly, it happened, all in the space of one second, the hood was TORN completely off its moorings by the wind, it FLEW up against the windshield, smacked into it and slipped off to the left, flattening itself like a piece of aluminum foil against the triangle formed by three elements—the wing, the side of the plane, and the diagonal strut that ran from the bottom of the fuselage out to the wing, which it braced and supported.

The hood flattened out against the triangle, pressed there by the rushing air. This destroyed the normal aerodynamics of the aircraft just at the time we were screaming out of control toward the ground as if we had been flung down from a sling.

"Pull it out!" Hal screamed. "PULL IT OUT!"

Johnny was grappling with the controls, struggling desperately, but he had lost control of the aircraft and we were beginning to roll as we fell.

Out the side window, right in front of me, I could see the hood of the engine PRESSED against the triangle as we dove downward. I could see the tremendous force of the air against the hood, as we fell further and further, plummeting like a sky-diver with a crippled chute, dropping helplessly down, out of the sky, end of our lives, so senseless. . . .

Until, with a kind of whoosh, the air CRUSHED the hood like a huge fist, PUNCHING it through the triangle, compressing it and FORCING IT THROUGH THAT SMALL SPACE, BAM-CRUNCH, followed by what sounded like almost silence as the plane ceased its spinning and began to respond to Johnny in the normal fashion, and he pulled it out of the dive, low over the Earth, and we leveled out, and all we could hear was the usual sound of the engine, a little louder than we were accustomed to because it was no longer shielded by its hood but open to the air in front of us. However, at that moment, it sounded merely like the purring of a cat to me. After a couple seconds, we all began to shout and to pound each other on the back, and I put my arm around Leslie and squeezed her into me and kissed her again and again, and we began to inhale and to exhale together with the joy and relief of those blessed and risen, like Lazarus, from the dead.

Chapter Twenty-four

People were running toward us from several directions as we descended from the cockpit. My feet planted themselves firmly, my toes curling as if they wanted to grasp the ground like fingers. I hugged Leslie once again, feeling so vibrant, so glad to be back on the Earth, the two of us, together and alive.

A local farmer pulled up in an old Chevy pick-up truck bearing the crushed hood of the airplane. The hood was larger than I had expected, seeing it now laid on the bed of the truck. The hood had fallen into the field behind his house. He told us that everyone in the area had been following our descent, so loud and alarming had been the din when we attempted to take the plane lower and simulate a landing.

Leslie and I headed toward Chinatown. We would eat at Wong's before we met up with our friends at The Roll Inn, a funky downtown R-&-B Club that Hal and I had discovered. I was driving along Rainier Avenue, still wired on the adrenalin. I couldn't ground my emotions. My moods were taking crazy swings, like wind-whipped laundry flapping on a clothesline.

On the radio, Eric Severeid was droning out one of his bland editorials, so middle-of-the-road that it lay completely between the two white lines. Suddenly, before I knew what I was doing, I began to bellow out the car window in this crazy, exaggerated Eric Severeid voice: "IT WAS THE BEST OF TIMES, IT WAS THE WORST OF TIMES! A TIME FOR BOLDNESS, A TIME FOR CAUTION! A TIME FOR RAPID CHANGE, A TIME FOR PATIENCE AND STABILITY! IN SHORT, A TIME LIKE ALL OTHER TIMES! AND YET, SOMEHOW, COMPLETELY NEW AND DIFFERENT!"

I must've been yelling pretty loud, because when I glanced at

Leslie she was looking at me as if I were mad. Then the guy in the car on my left angrily honked his horn at me. He pulled right in front of us, cutting me off. I screamed at him, and honked my horn: BEEP BEEP BEEP BEEP.

"Hey, take it easy," Leslie said.

"Yeah, take it easy. You're a good one to talk."

"What?"

Leslie was not one to miss any hint of anger that might be directed against herself.

"You know what I mean," I snapped.

"No ... no, I don't know what you mean."

"You could have gotten us killed."

"*What?*"

"Up in the plane, damn it. You know what I mean."

I glanced at her and saw her looking directly at me, her eyes bright and angry.

"No, I *don't* know what you mean. I don't have the foggiest fucking idea what you mean."

I recalled Leslie on Alki Beach when she had screamed at me and had banished me from her life. She was becoming agitated in the same way, her features twisted and vexed.

This only served to provoke me further. "That moron is practically tearing the fucking airplane to pieces and what're you doing? You're sitting there and saying, (I mimicked her in a gross, mean-spirited way), 'Wow! Oh, my goodness, this is thrilling. Oh, wow!'"

"That's *not* what I said!"

"Oh, WOW!" I continued, destructively. "Wow, wow."

"Stop the car!" she screamed. "Stop the fucking car! I'm getting out."

"I'm not stopping the fucking car!"

"Then I'll jump out. I mean it. I'll JUMP."

She opened her door and prepared to throw herself out.

"Ok, God damn it. You want out. I'll stop the fucking car and *let you* the fuck out!"

I swerved over to the curb. The station wagon behind me jerked away to avoid hitting the tail of my car. The driver blew his horn, cursing at me. I cursed back at him as he passed.

Leslie jumped out of the car and marched determinedly down the sidewalk. I sat there glaring at her back. There was so much voltage between us, I felt that if our eyes met we might be consumed in a flash of lightning.

She strode up the street in her tight skirt. For some reason this brought to my mind that day at work when she had fallen on her ass in the purchasing department and somehow—I don't know why—I began to smile. I thought of all the pain and misunderstanding she had been subjected to in her life, and I felt my sympathy go out to her, so determined not to let herself be falsely accused of anything ever again.

Then a big white Buick with four guys in it, guys who had no doubt taken a few TGIF drinks after work, slowed down and began to follow her up the street. I stepped on the gas and trailed them slowly. The guys wore ties but no jackets, technician-type guys like Johnny Flagon, crawling along at her pace as they admired her ass, she not conceding that they were there, although I could see that she knew very well exactly what was happening. Then one guy stuck his head out the window and he said, in an obnoxious, leering tone, "Ooowee, Honey, you going our way? I got somethin for you...." She spun around and gave him the finger and screeched at him at the top of her lungs, "FUUUUUUCCCKKKK YOOOOUUUUUUU," with a wild, harridan expression, staring directly into his eyes as if she were going to kill him.

"Hey...." the guy said, in an uneasy, startled, tone.

"FUUUUUUCCCCCKKKKK YOOOOUUUUUUU," she screamed again, walking TOWARD them, right into his face. They pulled away from the curb and drove off.

Leslie just stood there for a second, the underlying architecture of her anger softening. And then she began to weep. I could hardly believe it. Suddenly Leslie was standing there on the sidewalk, right out on Rainier Avenue, crying.

I stepped on the gas and pulled up beside her. Leaned across the seat and opened the door. She climbed into the car, not saying a word. She sat there for a moment, tears in her eyes, facing forward, trying to compose herself. Then she turned to me, and I couldn't explain why, but we both began to laugh. We laughed like crazy and we couldn't stop, she still crying at the same time, like a sunshower. I kissed the tears off her face and she shook her head as if to say, "Can you believe this?" and then she turned to me and we kissed each other's mouth, hard and passionately, in the car, in the early evening light, in the right lane on Rainier Avenue.

The band at The Roll Inn was playing "Night Train." The archetypical honky-tonk tune. The National Anthem of dives. I was on the dance floor with Leslie, grinding it out, both of us drunk on Thunderbird on the rocks.

Hal and Lilly and Vic and a girl named Fran were also on the floor, drunk on Thunderbird. The bar was jammed, and people were shouting, "Yes, Yes, Yes," at the band. The crowd was composed mostly of poor whites, and people from various minority groups, lower-echelon workers, derelicts, winos, downtown hipsters from the cheap hotels, and migrant poor, drowning the greasy hamburger sadness of their lives in the cheap sauce of one more Friday night.

When the band finished the set, someone immediately played a James Brown tune, "I Feel Good," on the fantastic, loud jukebox, and we all stayed out there dancing exuberantly together, the wasted and the sinking, gyrating luxuriantly in a kind of tribal rite that had sprung up in America, when people began to let go of their partners and to shake their asses to the insistent beat of African drums, a stone age ceremony that signaled the end of a certain white fifties sensibility forever.

I watched Leslie as she shifted into her other self, sticking out her behind and somehow letting it lead her around, as if she didn't know what it was going to do next. Leslie was a fabulous dancer. Many of the people were watching her as they moved around her. In her normal life, as pretty as she was, she would often stand with her shoulders forward, her chest caved in, as if to announce: I don't take any space, I need nothing, I am not a sexual being, I yield to you in Christ-like humility.

But once the drums started and the horns came in above them in blues-based chords, Leslie's shoulders would pull back, her chest would push forward, her ass would jut out, and she would get this insolent, sullen expression on her face and begin to move in a way in which most white girls did not move in 1961, her life energy now burning with a gypsy flame that was refracted by sapphires and rubies on its way to the world.

Everyone seemed to center their movements around her, like planets, and she reigned over the dance floor, the dark Queen of the Derelicts, the Empress of the Injured, and I was dancing with her, and something deeper and more comprehensive than the ego was moving me, some inner force akin to that which impels a flower to reach for the sun, and I wondered if I too had become trans-formed, because as I sweated and danced with these people — Negroes, poor Whites, American Indians and Chinese, the jobless and the jobbed, all of us sweating desperately and moving together in a pool of passionate energy—I felt so gratified to be able to *feel* again, to feel without restraint or reason, and it seemed to me that *all* of our hearts were aching to feel, and to share our feelings with the people around us, but especially with those who felt lost and despised and helpless in the world.

And then the juke box played "You Cheated," by The Shields, and I held Leslie close and we did the fish, moving against each other in the sequined light, but there was no way I could hold her close enough, there was such a small canopy of time left to shield the two of us from the long future in which we would be apart.

And then Ray Charles came on the speakers, "What I Say?" blast-ing loud enough for the angels to hear. Leslie and I stood still for a second. I placed my hand on her shoulder, which felt rusted and fragile suddenly as she stopped dancing and came back to herself. She caught her breath and smiled at me, the sweat running down her face, and I could see the warm life radiating from her, and I said, drunk and excited, "Ray Charles! Do you know what I would give to sing with the Raelettes? My life! I would give *my life* to be a Raelette," and I turned to the dancers and then back to Leslie, say-ing, "Doesn't anyone here twist?" and I began to twist, not in the normal white manner, but in the style I had learned in the bars on Green Street in Albany, in the red light district where the Negro prostitutes would go to dance, and although I never went to the whorehouses myself—I could never get past the HUMANNESS of

the women to somehow PURCHASE them—I did get to know some
of them at the bars, and they had taught me a Negro version of the
twist, and I began to do this Negro twist there in Seattle, at The
Roll Inn, to Ray Charles, a subtle dance with the action mostly in
your hands, which you held at your sides and rotated, as if each
held a screwdriver and you were turning in the screws in a syncopated rhythm as your body swayed slightly side-to-side in a kind of
echo of the twist, and I saw Leslie watching me, intently, her face
slowly beginning to shine, and then she began to move her body
to the music in the same way, and of course she had it down, she
could already do it better than I, and I looked up and saw Hal laughing as he and Lilly began to try it, and then Vic and Fran too, though
they couldn't pick it up in the Negro way as Leslie did immediately.
Then a couple of other people began to imitate us, and before the
song ended, everyone on the dance floor was doing various versions of this Negro twist, and when the next song came on, "Shout!"
by the Iseley Brothers, everyone started to twist again, and I looked
at Leslie, twisting away just like the prostitutes on Green Street, and
she caught my eye and gave me this big, luminous smile that passed
right into me, ravaging the defenses around my timid heart.

Just before midnight, we were back at our table, the six of us, drinking T-Bird over ice.

"This is a GREAT place," Leslie said.

Lilly and Fran agreed. We were all breathing deeply, our faces
glittering with little jewels of sweat that winked off and on in the
carnival of varied lights.

"Listen, do you guys know about Birdland?" Leslie said.

"You mean the jazz place?" Vic said.

"In New York?" I said.

"No. HERE!" Leslie said. When it became clear we actually had-
n't heard of a Birdland in Seattle, Leslie lit up like Times Square
after they ended the blackout at the close of World War II and she
said, "Well, you guys have really given me a gift here tonight. I mean,
this is a GREAT place. But now can I take you somewhere? I mean,
can I give YOU something you're never going to forget for the rest
of your LIVES?"

It was difficult for them to say no, but the others were committed to go to a party up on Queen Anne Hill, so Leslie and I continued on by ourselves. She directed me to Twenty-First and Jackson, in the Negro section. We parked on the street and walked toward a little old neighborhood moviehouse that posted a bare, unlit marquee.

"You're sure they're open? It's after midnight."

Leslie continued to lead me down Jackson and, sure enough, we could make out a weak light in the ticket booth, and some young Negroes standing around in the ill-lit vestibule.

"This was once a movie theater," Leslie said. "Then they turned it into a roller-skating rink, in the thirties, I think."

I bought our tickets and we ventured inside. We stopped in the lobby to buy her a coke. I stood in line next to her, unsteady from the drinking. I could see in the distance, through the open doors to the old rink, that the floor was level, not sloped down as in a normal moviehouse. On the little stage at the far end, a six-piece rhythm-and-blues band was playing a powerful riff over and over again, the trumpet and a baritone sax and a small organ bringing forth that sweet R-and-B moan that made you wish it would never stop because it *sounded so good*. The lighting was dim, and there was a barrier with a railing on top that enclosed the skating area, but I could barely make out that on the darkened floor there were over a hundred Negroes, kids along with older folks who had come in from the bars, and they all appeared to be skating slowly around the floor in a large oval, some facing forward, others facing backward, as they moved and did their New Orleans funeral-parade-like movements, all circling slowly clockwise as the band played its riff again and again:

Da Da Da DAA
Dum Dum
Da Da Da DAA
Dum Dum

All skating slowly in this perfect, lag-along, funky rhythm, around and around, nodding to each other as they passed, like some strange Negro Easter parade, not a single white person in the place, some with their hands clasped behind their backs like Dutchmen ice-skating on the frozen canals, all their heads bobbing as they circled along, and in my drunken Thunderbird perspective, it all seemed so perfect somehow, part of a vast set of magical American night-time mysteries that I could never come near to fathoming.

Leslie paid for her Coke. The Thunderbird was making me dizzy. All the people seemed so far away as I craned my neck to watch them in the distance. Leslie passed her Coke to me, and I took a long sip. She was supremely happy at having brought us here, the sole outsiders at this wonderful all-night neighborhood ritual.

She led me towards the rink. I struggled to focus my eyes, some-how having this feeling that in my drunkenness I was missing some-thing, some last amazing aspect of this incredible scene. When we reached the solid rail, I saw what it was: In my drunkenness in the lobby, I had not noticed the most important fact of all: NONE OF THE SKATERS WERE WEARING SKATES!

I could hardly believe that I had not noticed this before. Yet, it was true. All these dancers were circling the floor, no doubt just as they had done for years when Birdland had been a skating rink, only now there was a rhythm-and-blues band playing all night on the stage, and they were doing this perfectly contoured blues skat-ing, coolly and nonchalantly gliding along, BUT WITHOUT ANY SKATES.

I turned to Leslie and flowered into a huge grin. She had been absolutely right. I would never forget this sight, not in my entire life. She seemed suddenly to almost blush with pleasure as she bowed and said, "Monsieur," and I led her out amongst the skaters, and we joined in the flow, all-skate-slow, in a smooth glide around the floor, backwards and forwards, dipping and twirling in synch with the slowly moving crowd's easy slide, skating around and around with them to the slow blues sounds, skimming along through the late hours of the warm summer night amidst two hundred people without skates.

Chapter Twenty-five

Bill Thomson was surrounded by books—books in cartons, books in tall piles on the floor, books still in bookcases which stretched from floor to ceiling around the high-ceilinged living room of his Victorian house.

Bill was about forty-five years old. He had medium-dark skin and an intelligent face, with short, curly, graying hair receding from his large prominent brow. He wore rimless glasses, and he had an intense, piercing look.

He finished sealing a carton of books, and offered us a beer.

"Heineken," I said, as I read the label in the afternoon light. You didn't see many foreign beers in those days.

Bill nodded. "I try not to buy American."

I looked up at him, searching for a clue as to how to take what he had said. Leslie and I sat next to each other on the couch. The beer felt good going down, especially on top of the hangover I had acquired from the night before. There were several striking, violently colored, abstract expressionist paintings hanging on the walls in the few spaces between the bookcases.

Bill sat on a couple of cartons of books. "I like those paintings," I said. "They remind me of Willem DeKooning."

Bill's nodded. "Those're by Martha. My wife. She's in Oregon for the weekend. She went to school down at Reed. Now she's saying goodbye to some of her old friends."

"Bill and Martha are going to Africa," Leslie said. "Bill's been offered the job as director of a high school there."

"Leslie told me you were her professor in World History One, over at the U."

"Yes. Leslie." He couldn't help but smile affectionately in spite of himself.

Leslie smiled as well. "I was no historian, believe me."

"Leslie ... Leslie was a historian of that which never was and never will be."

"Oh, I don't know about that," Leslie teased him. Bill just nodded his head and took another sip of his beer. Leslie had spoken to me about Bill's deep rancor, yet he seemed affable enough. But I had seen my father open up in that manner too, at times, and Bill did remind me of my father.

"Are you going for long?" I said.

"We're not coming back." The barbed-wire determination returned to Bill's face.

"Not coming back?"

"That's what I said. Going, going, gone, like they say about a home run."

"You feel like Africa is your home?"

I don't believe he had thought of the term "home run" in that manner. He seemed surprised. He examined my face closely, as if he were taking care to evaluate me accurately. I didn't feel I had too much to worry about in that regard. Not from a professor who had recognized Leslie's special qualities and befriended her, in spite of the fact that he had obviously been hurt very badly by white people in his life.

"It's *going* to be my home," he said.

"Where exactly are you going?" I said.

"That I'm not gonna say."

"You're not?"

"Oh, I'll tell Virgil. In case he needs something. But not anyone else. We don't have any kids of our own." Then he remembered something. "You're the 'Danny' who helped him out?"

"He stayed with me a couple times. I wouldn't call it helping him out or anything. . . ."

"Virgil is smart. He should get himself a damn education. That's why I keep arguing with him." Bill spoke with force, moving his head slightly from side to side without realizing he was doing it. "With his ability, he could be out at the University. You have to be conscious, if you want to be free. You have to understand what's happening in the world." He set his bottle of beer down on a carton next to him. "That's where Leslie and I come to the parting of the ways. She thinks she cares about the world, but she doesn't care enough to really learn about what happened in the past."

"I learned enough to get an A in your class."

"Oh, yeah, sure. But I bet you haven't picked up a history book since."

"History is what happens in our mind, too. In our soul."

Bill turned to me. "Leslie wants everyone to be free, but I bet she's never once taken part in any social action." Leslie sat there, not responding. It was hard to tell what she was thinking or feeling. Bill was castigating her, but in an avuncular manner. He was still her professor in a way, prodding her, trying to provoke her into a dialogue.

"You want to change the world," Bill said to Leslie, "but you don't even take the trouble to find out what's going on. Or what led us to this fucked-up state we're in now."

Leslie continued to sit there silently. Then she said, "It's just that all that external stuff, it isn't what's really happening. It's all an excuse for not dealing with what's really bothering us. What's sick *inside* us. . . ."

She was trying to speak with authority, but you could see Bill had touched a sore point. She faltered a bit in her speech.

"See, that's white-people talk," Bill said. "If someone's fucking you over every day, right in front of your eyes, you don't need to find out in your 'soul' what's bothering you. You *know* what's bothering you. Some Jim-Crow redneck is bothering you. Sucking the very life out of you, until you want to kill him. And I mean that literally. Kill him. And not only him. All the goddamn hypocrites that surround you in this goddamn racist country."

He turned to me. "You know what finally got to me? World War II. When they drafted me and they put me in a goddamn segregated infantry company with a redneck white officer. I mean, I'll tell you man, that was the fucking last straw! And you know, by the time the U.S. went to Korea, there were STILL segregated units in the Army. That's why we didn't win that damn war. That wasn't communists against capitalists. It was just some poor yellow people who were determined to stand up to the goddamn whites."

142

Bill picked up his beer and took a sip. Leslie had said that Martha was the one who could defuse Bill's anger. The one person he really trusted. As he sat there amidst all the piles of his books, he seemed to be hearing her voice and trying to calm himself. I didn't believe he was angry with us personally. In fact, I felt Bill liked us. I knew I liked him. But something in Bill wouldn't allow him to let go just yet. He turned to me and he said, almost painfully, "Leslie here, she thinks she loves people, with all her talk about Jesus and Love and all that. But it isn't true." He glanced toward Leslie. Then back to me. "Now don't get me wrong. Leslie's always been one of my favorite students. She knows how I feel about her."

I looked toward Leslie. She was blushing slightly at the praise, and waiting apprehensively for what was to follow.

"But at bottom, she doesn't believe in people. Believe me. I know Leslie. We think alike in many ways. That's why she and I understand each other. Because she knows how mean and duplicitous people can be. They've been that way to her. She doesn't trust people one bit. That's why she can't *bear* to read the newspaper. It's too painful for her. It shatters her illusions about love and Jesus and all that shit. . . ."

Leslie was looking down, withdrawing into herself as she often did when she felt she was being criticized.

Bill noticed this and stopped. The room fell into silence and a cozy feeling subsumed us, the human warmth returning, amid the piles of books and the records.

Bill turned to me. "Well, Leslie knows I don't mean anything personal by all this. If I didn't like her, I wouldn't bother. It's just that you can't simply run away from things and hide in your own visions."

"I'm not running away," Leslie said feebly.

"Do you know about W.E.B. Dubois?" Bill said, speaking gently now. "Really. Do you know about Marcus Garvey?"

Leslie wasn't able to answer.

Suddenly Bill opened his compassion to her. You could see it in his face, and hear it immediately in his voice. "Well, I know you're trying. . . . Don't take it to heart. . . . You know me. . . . That's the way I express myself. . . . My friends don't have to agree with everything

I say...." He rose and pulled a record out of the bookcase. Set it on the turntable. "I just get lonely sometimes, I guess. I get to feeling like I'm surrounded by zombies."

I almost had to smile, watching Bill attempting to voice his good-will but always coming up with some tag like that one about zombies that made things ambiguous again.

"I just want everyone to get an education," Bill said.

"That's my problem," I said. "I've been to college for five years. Engineering school and then Wharton. That's my ticket out of The Bronx. But I don't feel I've learned a thing that can really tell me what to do with my life."

"Maybe it's time to start." Bill returned to his seat on the cartons.

I watched the record drop and listened to the beautiful, strange chords. "Gil Evans? ... Miles and Gil Evans?"

Bill nodded yes. I could see that I had impressed him by identifying the music so quickly.

"It's 'Miles Ahead.'" Bill seemed relaxed now. He was leaning back a bit in his seat on the cartons of books. We talked fervently about jazz for a while. I was feeling really good now. I opened up and told Bill my theory about jazz: That we were living through one of the greatest periods in the history of art, and that we didn't even know it. That just as people today listened to the Baroque composers, Bach and Handel and Vivaldi and Corelli and Albinoni and the rest, hundreds of years from now, people would be listening to Prez and Dizzy and Ben Webster and Bird and Coleman Hawkins and Sonny Stitt and Wardell Gray and Miles and Monk and dozens of others, all great native American musical geniuses.

Bill was nodding his head in agreement, but then he added sternly, "And how many of those guys you named were ever recognized by this Babylon country? How many were spit on and beaten up and ignored? Look at Bud Powell. Christ! They fried his brains...."

"But ... I mean, I agree with you. Everything you say is true ... but still, I think, it's ... maybe it's a different time now. A new generation is taking over. You can see it in the White House. JFK, he's different. I mean, look at his cabinet! Dean Rusk, at State. He's a Rhodes Scholar. And Robert McNamara at Defense. He taught at

144

Harvard. Even the undersecretaries. They're all top Ivy League guys. They're not gonna run around and bully little countries and shit like that."

I took a quick sip of beer. "And Kennedy, he keeps up with things. I read that he subscribes to a dozen newspapers and sixteen magazines. Ike . . . he would only read the paper on Sunday." I looked over at Bill. He wore a grave expression, even though he was listening patiently like a good teacher as I rambled on. I realized I was treading on his territory. Leslie just sat there without speaking. I wondered whether she was brooding about what Bill had said to her?

"Do you know his book, *Profiles in Courage?*" Bill said. When I nodded, he said, "Well, I hear he didn't write that. That it was mostly ghost-written by Theodore Sorensen."

I pulled up short. This seemed incredible to me, yet I knew that Bill believed it. He had a certain granite integrity you couldn't mistake. But here he was going a little too far. Perhaps even slipping into the tricky corners of paranoia.

"Are you sure that's true?" I said weakly.

"I can't swear to it. But that's what I hear. And they say his old man fixed it so he got the Pulitzer Prize."

We sat quietly as I tried to take this in. Bill was wandering way over the line now. People just didn't "fix" the Pulitzer prize. Or get it for books they didn't write. "I don't know," I said, hesitantly. "It's just that this seems such a promising time in America. . . ."

"Don't you see, man? This country can't be fixed. This country STARTED with slavery! It's bad at the root." But Bill calmed quickly. "Can I get you another beer?" he said, rising to get himself one.

"Do you have any scotch?" Leslie said.

Leslie's eyes were unfocused. Her attention was withdrawn into some unreachable cave within herself. She saw me looking at her, and turned away. Reached into her purse and took out a cigarette.

Bill returned with three more Heinekens, and a bottle of Dewars. Leslie poured a couple of inches of scotch for herself.

"I don't mean to tell you what to do," I said to Bill. "But . . . well . . . it's just that you're so eloquent. . . . I mean, maybe you could provide some of the leadership that people need . . . what with Martin Luther King and everything that's beginning to happen."

"You mean, why don't I go down south, back to where I come from, and get involved in sit-ins and so on?"

I nodded. Leslie began to take little sips of the straight scotch, using the beer as a chaser after each sip.

"Why don't you tell me why I won't," Bill said. "Just look at me for a second, and see if you can come up with an answer."

I looked at Bill. Straight into his pained and indignant eyes. And then ... his face began to shift. The curves and planes began to move as if ... he were turning into my father. I wondered if it was the Heineken on top of all that I had drunk the night before. I could see my father coming to the surface in Bill's face, around his fierce, dark, disaffected eyes.

"I think I know."

"What is it?" Leslie said. Her own speech was beginning to become slurred.

I took a deep breath. "Because if he goes to the South, and he gets involved in a sit-in, and some stupid redneck fucks with him, he'll kill the guy."

Bill's eyebrows raised, and in his expression I saw a certain higher estimation of myself. He exhaled slowly. "How did you know?"

I shrugged. I didn't want to tell him that he reminded me of my father. That I could see my father killing some guy who pushed him one step too far. He would choke a guy over a parking place at night, or fight with a junkie in the gutter, but he would never be part of a social movement. When it came to violence, my father was an independent entrepreneur.

"Oh, come on, Bill," Leslie said. "What's all this talk about KILLING someone." She seemed immensely disturbed. "I mean, criminey, let's get real...."

She reached for her glass and took another swig of the scotch.

Bill looked back at her coolly and said, with a quiet intensity, "I always carry a weapon."

"What?" Leslie said, nervously.

"I said I always carry a weapon."

"What do you mean? What kind of weapon?"

"A knife."

"A knife? What are you talking about?"

"Whenever I'm dressed, I carry a knife."

"WHAT?" Leslie was peering into his eyes. Waiting for him to say this was a joke.

Bill just nodded, with that grim look, almost a smile, that I had seen on my father's face when he was about to choke somebody. "What are you talking about?" Leslie said. She set her glass down on the table beside the couch.

"Just what I said."

"You mean.... Wait a minute, I want to clear this up. You mean you're carrying a knife RIGHT NOW? Here in your HOUSE?"

Bill nodded. The smile was attempting to trickle out of the corner of his mouth. "I told you, anytime I'm dressed, I'm carrying a knife."

Leslie's face was ashen. "Wait a minute! Are you telling me that when you were lecturing to our classes up at the University of Washington, you were carrying a KNIFE?"

"Was I dressed?"

Leslie's face darkened. She did not want to comprehend this.

Bill flashed a devilish smile. Now he was genuinely happy. His secret was out at last.

Leslie just sat there, staring absently at the books piled on the floor. A heavy silence settled on us like a collapsed tent. No one seemed to know how to proceed. Then Miles began to play "New Rhumba," and my spirits picked up. "You know, I took part in a sit-in once," I said, before I could stop myself. "I sat in at a lunch counter for two weeks. Then when they finally agreed to serve us, it turned out they didn't have what I wanted."

There was a sudden eye-of-the-hurricane silence. And then Bill burst out laughing. I turned towards him and saw that he was looking at me with a certain affection.

"You stole that," Bill said. "You stole that from Dick Gregory."

He continued to laugh. Leslie poured some more scotch and drank it. She seemed on her own wave-length somewhere, stunned by what Bill had revealed about the knife.

"You took a chance there," he said.

I nodded. "You know what I heard Red Foxx say once? It was at the Showboat in Philly."

Gerald Rosen

"The Showboat? I've been there. In the basement."

Again I nodded. In fact, Bill and I were both nodding now, in a kind of rhythm together. "I heard Red Foxx there one night. He said he went into a diner in Alabama and they said, 'Sorry, we don't serve any Negroes in here.' So he said, 'That's OK. I don't want to EAT any Negroes in here!'"

Bill rocked with laughter and we relaxed together, both sitting back and sipping our beers. Leslie was not laughing with us. She was leaning back on the couch, blowing smoke into the air and watching it rise above her toward the high ceiling.

The record ended and Bill moved to change it, putting on a Brandenberg Concerto. Number Five.

I looked at the large pile of books right beside my end of the couch. A stack of novels by American authors with names beginning with "F." Farrell. Faulkner. Fitzgerald. Daniel Fuchs.

I turned back to Bill. "Didn't you say you had Leslie in your *history* class?"

"That's right. World History One."

"But you have all these novels...."

"Well, literature's a part of history in a way.... I mean, everything that happens is part of the culture. Leslie's right in that respect. That's the way I teach history. I don't teach it as the history of upper-middle-class white men in Washington. I try to understand how everything fits together."

"That's exactly what I'd like to know," I said, excitedly. "You know, I learned all this specialized business and science, but what I wonder is, what does it all mean for me? For my life. And my death."

"That's what Kierkegaard said about Hegel. Hegel had created this whole incredible abstract system, but Kierkegaard asked what did this have to do with me, Søren, the hunchback, the single, lonely, suffering individual?"

"See, I wish *I* knew things like that. I mean, I'd *love* to understand things. Or to understand myself. That's what I never learned in school. How to understand myself. And ... I don't know ... but I wish I knew a way to ... contribute to humanity. You know what I mean? Maybe help other people or something...."

148

He nodded without speaking.

"I mean, I'm SO unhappy. But I feel almost silly complaining like this. I have a well-paying job and a solid future.... But I don't know, even rich people commit suicide.... You know, sometimes I wake up in the middle of the night and I'm scared to death that it all doesn't mean anything...."

I looked to Bill. I was hoping he would give me some way to proceed. He thought for a minute, looking down at the floor. Then he looked up.

"Sounds to me like you're trying to find *yourself.*"

"Yeah! That's it! That's it exactly!"

"Well, I'm probably not the greatest expert in the field of self-knowledge...." He smiled at his own expense. "Listen, you know what I mean when I say 'culture'?"

"Culture?"

"Yeah. Not high culture, but culture in general. In the anthropological sense. Why don't you give me a definition of it?"

I hesitated for a moment. I feared to disappoint Bill. I thought I knew what he was getting at, but I wasn't sure exactly how to say it. Then I blurted out, "Culture is what you feel outside of when you go to a *bar mitzvah.*"

Bill looked at me with astonishment for a fraction of a second and then he burst out laughing again. I could hardly believe it. Somehow I seemed to be winning him over in spite of myself.

"How would *you* define it?" I said, quickly.

"Well, not to get technical, I'd just say culture is the shared values and assumptions and beliefs of a people. And in your case, my thought is that that's the concept that can bring it all together for you. And I'll tell you something," he said, "they've got a whole department at Penn, right where you're going to school, that approaches American history from that angle. So, if I were you, I'd take a course there in the fall."

"But, I go to WHARTON!"

"I'll bet the folks at Wharton would let you do it if you push them. In fact, right there at Penn, they teach business history and history of science. Things like that."

"Business history? History of science?" I moved my head from side to side as I contemplated this. "You know, I never thought of that. I'm not afraid of that stuff. I wouldn't be at a disadvantage."

"And the history of literature. And sociology. And popular culture. Advertising. It all fits together."

"Man!" I said. "This is knocking me out. I might do this. I might take this course."

Bill smiled. "You'll do OK. . . . You're just starved for meaning in your life."

"Yeah. That's right. That's absolutely right."

"And I'll tell you something. I have a hunch that if you study American culture, and how each culture forms a particular kind of personality in people to perpetuate its values and institutions, well . . . I think you'll learn a lot about what factors went into making up *your* personality. . . ."

I felt I had been enchanted. Everything around me was shining in a way that I hadn't seen before. "Then . . . then, if I study America . . . American culture . . . I might come to understand *myself!*"

I drank my beer without saying another word, so enthralled was I by the possibilities opening up for me in my mind.

When I looked up and returned to the world, Leslie was standing and telling Bill she would stop by on Wednesday to say one last goodbye to Martha. But it all seemed so far away. I was stunned by what Bill had said to me. It had stolen my breath somehow. Yet it also seemed as if this was the first time I could really breathe. I thanked Bill as I left. I wanted to tell him that I was sorry he was going to Africa. That he was the one I would have liked to have studied with. But I knew that he would be a good teacher in Africa. That he would always be waking people up, pushing them into thinking and looking at themselves, whether he was in a classroom or just sitting around, playing his records and being himself.

Chapter Twenty-six

"**D**id I ever tell you about Donny Lang, the Canadian Negro guy Virgil and I met up in Vancouver one night?"

I was driving Leslie back to her flat. She was sitting silently next to me, drunk and sullen, but I was overflowing with excited soliloquies and arias brought forth by my talk with Bill.

"Donny plays the piano at an all-night jazz club we found. He's a *great* guy! He has these sad eyes, oh, God, I can't tell you how sad, and still, he played so beautifully ... I could hardly bear it. It was like getting all these wonderful birthday presents from someone who can't afford it...."

I hit the brakes as the light turned red.

"Anyhow, afterwards, in the morning, when the club closed, he invited us back to his house for breakfast with all the musicians and their girls. We were eating scrambled eggs and he asked me what I did, and I spilled it all out—Brannan, working on the missiles, my confusion and doubts, everything...."

Leslie didn't speak. The light changed. I stepped on the gas.

"Anyhow, he looked at me with this *unbelievable* weariness, I mean the kind you can't get rid of by sleeping, and he said, 'Well, Danny, God knows, I'm probably the last one to give anyone else any advice, but I'll tell you man, back in the war, on D- Day, I was there, with the Canadian Army, ...' and I said to him, 'You were THERE? On D-Day?' and he said, 'I was there through the whole European campaign, and I'll tell you one thing, Danny, I wouldn't spend my life working on missiles.'"

I pulled around a double-parked moving truck and continued up the street. "'No, Danny,' he said, 'I'd rather sweep the streets than do that.'"

The light ahead blinked to red, and I stopped again. Leslie was still not saying anything. I couldn't tell what she was thinking.

"I wanted to ask Donny about what Hal always says: How could they have fought Hitler without the planes from Brannan? But he'd already given me so much that night, and he looked so tired...."

The light changed, and we moved ahead. Then I brightened. "Hey! Wouldn't it have been great to get Donny Lang together with Bill to discuss all this stuff? Man! What a *conversation!*"

Leslie just sat there, smoking another Salem. This was unusual for her. She ordinarily smoked only about half a pack a month. "Yeah, Bill," she remarked, dourly.

"What's the matter?"

"What's the matter? Didn't you see him picking on me? He wouldn't get off my back."

"Picking on you?"

There was space for several cars in front of Leslie's house, but before I had completely stopped, she opened the door and threw herself out of the moving car, almost stumbling when her legs hit the ground.

"Hey!" I shouted, hitting the brakes.

Leslie regained her balance and strode swiftly away without looking back.

When I reached Leslie's flat, the door was wide open. She was seated at the kitchen table, already drinking from a long-necked bottle of Olympia Beer. "Hey, what's the matter?"

She turned toward me. Her chin was jutting out, her large gray-green eyes flaring over her strong cheekbones. "What's the matter? Bill was practically tearing me apart all afternoon, and you were so wrapped up in your own plans you didn't even notice a thing."

"He wasn't tearing you apart. He was ... goading you ... so you would respond to him and ... engage him in some way."

"Yeah, sure...."

"He was only trying to teach you something." I pulled an Oly out of the refrigerator. "Where's the opener?"

She picked up the steel church-key from the table and threw it to me. I caught it gingerly, trying to avoid the sharp steel point. I gave her a quick, acrid look but she turned away. I opened the beer and then sat on a rickety chair across from her. I took a small sip of the beer, but I realized that I didn't feel like drinking any more that afternoon.

"Teach me? He was trying to put me down, that's what he was trying to do."

"He wasn't...."

"He didn't listen to a word I said. All his talk about my escaping from reality and all that garbage. He's the one who's running off to Africa, damn it."

I didn't answer her. I was hoping she would begin to cool down, but her fury seemed to be growing as she examined the wounds of the afternoon, laid out under the bright lights of retrospection.

"Criminey! Who's he to put people down? It's guys like him that cause all the trouble, running off half-cocked to reform the world without ever taking a single look at themselves."

"I don't think...."

"All that talk about carrying weapons and shooting rednecks!" She looked directly into my eyes. She seemed on the verge of losing control."

"Wait a minute, maybe there is more of a reason to get involved these days," I said. She let out a dismissive grunt, waving my words off with the back of her hand, but I continued, "Maybe something really *is* happening. That's what I'm trying to find out. I don't want to just let my life pass and not be a part of something really important that's happening right in front of us."

"Happening?" she said sarcastically. "Nothing's going to happen until people look at THEMSELVES. Don't you see that? Violence isn't the answer. That's what your friend Donny up in Canada was trying to tell you. If we want to see the love at the heart of the the universe, we need to express that love in our everyday lives. In our *jobs*, for Pete's sake. Or else we'll just be going around the same circles of violence and getting NOWHERE! That's where all this hysterical running around and fighting always winds up. NOWHERE. DON'T YOU SEE?"

"HEY! There's no need to yell. Calm down. No one's threatening you. Bill likes you. And so do I...."

She continued to glare at me as she took a long sip of her beer.

"Maybe Bill's wrong about all the violence." I said. "But look at

Martin Luther King. Isn't he trying to do just what you said? To change the world through nonviolence and Christian love?"

"A lot you know about Martin Luther King."

"Hey, come on. Take it easy. You're getting all upset over nothing.... And it so happens I do know a thing or two about Martin Luther King. I've been sending him money for years. Remember the Montgomery bus boycott? Rosa Parks? I sent them my whole allowance for weeks."

"Your 'allowance'!" she said, almost smiling with contempt.

"Well, what were you doing? Fucking some guy named Phoenix or Tucson or something?"

"Maybe I was PRAYING, damn it! You ever think of that? Maybe I was working in the goddamn pea factory, packing frozen peas, and then maybe I was in Church, on my damn knees, asking God to forgive us for our sins and asking Jesus to have mercy on us and to grant us some peace and justice. You ever think of that? You think you're going to get something done without going to another level? A higher damn level!"

"You see? Maybe Bill *was* right. You don't really get involved at all. You just see us all as sinners or something and then you write off anything that decent people do to try to change things. You don't believe in the real power of love. Shit! What does love have to do with Cardinal Spellman in New York? Or with Catholic politics in Boston? What does love have to do with stopping goddamn birth control? I'm not even talking abortion, here. I'm talking about stopping fucking BIRTH CONTROL for shit sakes, so millions of hungry, unwanted babies can be born to suffer and starve all around the world. When has the Church ever made one single decision that wasn't based on its own self-interest? And then you talk about Jesus! What does Jesus have to say about all that, for shit sakes?"

"Jesus? Don't you talk to me about Jesus!" she shouted, standing up now, pacing about dangerously, unable to keep still, she was so filled with fury. "What do you know about Jesus? Or the Church? Nothing! That's what you know. You don't know BEANS about the Church...."

"Oh, yeah. Well I know one thing. I know the Church sides with the rich and powerful against the poor whenever it has a chance.

And against free thinking and the best minds. Damn it, look around. Who threw you out of the convent? Who put the goddamn books you like, Jean-Paul Sartre and Bertrand Russell, on the condemned list? I mean, how can you support that? Banning books. They might as well burn them, for godsakes. And they would. Believe me, they'd do worse if they had the power. What does Christ and love have to do with all that?"

She began to sputter, as if her tongue could not shape the stream of anger that was trying to burst out of her. And then she exploded. She moved up to the table, took her bottle of beer by the neck and and flipped it, backhanded, in my direction. I jerked my head and shoulders aside and the bottle sailed past me, spitting out froth as it skidded across the ancient, faded-yellow linoleum on the kitchen floor.

"Hey, DAMN IT!" I shouted back at her, showing her my teeth as my jaw tightened with rage.

Leslie whirled around and moved toward the old gas stove, where she had set a casserole dish that morning. She lifted the big dish over her head and slammed it down on the floor, smashing it into pieces that flew all over the kitchen. As if dazed, she stood there for a second, staring at the shards of glass that lay scattered around her on the floor like leaves of ice. She seemed to be trying to catch her breath and to collect herself so she could speak. She looked over at me while still breathing heavily, her chest moving up and down in a series of silent sighs.

"Look, you're never going to understand me," she said. "The Church is first in my life. Nothing is going to come between me and the Church. I'm going to go to church tomorrow morning. I need to go to Mass." She stopped talking to allow herself to calm down further. Then she began to speak in a more normal tone. "I'm sorry I put you through all this. But maybe it's good that it happened. Maybe it brought things out into the open. I don't know. I need time to think all this over." She bent over and began to pick up some of the larger pieces of glass from the floor.

"So you'd like me to leave you alone and not stay here tonight?"

She nodded. "I'd like to sleep by myself before I go to Mass. I have a lot of things to think about." She dropped a handful of the glass segments into the paper bag in the wastebasket under the sink.

I rose from my seat. I began to drift slowly toward the door.

"I'll see you at work on Monday," she said. "Just give me some time to think about all this. I'm going through a lot right now."

I felt my heart still beating rapidly. Felt the blood rushing through my arteries. It seemed to be chilling me rather than heating me up, like it did when my father used to beat me when something went wrong at his store, or after he lost a bet on a baseball game.

"I'm sorry," Leslie said. "I shouldn't have thrown that beer bottle at you.... I didn't really throw it to hit you."

I nodded as I edged toward the doorway.

"I'll see you Monday," she said.

Then, as I reached the door, I felt my feelings coming back, like when the blood returns into a limb that has been numb. I turned to her, and said quietly, "You know what I don't understand? I mean really. And I'm not speaking out of anger, now. I'm speaking as a friend. I don't understand how a person with your sensitivity, how a person with all of your brains, can put up with all that stuff I was talking about. I don't see how you can accept all that pain that the Church has caused you, all that ..." I didn't want to say hypocrisy, but she knew what I was getting at—"all that other stuff, just to be part of a church that seems to violate everything you believe in."

I remained standing there in the doorway. She appeared forlorn now. Faded and stooped and infolded, like a flower that hasn't been watered.

She looked up at me with a delicate, helpless expression on her face, breathing deeply in a series of sad sighs, as if a water millwheel were turning inside her, lifting up her grief and presenting it to the world a bucket at a time, and she said, "You'll accept a lot from someone who's got the keys to the only door you want to go through."

Chapter Twenty-seven

On Monday morning, I was seated at my desk doing some sophisticated mathematics. I had calculated how much money I made each day, hour and minute, and now I was dividing by sixty to figure out how much I earned each second.

When I glanced up, Leslie was standing beside my desk. Her mascara had run. She had been crying. "Do you have a minute?" she said plaintively. We chose a Sabena Belgian Airways 606, making our way up the stairs and into the first-class cabin.

Leslie sloped forward in her seat, her shoulders hanging down as if they were made of cloth. She apologized to me for her behavior on Saturday. I told her it was nothing.

"God, what a time I've had," she said. "It's like it never stops. Sunday morning I went to Mass. Then I went to the library. Later, Martha called, just back from Oregon. So I ran over on my bike to say goodbye."

"Was Bill on you again?"

"No. In fact, Bill was really nice to me. He even apologized!"

"He's quite a guy. You know, he reminds me of my father in a way. In fact, everyone I meet these days seems to remind me of my father—Bill . . . My boss, Jim Stilson . . . Bums I meet in the street who ask me for a dime. . . . It's weird. . . ."

"He liked you, you know. He told me so. Then he started talking about writers. About Yeats, for some reason. He said that Auden, in his poem on Yeats's death, wrote that mad Ireland HURT Yeats into poetry."

"Maybe Bill was talking about himself, there. That mad America hurt him into his eloquence. . . ."

Leslie still looked pained and vulnerable. Over her head, where the wall paneling of the airliner had been torn out, I could see the

157

differently colored wires running along like arteries. I left some space for her to begin to speak. When she didn't, I continued to fill in until she was ready.

"I don't know," I said. "I keep wondering what I'm going to do with my life. . . . I'll tell you the truth, I don't even think I'm cut out to be a really good alcoholic anymore."

I had caught her here, grinning in spite of herself, and it made me feel wonderful inside, cheering her up like that when she was feeling low. It made me feel better that anything else in my life.

Then she gathered her forces and began to speak. "It was my parents," she said.

"Your parents?"

"When I got home from Bill and Martha's. They were there."

"But why didn't they call?"

She shrugged. "They said they did call a couple times."

"But . . . they could have kept trying." Again she shrugged, looking sad and winsome. "Daddy has a meeting with the Musicians' Union in Seattle today, so they just drove over. They stayed the night with me."

"Was there a problem?"

"Well, Saturday night, after you left, a friend of mine from the old days, Bobby Valentine, stopped by for a minute. Bobby and I had made some homemade wine that first year, and now he had some bottles from his new batch for me. Well, when my parents came, I don't know, I guess I'd been crying the night before, and I didn't sleep well, and I guess I didn't look all that great, and I could see how sad my flat made them. I told them they could sleep in my bed and I would sleep in my sleeping bag on the kitchen floor, but when they went into the bedroom to put their stuff down, the bed wasn't made and I had my clothes strewn all over, the way I do, and there were all these bottles of homemade wine sitting there, and on the chair next to the bed was one of your ties. . . . I don't know, my father, he just started crying. . . ."

Here she began to weep. I reached into the pocket of my suit pants and handed her a handkerchief.

She sobbed, and kept blowing her nose into my handkerchief as I held my arms around her in the gutted airplane.

There was nothing to say. It was just another blowout on the road, as they say in sports. You have to pick up the pieces and move forward, and try again in the next town.

Finally she looked up at me and managed an embarrassed smile. "Criminey!" she said.

"It's no big deal," I said. I kissed her forehead lightly.

"I hate to make them suffer like that, but what can I do?"

"It's sounds to me like they're the ones who are making you suffer."

She stood up slowly. "God, how am I going to go to work?"

"At least you're not drunk." We shared a smile, remembering the time she had fallen on her ass in my office.

So began the smoother, downhill glide toward the end of my beautiful Seattle summer. One night we saw Fellini's film "La Dolce Vita," and then we stopped at the coffee shop we had gone to on the first night we went out together. Leslie was especially moved by the film's opening shot of the statue of Jesus, his arms out wide in a gesture of benediction, hanging from a helicopter while being hauled over groping modern Rome.

We agreed on how we preferred foreign movies to the popular American films. I told Leslie about films I loved—John Cassavete's *Shadows*, and *Breathless* by Jean-Luc Goddard, and a Russian film, *Ballad of a Soldier*, and she told me about her favorite, *Nights of Cabiria*, also by Fellini. And then I made Leslie laugh when I imitated Albert Finney's wild drunken speech from *Saturday Night and Sunday Morning*, acting it out loudly in the coffee shop, as if I were drunk myself: "I'm me and nobody else!" I shouted, in an English midlands accent. "Whatever people say I am, I'm not. Because they don't know a bloody thing about me. I'm a six-foot prop that wants a pint of beer, that's what," while people at other tables turned toward us with strange looks on their faces.

I told her how much I loved Thomas Wolfe's *Of Time and The River*, and of how I thought time *was* like a river, and then I recited the end of Dylan Thomas's poem "Fern Hill," where "time held me green and dying, though I sang in my chains like the sea," and although it was a weekday, and Leslie had an exam the next evening, we wound up staying together at Leslie's that night, as we both felt we had ventured too deeply into our feelings to separate and go our own ways.

Leslie continued to go out with old friends, and I would journey to various bars with Vic and Hal where sometimes I would meet other women, but each of these experiences at the bars merely threw a more beneficent light on my times with Leslie, and I always looked forward to seeing her again and resuming our doomed friendship.

We rarely spoke about the end of the summer. It was as if we had made an unacknowledged agreement to live peacefully in the short time we had left together, and to leave ourselves unscarred memories of each other, like rosary beads to work with our fingers during the long years in which we would be apart.

Chapter Twenty-eight

One day, late in August, a letter arrived at work from Mitsubishi:

Dear Mr. Daniel Schwartz:

We appreciate very much your letter and we look forward to business together between us if possible.

Please do not worry about your credit rating. As we say in last letter, we know Brannan. It is major airplane maker in the world. We have no problem doing business with you. We know your credit is outstanding.

Thank you for interest.

Sincerely,

XX

I decided it was time to end this farce, and to make a decision about the defense of the United States. I was too frustrated and hung-over to take this rondo any further. I determined that the Readiman missile would not use Japanese transistors. All over the country for the next two or three decades, people would be sleeping just a little bit more easily because of my ability to make the sound decision.

Then, almost before I could comprehend what has happening, I found that I had reached the home-stretch chorus of my growing-up blues, my last weekend in Seattle, the end of my days with Leslie Schmidt.

Chapter Twenty-nine

Leslie looked ravishing in her good white dress, the one she wore on all special occasions. She was tan from a weekend we'd spent on the beach at Lake Samamish. Her hair, longer now, hung dark, rich and mahogany, down past her shoulders, making her appear even taller than her five-foot, nine-inch height. I noticed many of the other engineers and businessmen at the inn glancing at her as we sipped our cocktails and chatted with those of the guests whom I had met during the course of the summer.

I had come to like many of these people. Some were guys I had played softball with, others I had met at work. The occasion was a dinner to honor my boss, Jim Stilson, after twenty-five years at Brannan.

Now that I had arrived at my final Saturday night, I had already begun to view my experience at Brannan in the nurturing light of nostalgia. We were gathered at a country inn just outside Seattle. The crumbled logs in the giant fireplace were not burning in open flame any longer, but continued to breathe orange in spots, lending the room a warm, couch-pillowed coziness, especially when you looked through the large windows at the misty rain falling steadily outside.

I was dressed up in one of my two suits, I was with Leslie, who looked gorgeous, and Brannan was picking up the tab. Everything was fine. The sadness of our imminent parting, the gin, the fragile crystal glasses, the fresh-smelling white tablecloths set with sparkling plates and heavy silver, and the hint of tragic memories in the process of being formed cast everything in a clear, Vermeer light that was so lovely it made you want to weep.

I introduced Leslie to Jim Stilson, my boss, and to several fellow workers. One man, Bunky Cardona, said, "Danny, there's one thing I've been wanting to ask you. About our first softball game...." He turned to Leslie. "Danny here had just come to play shortstop for us, and the bases were loaded with two out, and a guy hits a shot between short and third, a high line drive, and we don't know Danny from Adam, but he dives and he makes this incredible catch, I mean really unbelievable, back-handed, in the webbing of his glove, rolling over into left field, and coming up with the ball...."

I blushed slightly, recalling the catch very well. I saw Leslie looking at me with pride.

"But listen," Bunky continued, "he saved the inning, and maybe the game, and I mean we thought we had a pro or something, but then, the first batter in the next inning hits a little bouncing ball straight to him, and he drops it." He turned to me. "You know, when I saw that play, it almost seemed to me like you dropped it on purpose. To tell you the truth, I thought maybe you were afraid to have us think too highly of you or something." His voice trailed off, leaving the ball there for me to pick up. "I thought about that play a lot afterwards," I said. "But all I know for sure is I felt really embarrassed when everyone was making such a big fuss over me, talking about how I was going to lead them to the championship and all. I mean, I knew I wasn't THAT good."

Bunky laughed. He patted me on the back, and said, affectionately to Leslie as he walked toward the bar, "He's a nutty guy, this Danny.... But I'm glad we had him at shortstop."

Leslie smiled. She liked Bunky, but in general she was never comfortable with the rituals and formalities of the business world. I could tell that she felt awkward and out of place. In truth, she *was* out of place somehow, a kind of pre-Raphaelite beauty, set amongst the movers and shakers of the defense industry.

Leslie would never be at home in the world of society and manners. She would never entertain properly and say the correct things. She would always have a touch of the wild girl about her, the strange, beautiful outsider whose basic kindness and intelligence would not get a chance to shine in these surroundings because she would not reveal her best qualities, fearing they would not be recognized. And perhaps she was right.

Yet, beneath this fear, there was a stubborn integrity. At some hard center of herself, she wished to remain the daughter of Hog

Pete, a Catholic farm girl, living still, to a degree, in an age prior to that of the rational, skeptical, urban middle-class, a group before which she would often seem tongue-tied and frustrated.

I followed Leslie out to the deserted porch. I put my hand on her bare shoulder and kissed her. We stood there together, my arm around her, watching the softly lit, early-autumn rain.

I thought back to the beginning of the summer, when I had dropped that easy ground ball. I knew that Leslie would have dropped it, too.

When the moment arrived for the major speech, everyone in the room was drunk. The speaker was Bob Maytall, a florid, self-important, rich, local entrepreneur, filled with a large bag of orotund rhetoric about himself.

Bob was an important man in town, but in his own mind he was a kind of human Mount Rainier.

Seated next to Bob was his second wife, Myrtle—about twenty-five years younger than Bob, heavily made-up, with bleached-blonde hair, a low-cut gown and coarse features. Myrtle was extremely, staggeringly, unequivocally drunk out of her mind.

She passed through the banquet hall toward the ladies' room as Bob related endless anecdotes, each episode purportedly about Jim, but actually about Bob himself—his wisdom in originally hiring Jim, the opportunities he had given Jim, how much Jim had learned from him, etc.

Leslie fidgeted uneasily. It wasn't only Bob's monstrous self-regard, the sheer stupidity of his presenting his naked egotism in such an undisguised, uninteresting manner, but, from Leslie's angle, it was Bob himself, exactly the worst sort of boss to have if you were a sensitive young woman, the kind of man who had bullied Leslie all her life, talking suggestively, trying to fondle her—in short, a "pillar of the community" whose lack of insight into himself was as large as the giant faces carved into rock in South Dakota.

I turned to Leslie and whispered into her ear, "He's what my cousin Louie the Mook would call 'a legend in his own mind.'" Leslie gave me a weak smile, the kind you give your dentist when he tells you a joke as he's drilling.

Myrtle came wobbling back toward the dais. Between Bob and the large fireplace behind him rested a waiters' stand, a tripod with a round silver tray on top, filled with several dozen champagne glasses.

Myrtle passed behind the dais and, just as she turned herself slightly to slip unobtrusively behind Bob, her heel caught and she toppled like a tree onto the waiters' stand and RODE on it, impossibly ROLLING with it in slow motion as it tipped, and you could hear the glasses popping all over as they fell and smashed like tinkly fireworks, until the serving tray finally and irrevocably yielded and laid her, like a fish on a skillet, INTO THE FIREPLACE!!!!

Women screamed. People rushed forward. They dragged her out of the hearth disoriented, her gold satin dress blackened. Fortunately, she was not on fire. And she was unhurt—the luck of the drunk—although some guests doused her with champagne to make sure there were no living cinders adhering to her dress. Several people supported her, while two women brushed off her crushed dress and another attempted to console her, ignoring the fact that she wasn't completely conscious, standing there looking like Our Lady of the Bimbos.

Leslie and I sat in our seats, sipping on our wine, Leslie trying to hide a little grin.

At the end of the evening, after Myrtle had been propped up in her chair and Bob had shortened the remainder of his speech so that it lasted only twice as long as the Crusades, Leslie and I wound up in line behind Bob at the checkroom. The line was a long one. Everyone had brought raincoats. You could see Bob fuming. What was the point of having made all that money if you still had to wait in line for your coat with peons like me and Leslie?

Finally Bob made it up to the front. "That's mine. The beige one right there!" He leaned over the counter as if he were going to take it himself, although he couldn't quite reach it.

A timid, young girl was working the checkroom. "Do you have your ticket, sir?"

"*Ticket?* That's my coat! That one, right there. Just give it to me."

"I'm sorry, sir, but I'll need your ticket."

"TICKET? Don't you talk to me about a ticket. I told you that's my coat!"

"But, sir. . . ."

"Look, young lady. If you want your job, YOU JUST GIVE ME THAT COAT THIS MINUTE!"

The girl was almost in tears. Everyone was looking at her.

Bob shouted, "YOU GIVE ME THAT COAT! DO YOU HEAR ME? I KNOW MY OWN COAT, DAMN IT! YOU JUST GIVE IT TO ME RIGHT NOW!"

The girl stood there, too flustered to move. Bob fumbled impatiently in his pocket. He removed its contents, but there was no ticket. He shouted, "LOOK, YOUNG LADY, JUST GIVE ME MY GODDAMN COAT RIGHT NOW OR I'LL COME BACK THERE AND TAKE IT MYSELF!"

"Hey, calm down, man," I said, but he began to march toward the door on the side of the checkroom. "All right, all right, sir," the girl cried. "Here. Here's your coat."

Bob grabbed the coat out of her hands, and shoved his arms into the sleeves.

"It's just that there are so many coats, sir, and they told me . . ."

"GOD DAMN IT! DON'T YOU UNDERSTAND? I'M BOB MAY-TALL!" He shouted so forcefully that the girl moved backwards. "DON'T YOU THINK I KNOW MY OWN DAMN COAT? WHAT DO YOU THINK I AM, A COMPLETE IDIOT?"

"Hey, take it easy," I said.

He turned indignantly to walk away. Pulled the coat closed and started to button it. Stopped. Stood still for a second. Played with the buttons again. Spun back toward the girl, tore off the coat, slammed it down on the counter and said, "God damn it, this isn't my coat."

Leslie caught my eye and gave me a long, silent look.

The rain had stopped by the time Leslie and I arrived at Birdland together for the last time. We had changed our clothes back at The Palace, and had driven over with Hal following us in his own car. We "skated" for several hours and then, at about four in the morning, when the venue closed, we all stood outside in the damp air. Like us, the Negro kids from the neighborhood seemed hesitant to call it a night.

We were the only white people there. We had never really been taken in as friends by the people at Birdland—it was too much of a neighborhood place—but we had worked hard at showing them that we appreciated being there and that we would play by their rules, and by the end of the summer the regulars were familiar with us and would give us a smile when we arrived, or dance around us a little in a friendly fashion when we were on the floor.

This meant a great deal to me. I wanted to be accepted by the Negroes. To learn from them. I appreciated the chance to be with them on their turf, away from the normal white world, which I often felt was killing me as well.

Leslie and I lingered on the curb with Hal. A sports car came speeding down the street. Some of the Negro kids, who were standing in groups that overlapped the curb, moved back a notch as the little car roared toward us. It was Vic in his red Austin Healy, with the top down. We were about to shout out to him when he stepped on the gas and spun by us, almost hitting a couple of people. As he passed, he reached up and threw a beer bottle over his shoulder at all of us. It smashed in the street at the feet of some Negro girls. Several of the Negro guys shouted "HEY, MAN!!!" and they chased Vic down the street, his car fishtailing as he shifted gears and spun out.

I joined the guys in their pursuit, not wanting them to know that I was a friend of Vic's. We chased after Vic along Jackson Street, shouting and cursing at him, but he pulled away and disappeared up the hill.

I walked back with the Negro guys to the front of the theater where the crowd waited, most of them in the street now, trying to see what had happened. I was cursing Vic loudly along with the rest, and in truth I was furious at him, but I suspected that some of the people might have recognized him from the time he had been there with us a couple of weeks before.

We stood in front of the theater a short while longer. Then we walked up the street. At the corner, Leslie and I parted from Hal and moved quietly toward my car. I felt a heavy sadness. I had not been able to look any of the Negroes in the eyes as we left Birdland for the last time.

The next morning, about noon, Leslie and I were sipping coffee at her kitchen table, beneath the crucifix and the picture of the Virgin Mary on the wall.

Leslie had been in the shower when I awoke. We had not said a word about my leaving. Now we sat there quietly, avoiding each other's eyes. Sipping the coffee. Buttering slices of wheat toast. Speaking in flat tones. About Vic at Birdland. And the dinner at the inn. We spoke of everything but what was really on our minds: our separate futures and the America-sized separation that loomed before us.

I honored Leslie's wish that we not talk too much about this. Then the time for me to leave approached.

"Can you pass me a little more milk?" I said.

Leslie moved the milk toward me without speaking.

"Well, it's sure been a great summer," I said.

She nodded.

"I know you don't want to get sentimental. . . ." I said.

"Oh, it isn't that. . . ."

". . . but, really, I'll never forget you. These weeks . . . they've been the best weeks of my life. I've learned so much . . . had such great times." I picked up my spoon. Stirred my coffee. Leslie looked so shy and pretty and sad, sitting there across from me. I tried to memorize the way she looked at that moment. "I've never had a friend like you before. I mean, a girl who was my closest friend . . . and . . . and my girl friend at the same time . . . if you know what I mean. . . ."

She nodded bashfully. "I've had a great time, too."

She was not saying much. Because she liked me. I knew that she liked me. This was painful for her.

"I mean, someone I could really talk . . ."

"I know. You don't have to say it." We sipped at our coffee. I moved my gaze around the room. The ancient gas stove. Her battered old bicycle leaning against the wall. I couldn't believe that I would never be seeing Leslie again. But it was true. It was finally happening.

"I'll never be the same," I said, quietly.

Leslie lit up a cigarette.

"But somehow," I continued, "in some strange way, I feel I know less than when the summer started. You know what I mean?"

"You mean you're less certain about things?" She exhaled smoke lazily into the air above our heads. The room lay perfectly still. The sun filtered in through the light curtain on the kitchen window. There were no cars passing on the street. "Yeah. That's it." I watched the smoke rise. Looked carefully at Leslie, sitting there. I so much liked the way her long, graceful neck rose out of the clean, washed-out, thin white sweatshirt she was wearing over her jeans.

"I mean, God ... look at all the people I've met. And all with different ideas. And damned if they don't all make sense when you hear them. I just wish Bill hadn't gone to Africa so soon. I would have *loved* to have talked to him about what Virgil always says. About peace being the way and all that. And, shit, wouldn't it have been *great* to hear Bill and Donny Lang up in Vancouver talk about violence! Man, those two guys ... I didn't know what the hell to say to either one of them."

"Oh, you did OK." She gave me an affectionate smile.

"No. I don't think so ... You know, Virgil once told me that after he quoted Martin Luther King to Bill, Bill snapped, 'You want to see where our people have protested? Just look wherever there's a swimming pool in the ghetto. That's the history of Negro protest in America. Create a riot and they give you a pool.' Then Virgil looked at me as if I could say something about this, but really, what do I know? ... "

"I wish *I* knew," she said, releasing a sigh. "You know me. I believe that love and eternal life are at the heart of the universe. Not death and nothingness. But you can't say that to anyone these days. They think you're a creampuff."

I finished the last piece of toast.

"You know," I said, "I was awake last night, thinking about everything. ... God, sometimes people are so amazing. ... I mean, look at Virgil. ... He doesn't have a bass, so he plays an imaginary one. ... And yet it's *not* just imaginary. ... It's *good*, in a way. ... And the people at Birdland. ... They lose their skating rink, so they make believe they're skating. ... And yet, it's not just imaginary. ... You know what I mean? ... It becomes a kind of dance. ... "

She said nothing, but I knew that she understood what I meant.

I continued, "Look at the Negroes. They have so little, but if they have a problem, they don't always just mope and all.... Sometimes they imagine their way out of it.... I wish I could learn to do that.... You know what I mean? To really *imagine* some solution to my problems...."

"Which problems are you thinking of?"

"Loneliness ... death ... how to find a path in my life that has some meaning...."

We sat there quietly. I sipped at my coffee. I looked at Leslie's slim, graceful features as she lit herself a cigarette. I didn't want to walk out the door.

"You'll be studying theology at Seattle U. in the fall?"

She nodded. "I'm going to study the *Summa*. With a priest you'd like. Father Orleans. He has a bowling team. 'Orleans' meanies.'" She smiled. "He's a crazy guy. He hates the Jesuits. Every time he mentions the Jesuits, he goes 'khatouuiee,' as if he's spitting on the floor."

I smiled along with her. I knew nothing about the Jesuits, or how they fitted into the scheme of the Church, but I enjoyed watching her tell the story. "Well, we better get moving," she said, rising.

I rose along with her.

"Yeah, might as well shove off," I said.

"Don't forget this," she said, running into the bedroom and snatching my blue tie, which had been on the back of the chair in there all summer.

"You can keep it if you want."

"Naw," she said, handing it to me.

I tossed the tie around my neck. Enfolded her in my arms and gave her a final kiss.

I pulled away and took her hands. Held her at arms' length and looked at her for the last time.

"Will you answer if I write?"

She shrugged. There were the beginnings of tears in the corners of her eyes.

"You won't mind if I write?"

She shrugged again. Not trusting herself to speak.

"Well, maybe I'll drop you a line now and then. Just to see how the philosophy of love is doing in the world...."

Her eyes glistened as she smiled at me.

"Good-bye, Leslie," I said, looking into her eyes. "I'll never forget you."

She turned her gaze down toward the floor. She was at her most beautiful at moments like this, when she was shy and filled with unvoiced sorrow.

I began to choke up, so I turned and walked out the door.

Chapter Thirty

Vic and I left Seattle on Monday morning. Hal stood glumly outside The Palace, desolate as an orphan, already drinking. In Montana, my car broke down and we were pushed for miles by two cowboys in a pickup under the Big Sky, with thousands of mosquitoes attacking us, thick as the stars.

At Glacier National Park we came upon a mountain lake so blue under a sky so pure we burst out of the car with our musical instruments and began to wail like madmen, with Vic playing his amazing runs on recorder, and me pounding out rhythm on a conga, neither of us acknowledging how much we loved it when amazed tourists stopped their cars to watch "the beatniks."

In North Dakota we witnessed an accident between a tractor and a truck, with both drivers hurt. We drove furiously to the state police barracks eleven miles away to summon help because, incredible as it seemed to us, none of the farms between the crash site and the police station had telephones.

In Chicago, the two of us went over to McKee Fitzhugh's funky little club in the heart of the South Chicago ghetto where, astoundingly, we caught a group that featured two of the finest saxophone players in the history of the world—Sonny Stitt, the great alto man who sounded so much like Charlie Parker, and Gene Ammons, recently out of jail—playing some of the greatest tenor either of us had ever heard. After the club closed, we were so excited that we tried to buy some marijuana from two Negro guys our age whom we had met at the bar, Vic saying, "We need to get some boo, man. We have got to get ourselves some boo."

We gave them ten bucks and walked with them through the back streets of the South Side of Chicago until they entered a run-down apartment house and disappeared. We ranted for a while about the injustice of it all, but they were nice guys, actually, and it was hard to stay pissed-off on a night when, for the price of a couple beers, we had chanced upon one of the great musical events of our lives.

Much of the time we had been at McKee Fitzhugh's, I found myself thinking about Leslie. Whenever some hipster with a crazy hat that she would have dug walked in the door, I wanted to nudge her with my elbow. Whenever Sonny Stitt or Gene Ammons played an incredibly fast run or a beautiful phrase, I wanted to turn to her, the lone white girl at the bar, and bob my head with hers in time to the music.

Thinking of Leslie made me realize how much more great art means when you can share it with your friends.

I dropped Vic off in New Jersey, then showed up at my family's four-room apartment in The Bronx and rapped with my brother Barry, while my mother alerted the approximately four thousand relatives who lived in the building that the prodigal son had returned.

I waited up for my father to come coughing down the street, home from his store in Harlem at midnight. I had missed the habitual crazy-linebacker expression on his face, the warmth he would sometimes show toward me at unexpected and wonderful moments.

When he walked in the door I could tell that he was glad to see me. I ran up to him and shook his hand. "Well, you're home." He scanned me up and down. Smiled. "You had a good time?"

I nodded.

He looked me in the eye and said, expectantly, "Did you save up a lot of money for the fall?"

Chapter Thirty-one

Back in Philadelphia, I entered my second and final year at Wharton. In May I would have the M.B.A.

I was rooming with Ritchie Hotchkiss in a large apartment building situated above the basement bar I liked, the one I called "The Inferno," from which they threw the rowdy patrons *up* the steps into the street.

I was studying madly and getting straight As, but I had little enthusiasm left for any activities outside of my work at the university. Sometimes I ventured out to a mixer or on a date, but a familiar sadness clung to my days like moss.

I drank far too much, and I was beginning to feel like a ragged collage, an assemblage of scraps and fragments loosely glued together, in danger of coming undone.

Often I would drink by myself in my room at night and think about my my wonderful cross country summer.

October 20, 1961

Dear Leslie,

Hope this letter finds you well and absorbed in your studies of Thomas Aquinas. I'm reading as much as I can along those lines, though I'm afraid I've got little spare time. I am reading my way through Dante, The Divine Comedy, *a couple sections at a time, each night. The first part,* The Inferno, *reminds me a little of The Bronx. (Just kidding! Please, Officer, stop me before I joke again!)*

I hope you got my earlier two letters. The first about the trip back and the second about that fabulous Coltrane show at the Village Gate. My God, Coltrane and Eric Dolphy, playing together with Elvin Jones and McCoy Tyner and two bassists! I kept saying to myself, "This is history! You're see-

ing an historical event!" And who could believe that Vic would show up? It seemed like the spell of Seattle wouldn't let go. The only thing missing was for you to arrive on your bike and pop in the door in your jeans and sweatshirt, carrying one of your precious books like God and Philosophy *by Etienne Gilson, and pull up a chair and have a beer with us.*

(If only there were some way to keep the summer going—the music, the talk, having someone to sleep with, someone who was my closest friend and confi-DANTE.)

Anyhow, the Wharton School let me take that course in Twentieth-Century American Culture that Bill Thomson recommended. I love it, I'm reading like mad, but I find I can't fit back into the social life at the college. I seem to have forgotten the social games, or to have lost the desire to play them.

I miss you a great deal, my friend. I often wonder why life has to be compartmentalized into a mature "day" half, where we suffer, bureaucratized, silent and alone, and another "night" half, where we let our true spirits out to breathe. But I'm getting maudlin. Must be that Gallo port I've been drinking. I think I'll close and play Johnnie and Jo's "Over The Mountain" twenty times, and dance the fish by myself and pretend I'm dancing with you.

I hope you're making progress in your quest to bring love back into the industrial world.

Take care of yourself, Pal.

Love,

Danny

P.S. I keep thinking about how Hal always used to call me "Mahatma Gandhi in a Cadillac." I guess there was some truth in it, and that was why it annoyed me so. I've been reading some Hinduism. I wonder if the vision they talk about is the same one that St. Thomas saw. The Hindus say that what stands between us and God is our ego—our selfish craving and defense systems that seperate us from others and from God. But how to get beyond this state? I read where the Buddhists talk of right work as part of the process. Work that doesn't feed our selfishness and our defenses. I guess if God is love and forgiveness like you say, then all this doesn't mean so much in the end, but I keep thinking that somehow it's central for me. But what is my right work?

175

Gerald Rosen

* * * * *

November 10, 1961

Dear Leslie,

It's Friday night. Since I finished my studying, I've been reading T.S. Eliot's "Little Gidding," and drinking Gallo port by myself in my room, thinking of you while playing "Earth Angel" four hundred times.

You know how T.S. Eliot says that he traveled around until finally he came back to the very place he started from, but now he understood it for the first time? Well, this summer I, too, did some serious traveling, and now I, too, have returned to the place from which I started, only now I don't understand it for the first time.

Don't take any wooden Jesuits.

Love,
Danny

Chapter Thirty-two

November 28, 1961

Dear Leslie,

I received your change-of-address card. Unless I'm mistaken, that's in the U. District. What's happening? Are you still going to Seattle U.? Are you transfering back to the U. of Washington? Please send me your phone number.

I had the most awful day Saturday, a day that was typical of what's been going wrong for me here. Two married friends of mine and their wives fixed me up with a date, and she was all wrong for me. We didn't connect at all. She only wanted to go out with me because she had heard I was first in my class.

We wound up that night at a posh fraternity party, the kind I hate, where the brothers are wearing tuxedos and they've got this old Negro man dressed up as a butler or something, to sweep the floor between dances. My date was dancing to a crappy Lester Lanin-type band with some fraternity guy she knew, Preston Schuyler, so I went over and said a few words to the old man, he looked so sad standing there. He told me he cooks for the fraternity every day, and yet here were all these guys, and they wouldn't even acknowledge they knew him, for God's sakes! You could see he was lonely and out of place, and that was the way I was feeling too, in my old sport jacket that I've had forever, but for the first time that evening, I began to feel good. I'd found someone I could talk to.

But when we got back to my friends' house, my date started shouting at me, and everyone was saying that my jacket was out of style and that I shouldn't have talked to the butler, and then my date started bawling, and everyone was looking at me as if somehow I was responsible.

But listen to this: The night before, I had gone to hear some jazz at the Showboat, by myself after the library closed, and who sits down next to me at the bar but Fats Domino! He's a great guy. We had a terrific conversa-

tion! And listen, I had no trouble with Fats Domino. He wasn't saying my jacket was wrong, even though it was the same jacket! He didn't give a shit about my goddamned jacket! And the same damn thing happened at Bryn Mawr that time I met one of my heroes, the Irish playwright Brendan Behan. (He was sober, if you can believe it, and I was drunk.) After his performance, I leaped onto the stage to thank him, and he invited me into his dressing room, and we had a real talk, I mean, a great talk. He didn't care what kind of sport jacket I had on, believe me, and before he went out to meet the girls again, he took out a cigar and told me he wanted to give it to me because he had stolen it! and then, he told the girls I was his "good friend"! But the next week I was banned from the campus for supposedly insulting this famous author. Well this is exactly the opposite of what was happening, but try to explain this to anyone! Aggggggggghhhhhhh!

Hey, listen, kid, I miss you. I'm isolated here. Like in High Sierra, *where Humphrey Bogart winds up on top of the mountain cornered, by himself, but he's so high even the cops' bullets can't reach him.*

I'm holding out. But I need help. My supplies are running low.

Stay in touch, my friend, my sister, my double.

Yours, as always,

Beau d'Lair

Early in December, about a week after I sent the letter, Ritchie Hotchkiss hurried into my room.

"You've got a phone call. It's a girl."

"A girl?"

"Sounds like long distance."

I picked up the phone in the living room.

"Oh, Danny, something really awful's happened."

"Leslie? What wrong? Are you OK?"

"It's not me. It's Hal. Oh, Danny, this is so hard to talk about, but I had to tell you. . . ."

"What is it?"

"Hal ran over a little boy. It happened about two weeks ago. I didn't hear about it for a few days."

"What? Is the kid all right?"

"No, Danny. It's terrible. The boy died. He was about four years old."

"But how did it happen? Was Hal drunk?"

"I don't think so. It was in the morning. He ran a stop sign and he hit this kid who was crossing with his mother."

"Is the mother OK?"

"Yes. But Hal . . . he's shattered. The kid's parents have been real good to him. They belong to some kind of Christian sect and they've been praying for Hal, and they've been really trying to help him."

"Have you seen him?"

"I've been studying real hard at school, and what with work and all I haven't seen much of anybody. But of course I rode over to his place on my bike once I heard."

"How is he?"

"It . . . it was like he was all empty inside. He kept saying, 'My life is over. My life is over. All I've got is these people who are praying for my soul.' I stayed with him for hours. I cooked him a dinner. I was afraid to leave him alone. But finally he told me it was OK to go, and then I went back a couple days later and he wasn't there. I checked up on him at work, and he hadn't shown up."

"Where was he?"

"Well, that's just it. He's disappeared. I spoke to his boss, and they're worried about him, too. His car was found down by Pete's. Danny, that's near Puget Sound. . . . You know he can't swim."

"Wait. . . . Look, don't assume the worst. That's near the train station. He probably took the train somewhere. Or one of the ferries to one of the islands, to take some time to get himself together or something. . . ."

We sat there in silence, listening to the miles of wires and the wave guides humming between us.

Finally, I broke the silence. "Well, there's nothing you can do. . . . You know Hal. . . . He's probably holed up somewhere, feeling guilty. . . . He'll be OK," I said without conviction.

"I sure hope so."

"Hey, listen, how are you? I mean besides this thing with Hal."

"I'm OK, I guess."

"I got your card. Are you living in the U. district?"

"Yeah. I've got this new roommate. A nursing student. Susan. She's Jewish. She's real nice. I know you'd like her." She paused for

179

a second, and I felt a little better suddenly, hearing her imagining me back in her life, thinking about whether I would like her friends or not.

"I always seem to wind up with Jews these days," she said, and I could tell she was smiling weakly as she said it.

"Are you still at Seattle U.?"

"Yeah.... But I'm not going to go on with the theology.... I'll tell you about it sometime. I may transfer back to U.W. I think I'm going to be a high school English teacher."

"Really? Wow! Everything seems to be changing these days. I don't know what I'm going to do, myself. I've only got a couple months left to decide, before the job interviews start. And I've got the Army to think about, too. I just got a draft notice. But listen, that's for some other time...."

"Yeah, I better run. Did I tell you I'm quitting Brannan? At Christmas. I've got some money saved up. Maybe I'll work part-time waitressing, and study lit. I don't know. I'll work something out. I have to make a change."

"Leslie, listen.... There's so much I want to tell you, I don't know what to say first.... It's great hearing your voice. God, I wish we could really talk." She didn't respond, so I continued, "Listen, I really miss Seattle. I miss our times together, and our talks and all.... How about if I come out there for Christmas? You sound like you could use someone to talk to, what with Hal and everything. Maybe we both could use some time together."

Again there was a silence on the line. I sat there listening to my heart beating under the singing of the electricity.

"Listen," I said, "if I can scrape together the fare for a cheap ticket, would you be pissed if I showed up on your doorstep at Christmas?"

"Pissed?" she said, gently. "Oh, Danny, how could I be mad at you for something like that?"

"Wahooo!" I shouted as I hung up the phone and Hotchkiss came into the room, smiling, ready to hear all the dirt. As I related to him what had happened, I felt the strangest mixture of sadness and happiness. I was seriously worried about Hal. But at the same time,

I was just beginning to realize that something had happened between Leslie and myself. She had reestablished the connection. She had called me, 3000 miles away, when she was in trouble.

I was back in Leslie's life. And she would not have opened herself to the pain of another separation for merely a week of fun and talk.

"And she's not studying theology anymore," Hotchkiss pointed out.

"I'm going to Seattle!" I shouted. "I can hardly believe it. Yahoooo!"

Hotchkiss stood there beaming. He reached into his wallet and handed me a fifty.

I looked at him, puzzled.

"To get you started on your airfare."

"Oh, I don't know...."

He pressed the fifty into my hand. "Chalk it up to class guilt," he said lightly. "You'll pay me back in the spring."

I took the money and thanked him.

"That's OK," he said, smiling. "You know, you look truly happy for the first time since you've come back."

Chapter Twenty-three

On Christmas morning, Leslie answered the door of her flat wearing a loose-fitting, thick, baggy, aquamarine sweater, no doubt from the Goodwill. Behind her, a beautifully decorated tree unfolded like a little ballerina, offering colored globes and bangles, twinkling lights, striped candy canes and large stars.

"Leslie! It's great to see you."

She looked into my eyes, smiled, and handed me a delicate silver and red Christmas tree ball. I moved forward into the doorway and hugged her to me, I can't say for how long, carefully holding the fragile glass ball away from us. The Christmas tree in the background shed light around her like a nimbus. Her hair was longer, a deeper brown than it had been during the summer. She seemed thinner when I held her; I could feel her ribs through the heavy sweater that she wore over her jeans. Her skin glowed with a wan luminosity, like pearls in candlelight. She had, no doubt, been working and studying hard. Her whole being was less earthy, more fragile, than when I had known her in the flare light of the drunken summer.

"God, it's great to be here!" I said. "I've been getting higher and higher all night. I couldn't sleep a wink all the way across country."

I handed her the Christmas-tree ornament, picked up my old suitcase and followed her into the apartment. She hung the silver and red ball back on the tree. "You wouldn't believe the cheap flight I found." I set my suitcase down near the door, which was at the corner of the large room. At the far end there was a kitchen and a small dining table. "The plane made eight stops."

"Eight?"

"Great Falls, Butte, Yakima, Bismarck. I've been in every one of them in the last twelve hours. The stewardesses couldn't believe it.

No one takes that flight all the way across."

I dusted snow off the shoulders of my parka, and set it down on the couch. Then I took Leslie in my arms again, and whirled her around as we both laughed breathlessly.

"This big room is mine. My roommate Sue sleeps over there." She indicated a bedroom off the large main room.

"Where do *you* sleep?"

"Here." She pointed to the sofa. "It's a convertible."

I must've looked a little surprised that she didn't have a bedroom of her own, because she explained, "Sue pays more of the rent this way. The bathroom's in the hall, but we only share it with the couple next door."

"Is Sue here?"

"No. She'll be back in a week."

I collapsed down onto the soft, old couch. Leslie remained standing. Happiness shone from her face.

"It seems like a pretty nice place to me."

The room had a cozy feel to it, with worn Persian rugs on the floor, lots of books and various pieces of heavy old furniture filling the space. In fact, with the glittering lights of the tree, the orange glow of a Japanese paper lantern, and the flames of three candles burning on the mantel, it seemed as though we were on another planet somehow, one a little more magical than the Earth, a little more like home.

"I love the tree."

She blushed slightly. "I wasn't sure if you celebrated Christmas. But then I figured, what the hell...."

I thought: I'll bet she's been excited about my coming, but she has a hard time saying it directly. The tree was her way of telling me.

She picked up my suitcase. I wondered if she would carry it into Sue's room, but she just set it up against the side of the convertible sofa.

She put a kettle on the stove. I joined her at the kitchen end of the long room and sat at the little table.

"Have you heard anything about Hal?"

"Nothing since I spoke to you. When his parents came out here,

I went over to his flat to see them. They're real nice. Totally devastated by all this. They paid his rent for a few months, and they're going to keep the apartment for him. But that's it. Nothing about Hal himself."

I let the subject drop for now, and turned my attention back to Leslie. It was difficult to know how to respond to each other after several months. I think we were both glad for the chance to immerse ourselves in the ordinary simple ceremonies, the taking of tea together, the spreading of rich strawberry preserves on toasted English muffins. Seattle had come to seem to me more like a dream than a real place one could actually return to. Yet here was Leslie, in the vibrant, living flesh of her actual embodied presence. And every now and then I would catch her opening up her generous sunflower smile.

We strolled over to the University, which was situated about a quarter mile from Leslie's house. Seattle had always been like a pretty young girl in my imagination, and now she wore a shawl of bright, melting snow in her hair. We gazed into the windows of the bookstores on University Way. Leslie looked spirited and pretty, wrapped up in an old peacoat, a knitted navy-blue sailor's watch-cap on her head, her breath turning to fog in the nippy air. She smiled at me shyly whenever our eyes met.

We proceeded onto the grounds of the University itself, ambling past the totem poles and the rows of stately sycamore trees. I was surprised to see tended flowers still alive and in bloom. "Today's colder than usual," Leslie said. "It doesn't usually snow here."

"I hear it rains all the time."

"Lightly, most of the time. Often just a kind of mist." She was almost whispering, her voice like a tender rain.

We strolled over to the "Red Square" at the center of the class-room buildings. Mount Rainier was not visible in the overcast sky, but it didn't matter to me. I knew it was there behind the clouds. I knew things were all right.

We returned to the house and sipped at warm brandy. There was little to say. Nowhere to get to. We were completing the process that had been our destiny since we had sat next to each other at orientation that initial day at Brannan.

Leslie cooked us a beef stew. We drank burgundy wine. I gave her the presents I had brought: A forty-five doo-wop record of Clyde McPhatter and the Drifters singing "White Christmas," which made her laugh, and a more serious record, an LP of John Coltrane's "My Favorite Things," which she loved and played twice through, along with a boxed set of Pablo Casals playing the six Bach "Suites for Unaccompanied Cello," which so moved her she ran over to my chair and gave me a long kiss on top of my head.

But the pinnacle of the evening arrived with the present she had bought for me. Wrapped in red paper, under the tree. Gil Evan's LP "Out of the Cool." I had never heard it before. It tore me apart with its sad beauty. That Leslie could have found such a record! I felt so warm inside, it almost seemed that my life was happening to someone else, someone who was happier than I could ever be.

We opened up the sofa, took off our clothes and lay in it together beneath the soft comforter, between the fresh, cold sheets. I was tentative in reaching out to her at first, as if I were still holding the fragile Christmas-tree ornament in my hand. I knew how volatile Leslie could be, and as much as I yearned for her body, it was love that I hungered for, although sex had its powers too, of course, its philtres and potions, and when we finally made love to each other, gently, cautiously at first, and then without the limits we had observed during the summer, it seemed less a sudden jump to a higher level in the history of our relationship than a simple acknowledgment of the profound intimacy into which we had already moved.

We spent the next couple of days in complacent supplication to the ordinary. We spoke of Hal several times, even ventured over to his apartment once on the bus, but it was still empty, as we expected. We talked little of ourselves in any serious manner, listening to a fine new Negro radio station that Leslie had discovered, soaking ourselves in a contentment we had glimpsed at times during the summer, but now without the fights, the haggard drunkenness, the strident reaching for the undefined.

On the fourth day, we ventured over to the familiar downtown streets, and the sun broke through, and the very air we breathed seemed to float motes of hope that danced and glistened in a Vivaldi concerto of light.

That evening, with the air smelling piney and new, we walked through a soft, misty, Monet rain from the Pike Place Market, where we had eaten a fish chowder, over to see the movie of *Breakfast at Tiffany's*, with Audrey Hepburn. There was something synchronistic, almost magical, in the way that Holly Golightly seemed to project so much of Leslie up onto the large screen, both women so pretty and bright and full of life, arriving in the big city from nowhere farms and winding up at the vortex of various eccentric people and chaotic events. But there was a large and most revealing difference between Holly and Leslie as well. Leslie had known, somehow, right from the start, that the kind of diamonds she was seeking would never be sold at Tiffany's.

The next day, after we read together through most of the chilly afternoon, sipping tea with a touch of brandy while Casals played Bach, our conversation finally drifted out of the sheltered harbor we had constructed together during the past few days.

"Boy, this thing about Hal is really something, isn't it?" I said. I was sprawled on the sofa, across from Leslie. "I mean, Hal had everything going for him, and then, in two seconds, it's pretty much all over.... I don't know what to think about it...."

"That's what they don't teach us in school. How to deal with really serious things." Her voice drifted off. She stared blankly across the room into space.

"And it's so unfair that it should happen to Hal," I said. "I mean there are so many bad people in the world.... You know, I've been really haunted by all this.... I mean, if there is a God, how could He let something like this happen?"

Leslie turned her head toward me as I continued to speak. "Finally I bought a copy of the Bible. I opened it up and read from different places in the Old Testament, at random. And you know, what happened to Hal, it seemed to fit right in there. Because what the hell is the Old Testament about anyhow? God tells the Jews to smite this people, and then that people, and then he himself drowns a bunch of people, and then he smites some other guys.... I mean it...."

"Oh, pshaaw!" she said, lightly, not following me into the dangerous area of our dissimilar backgrounds and aims. But I pushed ahead. "You know, sometimes I don't have the foggiest idea of how people can really believe that Old Testament stuff. The picture they draw of God in there ... angry ... vengeful ... I'll tell you the truth, I don't find Him to be even one-tenth as intelligent as Albert Einstein...."

The trace of a grin snuck onto her face in spite of herself. She straightened up in her chair. I knew she couldn't resist taking the bait. And yet there was no denying we were circling closer to the dangerous hot sun at the center of our relationship. "But don't you see?" she said, "that's why Judaism NEEDS Christ to complete it. Jesus brings the very mercy and forgiveness that you're so sorely missing in the Old Testament."

When I didn't respond, she added, "Everything in the Old Testament leads up to the appearance of Christ. There are signs of his coming all over in the text."

"Yeah," I said. "Nietzsche says that every time some Jew picks up a wooden toothpick in the Old Testament, Christians see it as a sign of the coming of the cross."

"Did Nietzsche really say that?"

"Pretty much," I said, caught in my exaggeration, but happy to see her smiling. "But not as colorfully."

"I thought so...."

There was love in her eyes as she looked at me. I took another chance. "You know, I did some reading on St. Thomas myself, this fall." She registered surprise.

"He was a brilliant man," I said.

"Was he ever! You don't see people struggling to put the whole world into a single system of thought anymore. I mean, he really tried...."

She stopped, the circumference of her language defeated by the magnitude of what she was envisioning. The *Summa.*

"Yeah, I think I know what you mean." Then I added, as gently as possible, "But you know, there is one thing that troubles me. I mean, here's this man, St. Thomas Aquinas, one of the greatest minds in the history of Catholicism, and yet ... well here's a quote I read of his." I reached into my wallet, and pulled out a ragged piece of paper, which I now began, perhaps unwisely, to read: "Here, this is St. Thomas: 'The blessed in heaven will see the punishment of the damned in order that their bliss will be greater.'"

Neither one of us spoke. I crumpled up the little piece of paper and stuffed it into my pocket. Leslie looked up toward the ceiling, wandering alone in her thoughts. When she turned back to me, she had an expression of the deepest seriousness on her sad face. I thought I had never seen her look so beautiful. She said simply, "I know what you mean. And there's not much I can say." There was a profound, dark sorrow in her eyes. "But I do have to tell you that if you're thinking that any statement by anyone, however mistaken or sadistic, is going to take me away from Christ and His Church . . . ."

She didn't finish. Yet, although her stubbornness was familiar to me, her tone now lacked a certain hard fire.

"Things aren't going to be easy for us. . . ." she said, almost swallowing her words.

"For us!" I thought. My spirit quickened.

"This all relates to my leaving theology. You see, I really studied this fall. I studied as if my life depended on it, and believe me, in a way, it does. . . ."

"I know what you're saying. I mean, I don't understand how people can just go ahead with their lives, knowing that someday they're all going to . . ."

"Wait. Let me finish for a second. What I found in studying St. Thomas . . . see, near the end of his life, St. Thomas had a vision. An overpowering vision . . . and after that, I don't think he ever really wrote in the same way again. . . . After he had this vision, he turned to all the books he had written, all those marvelous . . . those jewels of the human intellect, and he said, 'It's all straw.' Can you believe it? The author of the *Summa,* pointing to it and saying, 'It's all straw'?"

She rose up as if to ground her excess energy somehow, and then sat back down, this time on the arm of her chair. "You know, that dead-end where St. Thomas was . . . that seemed to me to be exactly where I had come to. But I hadn't had the guts to see it until I read about St. Thomas having that vision and saying what he said."

She dropped her arms to her knees. "Somehow, I'd already had it with that kind of scholastic thinking. Because when I thought about all the books I'd been studying, it seemed to me that all I kept feeling was, 'You can't get there from here. Not along this road. Not through the intellect alone.'"

"How *do* you get there?"

"Through having the vision, I guess. I don't know. . . . Through meditation? Through the heart? Through loving all of creation, without exception?" She gave her shoulders a little shrug and said, almost questioningly, "Through forgiveness? . . . Through following the path of Christ."

She slid back down into her chair.

"And so you decided to leave theology and to study literature instead. . . ."

She nodded. "There's something humble about literature. It doesn't make great claims. It pretty much sticks to the material world, which is the arena in which we have to fight our battles while we're here, isn't it? All the chaos and crap of everyday life."

"Well, it's certainly easier to make a living teaching English," I said, trying to lighten things up a bit. "There's not much of a demand for theologians these days."

She nodded. "And we do have to make a living."

"Don't I know it. 'Render unto Caesar that which is Caesar's,'" I said, knowing it would get her to smile as she always did when I surprised her by quoting from the New Testament.

"Render unto Caesar that which is easier," she said.

Chapter Thirty-four

"Things aren't going to be easy for us." Leslie's words kept rising to the surface of my mind like the bubbles in a glass of Gallo Port and Seven Up. But what exactly had she been referring to? The remainder of the week? Our lives together?

Leslie was standing at the sink, preparing the Pacific red snappers for broiling with butter and lemon. I stood next to her, peeling potatoes. "You know, that's a traditional Christian symbol," I said.

"A fish?"

"No, Pacific red snapper broiled with lemon and butter." I dropped the potatoes in a pot of water on the stove, and turned the gas flame up to full volume. "It's great to be here. I'm really glad you called me in Philadelphia."

"Did you say something about the Army on the phone that time?"

"Yeah. I got my draft notice. I have to report for a physical when I get back."

"Do you think you'll pass?"

"I don't see why not."

"So you'll go in for a couple years?"

"I don't know. . . . I can get out in a second if I want to. All I have to do is work for a big corporation."

"Are you going to interview for those kinds of jobs?"

"I don't know." I grasped a long carrot and began to shave it with the potato peeler.

"Do you want to go into the Army?"

I shrugged. "In a way, I really do feel like everyone should serve." I turned on the faucet and held the scraped carrots under the cold water. "A friend of mine says, once I've got the Wharton M.B.A., they'll let me go right into the Medics as an officer. They call it a 'direct commission.' The only catch is that you have to sign up for three years. Maybe I could save my money and use it to go back to school."

"And if there's a war?"

"Then I'd run an aid station. Right up near the front. . . . At least you're helping people. You're not trying to kill anyone." I dropped the carrots into the boiling water. "In any case, I don't see war as being very likely. Sure, there's all this Berlin crap, but if that comes down it'll go nuclear, and we'll all be killed anyhow. . . . God, you should see what's going on back East. Everyone's building fallout shelters. Governor Rockefeller wants them all over. . . . Right now they're building one at Rockefeller Center. I guess that way you're OK if there's an atomic attack while you're watching the Rockettes."

She set the fishes on the hot grill, their cold flesh sizzling.

"Actually, this isn't a bad time to go into the Army," I said. "There's really not all that much trouble in the world. I mean there's Laos. . . ."

"Where?"

"Laos. The old French Indo-China. I think it's part of Vietnam or something. But we'll never get involved in that one. Not with President Kennedy at the helm." I poured us each a jelly glass of white wine.

"To the first Catholic President," I said.

She smiled and touched her glass to mine. We sat down across from each other at the old, slightly chipped table. "I've really come to like Jack Kennedy," I said. "I know he hasn't been able to get all that much accomplished so far. He's got to go slow, to keep the Southern Democrats in line. But his heart's in the right place. . . . I don't know. I just *like* him. Have you ever seen any of his press conferences?"

"I don't have a TV."

"Well, I hardly ever watch it myself. But you should see him. They have this old lady, May Craig, from some newspaper in Maine, and she always brings up some crazy thing that's embarrassing, and Kennedy, he plays off her like a comedian with his straight man. It's great to watch. He's hilarious. You know, I've always respected Presidents and all—I mean, let's face it, it's one tough job—but Kennedy, he's the first President I ever thought I could be friends with. . . ."

She laughed.

"No, I mean it," I said, blushing slightly.

Leslie sipped at her wine. I was afraid that I had been silly, going on about President Kennedy like that, but she seemed to be enjoying herself.

"You know, I don't follow this stuff very closely," she said, "but I was just talking about President Kennedy last week."

"Oh yeah?"

"Remember that Swami I used to know? The one who left for India at the beginning of the summer?"

"The Hollywood guy?"

"Well, he's not exactly a Hollywood guy. . . ."

"Wasn't he the one who dated Marilyn Monroe?"

"He was her friend, yes. Anyhow, he was in town for a few days, and we had a cup of tea together before he went back to India. And, you know, he told me something real interesting."

"What's that?"

She stood up and continued to talk while she turned the fish over. "Well, I know it sounds strange, and maybe I shouldn't repeat this, but between you and me, he told me that Jack Kennedy is having an affair with Marilyn Monroe."

She slid the tray back into the broiler and returned to the table. I stared at her to see if she could possibly be serious. "Are you joking?" I hoped she would break into a smile.

She shrugged. "That's what he said."

"Wait a minute! Wait one cotton-pickin' minute. Are you telling me that some Swami told you that John F. Kennedy, the President of the United States, the husband of Jackie Kennedy, is having an affair with Marilyn Monroe, and you *believe* it!"

She smiled bashfully. "I don't know. I'm just telling you what he said to me."

"But . . . but, this is unbelievable. I mean, it's so obviously one of these crazy rumors that . . . well, I mean, why not Jayne Mansfield? Why not have the President dating Jayne Mansfield?"

"Swami said that Jack Kennedy *is* trying to sleep with Jayne Mansfield. But she's married and all, so he's having more success with Marilyn Monroe. He says Marilyn Monroe really likes Jack. She wants to marry him."

"What? *Marry* him? But Leslie, . . . don't you see? I mean, this means that Jack Kennedy has made himself the rival of Jayne Mansfield's husband, Mickey Hargitay, 'The Hungarian strongman'!" I began to laugh cynically. "You're saying that John Fitzgerald Kennedy, the President of United States, is trying to sleep with the wife of a Hungarian Strongman, and he's also balling the ex-wife of Joe Dimaggio, for God's sakes."

I swallowed the rest of my glass of wine.

Leslie looked a bit worried. "I was just saying what Swami told me. . . . Like I said, I don't follow this stuff. . . ."

I poured myself another glass of wine. "Listen, I'm sorry," I said. "Maybe I do make too much of Jack Kennedy. . . . It's just that I *like* him somehow. I mean, I want to like *somebody*. . . ."

"I know," she said. "I was just being contrary." She reached across the table and poked her finger into my ribs. "Come on, let's see a smile. It was a juicy rumor, you have to admit it. Come on," she said, continuing to prod me in the ribs. I pulled away, smiling. Then we both began to laugh.

"Boy, that was a great dinner," I said, leaning back and patting my belly.

Leslie's face filled with pleasure.

"Did you say something before about going back to school after you graduate?" she said. I nodded. "I really like this course in American Culture. The one Virgil's uncle Bill told me about. Hey, you remember when Bill asked me to define 'culture'? Well, if he ever writes, tell him I figured it out: A culture is a group of people who have decided not to see the same things together."

The coffee began to boil. I rushed over and turned down the flame. "Seriously, though, studying liberal arts . . . that's what I want to do with my life. You know, understand things. How we got here . . . how to live . . . How to die," I added quietly.

"Maybe you should meditate. . . ."

"I don't rule it out. . . . I know so little about everything that really matters. . . ."

We sat quietly. I leaned back in my chair. She lit up a cigarette. I watched the white smoke rise through her soft brown hair. "I've been thinking maybe I could go on for the Ph.D. Maybe I'll give up all this engineering and all, and become a teacher. Serve humanity or something," I added, smiling shyly, embarrassed to say it.

We sipped at our coffee. Leslie seemed lost in her thoughts. I wondered what she was thinking.

After a few minutes, I said, "Hey, wouldn't that be great? If you were studying literature and I was studying American Civ.? God, the conversations we could have!"

She smiled, not saying anything.

Chapter Thirty-five

"I can't believe we were walking around in our shirt sleeves in Portland at the end of December...." I was seated on the couch, Leslie slouched in her favorite easy chair.

She nodded. "It's mild like this quite a bit here. Hey, wasn't Virgil looking great?"

"Managing Flora's cousin's store is really bringing out something in him." I finished my brandy. "Why'd Flora transfer to Portland State, anyhow?"

"She wants to teach down there, where she grew up. Virgil's pretty much putting her through college."

I smiled, thinking of Virgil during the summer. His great imaginary bass solos and all. "He's a helluva guy," I said. I glanced over at the tree. The colored lights strung through the branches were twinkling like little end-rhymes. Leslie looked warm and content, ensconced in her chair, the Mexican Indian shawl wrapped around her shoulders subtly reflecting the blinking lights on the tree.

Later that night, after we made love, we lay awake on the sofa-bed, my arm beneath Leslie's wide but slender shoulders. The Gil Evans record Leslie had given me was playing on the phonograph. Thick sandalwood incense candles joined the Christmas tree lights in filling the room with a scented, warm glow.

"You still awake?" I said.

"Yeah."

"I was just wondering about something.... Is it true that the Pope's supposed to be infallible?"

She chuckled. "What got you on that? The Pope?"

"I don't know.... I was just thinking...."

"Well ... he's just a person. He's not a God or anything. He can make mistakes like anyone else.... It's just when he speaks *ex cathe-dra,* that means 'from the chair,' or the throne, that he's considered infallible. It's only on matters of Church doctrine and stuff like that."

She looked at me with curiosity.

"I don't know.... I was just letting my mind wander."

She turned back toward the ceiling. We both lay there, breathing the heavy, perfumed air.

"I don't know that much about Catholicism." I summoned my courage. "Like, I mean, I don't even know whether a Catholic can ever marry a guy who isn't Catholic...."

She hesitated a second. Then she said, tentatively, "Yeah.... It's possible.... I mean, the Church doesn't recognize any other kind of marriages. Civil or anything...."

"So how do they do it?"

"He takes some instruction. He doesn't have to convert or anything. And then he has to sign a statement saying he'll agree to bring the kids up Catholic...."

I could hear Leslie breathing slowly beside me. Waiting to see what I might say. After a while, her breathing began to slow and to deepen, and I knew she had fallen asleep.

I lay awake thinking about bringing my kids up Catholic, with nuns and sin and all the Old-World baggage that had been passed down to us like ancient steamer trunks in the attic. When I had asked Leslie about Catholic marriages, I felt the whole room tremble.

"Time to get up." I looked up at Leslie, already dressed, standing beside the couch. The air carried the delicious singed odor of fried potatoes and scrambled eggs. "It's almost noon," she said. A hazy sun shone through the dust on the window behind her. Apparently the warm weather was holding. Leslie was wearing an old pair of shapeless beige pedal-pushers that I remembered from the summer, and a light-green print cotton pullover shirt.

After I finished breakfast, I said, "Can I ask you a question? It'll take a couple minutes."

She nodded.

"And listen, whatever happens, will you promise not to answer definitely? I mean, just think it over, and we won't mention it for a while, OK?"

She nodded again.

"Well, last night, I was thinking a lot.... I couldn't really sleep.... And I had this idea, after seeing Virgil and Flora and all...."

"What is it?" Her voice was soft, like flannel.

"I was thinking about my future, and I made a big decision. I'm definitely going to become a teacher."

"I thought that was where you were headed," she said quietly. "It's funny, but back in the summer, when Hal used to call you 'Mahatma Gandhi in a Cadillac,' it would get you so mad.... But somehow he did push you into looking at your life.... And now you've changed your path. Only in exactly the opposite direction to the one he wanted." She smiled.

"I ... I want to have a job where I can go to work every day knowing that my aim is to help people. Does that sound silly?"

"No, not at all." She moved toward the other end of the room where she picked up her purse. "I'm just getting a cigarette. Keep talking."

"Anyhow, I'm going to go into the Army. For three years. I'll ask to be stationed in Massachusetts. And then, I'll apply for a fellowship to Penn in American Civ."

She struck a match and lit up.

"I'll study every night in the Army. Nothing's gonna stop me. I'll buy college textbooks in history and art and philosophy and I'll begin with the Ancient Greeks and I'll work ..."

I saw her smiling gently and realized I was gritting my teeth as I talked. I smiled along with her.

"Anyhow," I said, "what I'm leading up to is ... well ... I thought that you might want to go along this path with me."

She peered somewhat helplessly into my eyes. Quickly I began to talk. "I could put you through school while I'm in the Army. You can go full-time. We can be together this spring. We'll never have to be separated again."

She blew some smoke in a perfect smoke ring, and watched it rise toward the ceiling.

"You mean get married?" she said, finally, as she turned back to me and looked into my eyes with no expression on her face.

I nodded yes. She blew another perfect smoke ring. Watched it rise and lose its identity as it blended into the air above. Then she moved her chair back a touch and turned sideways in it, creating a little more distance between us, a kind of escape route. She was not a girl you could push. Yet her face did not appear to be angry. She looked more like a person who had been spun around by a strong wind and needed time to re-orient herself.

I rose from my chair. "Well, I asked you not to respond, and I want to thank you for hearing me out."

She couldn't resist a wry smile. As she rose from the table, I thought I could see a certain sympathy for me in her glance. She knew I had taken a risk, and in the name of both of us.

Chapter Thirty-six

The prodigious jukebox at the Roll Inn was pouring forth loud music, and some of the dancers were doing the twist. Leslie turned to me, and said wryly, "The natives have really become attached to the twist since you brought it out here from the East."

We were sitting by ourselves in a booth in the corner, nursing a couple of bottles of Oly, hardly saying anything. After a while, we got up to dance. A tall Negro man played "Fever," by Little Willy John, on the jukebox. The heat in the Roll Inn was turned up too high. Leslie flushed with warmth in her heavy turtleneck, the gypsy fire glowing within her. She moved her ass in a way that allowed her hot stubbornness to come forth, the sullen independence that made her so much more formidable than if she had been simply pliant and agreeable.

We did a mashed-potatoes to "Please, Mr. Postman" by The Marvelettes, a slow yearning dance to "Will You Still Love Me Tomorrow" by The Shirelles, and a fish, tight against each other, to "Sleepwalk" by Santo and Johnny. When we returned to our booth, Leslie fanned herself with her hand.

"Whew! It's sure hot in here."

We sat for a while without speaking. I shredded the label on my Oly bottle with my fingernail. Leslie rested her chin on her hand and looked absently across the club. The dancers were moving together in a slow bop to Lloyd Price's "Stagger Lee." Then the juke box played "Tossing and Turning" by Bobby Lewis. Leslie turned to me and said, slowly, "I could never go to school in Massachusetts."

"What?" At first I didn't know what she was talking about, but then I realized, with a rush of adrenalin that shook me, that she was responding to what I had said to her that morning.

"Massachusetts. I could never go to college there."

"But why not?"

She girded herself. "I can't compete with those kids back East. I'm not the person you think I am. I'm just a girl from a farm in Idaho."

"I know you're from Idaho. That's one of the things I like about you."

"I was raised with sheep and hogs. When my grandparents came out west, Idaho was Indian territory."

"So?... Where were my grandparents at that time? Poland? Lithuania? I don't know. None of my aunts or uncles will even talk about it."

She looked at me with a pained expression. "But . . . I mean, my mother, she didn't have *shoes* when she was a girl. . . . How can I go back East? They'll never . . ."

Her voice trailed off.

"God, where do you think *I* come from? Debutant parties and charity balls? Why are you being so down on yourself? You're going to be a teacher. What's wrong with that? I mean, *Socrates* was a teacher, for God's sakes!"

The blazing gypsy had disappeared, and Leslie's face took on a delicate quality, like cut glass in the colored ambiance of the Roll Inn's ricocheting light. She was now the bright, shy, somewhat fragile girl whom they had made fun of in high school because she couldn't afford to buy the right clothes.

"But the kids there, I mean, they were brought up on Thoreau and Emerson and Hawthorne. Where do I fit in? Criminey, can't you see? I'm from nowhere. My father watches Lawrence Welk. That's the limit of our culture. . . ."

"What're you talking about? Your family has a band. You grew up with music all around you!"

"Yeah. Country musicians coming to shoot my father."

"But don't you see how rich that is? And you have great taste in music. You can play any instrument. I've seen you."

She shook her head, afraid to believe a word of what I was saying.

"Listen," I insisted, "don't you see? You did well at the University of Washington."

"But the University of Washington . . . I mean, it's just a Western school. . . ."

"Just a WESTERN school? What are you TALKING about? The University of Washington's a fine university. Anyone knows that!"

Leslie sat there quietly, making a slow ring in the water on the table with her finger. But on her face there was a certain relief.

As I caught my breath and pulled myself together, I realized what had just happened. If Leslie's worst fear of marrying me was that she wouldn't be able to make it at a state college back East . . .

"Do you guys want a couple more?" The stocky waitress picked up our empty beer bottles. Leslie straightened up, startled out of her reverie. She turned to me. "Would you be interested in going out for a little air, Danny? It's awfully stuffy in here."

Downtown Seattle was quiet and deserted. There were virtually no shops open. The streets were deserted and dark except for the street lamps whose yellow light was diffused by the thick fog that had settled over the city.

Leslie wore a pained expression on her face. I reached for her and held her to me and kissed her, but she continued to look troubled. We began to straggle, a half-step at a time, up the brumous street, just moving for the sake of not standing still in front of the Roll Inn.

"You know you shouldn't be concerned about school back East."

"But how can your family accept me? A German Catholic peasant. . . ."

"Don't worry about my family. I mean, sure, they'd find it easier if I married a nice Jewish girl and raised two nice shiny Jewish kids, but that's not what's happening for me in any case. They'll love you once they meet you. You're not a Catholic or a German or . . . anything but yourself. How could they help but like you?"

"I don't know about that. . . ."

"Well, I do. That's one thing about my parents. They always come through when the chips are down." She didn't respond. Continued to look pained. We came to a corner near a movie theater. Stood under the red traffic light which, along with the rest of the scene in the soft gray fog, glowed like an Impressionist painting.

"You'll like The Bronx. I mean it. You'll finally see all the people I've been telling you about. My crazy cousin Herbie."

The light changed and we walked slowly across the deserted street.

"You know, he once reported a dead pigeon to the police. I mean it. In Greenwich Village." I told her the whole crazy story to cheer her up. A tiny smile slipped onto the corners of her mouth.

We were now in front of another movie theater. The Coliseum. A man in a bowtie was tallying up some figures in the ticket-seller's booth, a lone inhabited island in the thickening sea of fog.

We continued to stroll along the sidewalk. It was hard to know where we were. We were proceeding slowly through a world without external parameters of location, guided only by the lights of movie theaters.

"And my cousin Louie the Mook," I said, to keep her from retreating into herself. "He's unbelievable. I call him the Indomitable Buffalo, with his powerful hunched shoulders and all. You won't see any mooks in Idaho. Not by a long shot. If you want to see a mook, you've got to go to his natural habitat—New York City...."

I put my arm lightly around her shoulders. She seemed to be brightening a little. We stopped for a second, and I gave her a squeeze. Then we began to float down the street again. I didn't know where we were exactly, but I wasn't concerned. It was just me and Leslie, blinded by the fog, deciding whether we would be lonely or not for the rest of our lives.

"Why don't you say yes?" I said, suddenly. My words sounded muffled in the fog, like in a big synagogue.

"But our backgrounds ... they're so different." The strained yellow streetlights seemed to drain the color from Leslie's troubled face. "You still think I'm going to give up on Christ. Or the Church. But I'm not going to."

"All right. All right. I'll take the lessons from the priest. I swear. I'll sign the papers. I'll make all the promises...."

"I believe in Jesus." She began to drift up the the street again, giving herself a little space. I moved along with her.

"But what is it that Jesus stands for?" I said. "Love one another. Isn't that what you've always said you believe in? That love is at the heart of the universe. Well, I believe in it, too." We took a couple steps in silence. Then I said, "I know it sounds corny, but since I met you, Leslie, I've come to believe that love is possible on the Earth again. Somewhere along the way, I'd lost that.... But then ... somehow ... I began to think that maybe what I'd always really wanted ... that it might be possible again.... And I thought ... I thought that you believed in that, too."

I put my hand gently on her shoulder. She turned and looked into my eyes.

"I love you, Leslie. Let's not go our separate ways again. So what if our backgrounds are different? For once in our lives, let's bet it all. Let's stake everything on the possibility of love."

Her face still revealed her apprehension, but she said, looking down, so quietly that I could barely hear her, "OK."

"You mean it?" I said, looking desperately at her.

She nodded shyly.

"YAHOOOO!" I shouted suddenly, loudly, down the street, into the cushioning fog, my voice dissipating against the millions of tiny droplets of mist that floated around us while I grabbed her and pulled her toward me and hugged her and kissed her, and she looked incredibly shy, but after a while, a little fog-lit smile came onto her face, a winsome smile that she no longer attempted to hide.

When we came back to the Earth, she peered around us. "Do you know where we are?"

I looked up and down the nearly opaque street. Shook my head. "I don't have the foggiest idea," I said. "Not the FOGGIEST!"

She gave me her big Idaho smile this time, and I looked up and I said, "All I can see are stars," and I put my arm around her, and we began to walk ahead until we came upon the Paramount Theater, the marquee dark and the front area deserted, but the lobby still weakly lit like an Edward Hopper painting in the shrouded, damp air.

"You know how to get us home from here?" I said.

She nodded. Her face was suffused with a deep and somehow timid happiness, which shone peach and gold in the heavy white fog—downy clouds which, it seemed to me, had journeyed to the troubled Earth solely to soften the edges of our tremulous discourse.

Chapter Thirty-seven

Feb 7, 1962

Dear Leslie,

My folks did finally come through. My brother Barry told me they first called two meetings of all the aunts and uncles and cousins to discuss whether to throw me out of the family or not. But I think my parents were less concerned with the purely religious angle than with satisfying the relatives and neighbors. Still, it was pretty painful—to think of them debating whether to throw me out of the family or not. But they did come through. All they ask is that we undergo a civil marriage first, and then we can be married in church, to satisfy your folks. That seems reasonable enough. In fact, my father, incredibly, has been talking to a priest he knows in Harlem, near his liquor store, to arrange the church wedding for us. If you knew what a large gesture this is, my father setting up a Catholic wedding for his son, you'd be really proud of his generosity in this regard.

I know they're going to love you.

I've begun my lessons with Father Moynan here at the University, which so far are relatively painless. (You get used to being stretched on that cross after a while. You build up strength in your wrists.) But seriously, on the first day, the question of sin came up, and I asked whether he meant venial sin or mortal sin, and he burst out laughing and he said, "If you know those kinds of distinctions already, these lessons are going to be a snap."

He's a good guy. All is going well. Yes, your mother can call me at any time. I promise to seem rational on the phone.

Can't wait to see you. It's going to happen.

Love,

Danny

P.S. I've returned to reading Dante. The Paradisio. *Love it, like the other two.*

Everything I wrote to Leslie was the truth, but I did not tell her how strange it all seemed to me, entering the Newman Club and talking to a priest about Church matters. In the world in which I grew up, there were no pictures of Christ, no Virgin Marys, no crosses, no saints, no incense, no New Testament, no Easter, no Christmas, no Holy Trinities or virgin births, and no interest in any of this, whatsoever. These were all fictions or, to put it less politely, lies, the concerns and delusions of our historical oppressors.

I did not *like* going to my lessons. Although I enjoyed talking to Father Moynan, I could not forget that I was being forced to attend. Blackmailed, so to speak.

I discovered nonetheless that there was much to be learned from Christianity. I hadn't lied to Leslie when I said I liked Father Moynan, a charming man who was doing all he could to make this easy for me. Yet I felt apprehensive, fearful, ashamed, and even traitorous when I began. After all, it had not been Muslims or Hindus or Buddhists who had been killing Jews for thousands of years but Christians, for all their talk of loving your neighbor and such.

Yet Catholicism was largely responsible as well for much of the beauty that attracted me to Leslie, for the way she had of deepening every question by moving it from the plane of thought to the depths of soul. For her tender notions of the primacy of mercy and forgiveness, and love at the center of everything.

And Christianity was at the root of all the music that I most loved—that music which was my dearest consolation and trusted source of strength in my desperate and lonely times—not just Johann Sebastian Bach but jazz, and rhythm-and-blues, and rock-and-roll as well, all of which stemmed ultimately from the spirituals of the Negro churches of the South.

And the civil rights movement, which meant so much to me, also derived from these same Christian churches. After all, the leader of this movement, the one person whom I most looked up to, was *Reverend* Martin Luther King.

Nonetheless, in the same stubborn way in which Leslie would not let go of her ties to her sweet Jesus of mercy and love, and her St. Francis, and the beauty and ritual the Church offered her, I found there was much in my Jewish heritage that I was not going to let go of as well—a respect for independent thought and uncoerced individual moral judgement, a skepticism toward any man who said he was God or said he spoke for God, a suspicion of immoderate, life-denying Puritanism, and a resistance toward any centralized, autocratic organization that attempted to indoctrinate people as children and to tell them what they should think and do as adults.

At bottom I was still a secularized Jew, an American, a child of the Enlightenment, a student of science. I would not turn my mind over to anyone. Not for any price. Never.

Yet, I did yearn for something of the sweet, soul-stirring spirituality, the deep mystery, the belief in mercy and forgiveness as a supplement to the justice of the Old Testament, for all those things that Leslie embodied for me, those ancient balms that constituted a large part of her loveliness, her fascination.

And I was becoming fascinated by the Buddha, who said amazing things like, "The ocean has only one taste—the taste of salt. The truth has only one taste—the taste of liberation."

I was confused, but exhilarated, for I knew that Leslie and I were choosing a path which offered the two things we needed in our lives: the time to study and learn, and the freedom to change.

The winter stretched long. For months, the snow lay around on the streets of Philadelphia doing nothing, as if suffering from what we would now call chronic fatigue syndrome.

Finally, in the middle of April, Leslie and I rushed into each other's arms at the airport in South Philly. I pressed her close, feeling the soft fire of her body against mine, smelling the smoky pines and firs in her hair, and she clung to me as if I were a single floating log in the tumultuous Snake River of her life. I could see the pale cast of apprehension beneath her smile. She carried herself like a beautiful thoroughbred colt—sleek, alert, ready to bolt at any second.

Neither one of us had our feet on the ground. Leslie in Philadelphia! I couldn't make it seem real. It was as if a pair of giant cymbals had crashed together from opposite sides of the country and the vibrations were resounding all around us, shaking everything in the terminal.

Suddenly, I was no longer the solitary, lonely outsider. Now I

MAHATMA GANDHI IN A CADILLAC

had my own girl, an extraordinarily pretty girl, looking fresh and bright and vital as the West as she walked at my side through the airport. My bride.

We headed toward West Philly on the Schuylkill Expressway. "I got us a furnished apartment. Some guy down the block left school, and the old landlady rented it to me. She lives right downstairs."

Leslie nodded. But she seemed on sensory overload. "I just hope I'm doing the right thing."

"What do you mean? Of course you are."

"It's such a long way.... Your family ... my family."

"Come on.... You know we're OK.... It's like the Moonglows sing: 'We go together, like two straws in a Coke. Why not come over, and you'll meet my folk.'"

She smiled weakly. I put my arm around her. "You'll have a great time here. We'll drive up to New York tomorrow for our two weddings, and then you'll have a month to get to know Philadelphia. I'll show you the art museum. The crew races on the river."

She sat there, seeming to accept this as her fate. We left the expressway, and I pointed out Franklin Field and Convention Hall, but I don't think she was interested in sports stadiums at that moment.

There was a parking place directly in front of the three-story building which was to be our new home.

"See," I said. "A parking place. You don't know what this means. It's all magic."

I lifted her old, bulky suitcase from the trunk. A thin, bearded man walked past us on the sidewalk, dragging behind him a ten-foot-long cross that was hooked over his shoulder. At the base of the heavy cross, where it met the sidewalk, he had affixed a little rubber tire, to make it easier to pull along.

Leslie looked at me with a twinkle in her eyes.

"Welcome to the East Coast," I said.

As we turned into my street, Nelson Avenue in The Bronx, treeless, with bare six-story buildings on either side, I was singing "April in Paris."

I parked in front of my parents' apartment house. All around us, excited yentas began to pound on their drums to alert the neighborhood that I had arrived with my *shiksa* bride. I didn't care. All I could hear was beautiful music. My mother welcomed us into the house with open refrigerator. She set out heaps of cold cuts along with forty-five types of Kraft cheese from Daitch's Dairy, cakes and pies from Zaro's bakery, and various kinds of Hoffman soda. We joined several of my aunts and cousins from the building for an introductory feast. Leslie looked so pretty in her slim blue skirt and sleeveless white blouse, that I was floating on my happiness and pride like Mercury, with wings on my black Florsheim shoes. And Leslie herself responded with the warmth and shy good nature she was capable of whenever she felt a hope that she might be accepted by the people around her.

In the middle of the afternoon, when the guests had left my mother and Leslie and I sitting in the living room, I leaned out of the window, and there, at the end of the block, on his stoop, reading a book, was my cousin Herbie!

"Herbie's back in town?"

"For a few days," my mother said sourly.

"What's the matter?"

"He's driving his mother crazy, that's what's the matter. I hate to say it, but he should stay in New Orleans if that's the way he's gonna be." She turned to Leslie. "I have nothing against Herbie. Ask anybody. But he's twenty-four years old now. He's gotta grow up and act nicer to his mother and everyone." She turned back to me. "Listen, just forget about him, Danny. Leslie's already met enough people."

"Whaddya mean? Herbie's gotta meet Leslie, or he'll never forgive me."

"I don't mind," Leslie chirped. "I'll just change into something more comfortable." She hopped up and went into my bedroom. When Leslie re-entered the room, she was wearing only jeans and her white, sleeveless blouse. No shoes or socks.

"You ready?" she said.

"Your shoes, dear?" my mother said. "You'll need them in the street."

"No, it's OK," Leslie said blithely.

"But . . . you'll catch a cold. . . ."

"No. It's warm. I'm used to it."

"But . . . but, dear," my mother turned to me with a worried frown. "She'll step on something, Danny. . . . Some broken glass."

"It's OK," Leslie said, moving toward the door. "I'll be careful."

I could have turned to Leslie and said, "Just put on some shoes, OK? Everyone in New York wears shoes on the street, and you're making my mother uncomfortable," but I was so unaccustomed to my new role as husband that I wasn't sure how to respond, especially when Leslie was going to meet Herbie, whose beatnik ways she had heard so much about.

And really, I thought, what's the big deal, going barefoot down the block on a warm spring afternoon?

The neighbors didn't agree. I saw them gloating at their windows. Leslie didn't notice. She was entranced by the chaos and the rich fecund smells, the noise and teeming life of the copious Bronx streets.

Herbie was sitting on the stoop of his apartment house reading Celine. *Death on the Installment Plan.* He looked up as we approached and immediately I saw he was impressed by Leslie. In fact, he couldn't take his eyes off her.

His face was bloated and puffy. He was on his Marine pension now, and I had heard that whenever a check arrived he would go out and eat huge meals, often one after the other, until he was ready to burst.

He didn't seem the least bit surprised that I was back, but he did seem astonished that I was standing there with such a pretty girl—a girl with no shoes on, my new pal, my bride.

"Herbie, this is Leslie."

He nodded slightly and said, holding up the book, "You wanna be depressed, just read Celine. I mean, he's great, man, but whew! Can he bring you down! He really tells the truth! And we can't bear too much of that, man."

"I don't know about that," I said, smiling toward Leslie, who seemed to be enjoying herself, her eyes bright and wide-open. "I think the truth is turning better these days. I've got lots of hope."

"I can see why," Herbie said, appraising Leslie in a not-very-

209

subtle manner.

Leslie blushed, but did not look away. She would not be pushed.

Herbie began to talk about the existentialists, rapping quickly, using all kinds of large Latinate words. "They know where it's at," he said, finally. "Life is meaningless, so you better get it while you can." He turned to me. "Eternity comes only once, you know, man, in spite of what they teach you at Wharton."

"How do you know that?" Leslie said, quietly.

"Know what?"

"That life is meaningless. How do you know that?"

"Yeah," I said, grinning with delight.

"Look around, man. Just travel a little and look around." He turned to Leslie. "I been out to the Coast a few times. Frisco mostly. City Lights Books. Dropped some bennies with the crowd at the Co-existence Bagel Shop. Danny, here, he doesn't travel much. He thinks he can get it all from his professors." He jumped up and fondly punched me in the shoulder, beginning to spar with me.

I blocked his light punches. There was a friendliness to this old ritual, yet he seemed to be having a problem trying to relate to me now that he could no longer advise me on how to succeed with girls, since I was with this girl who was obviously all right, by his standards as well as my own.

"I went to San Francisco, too. Last summer," I protested. "I went to City Lights and all the rest, man." I leaned to the right and looped a soft left hook, which he blocked as I meant him to.

"Yeah," he said, sarcastically, "to work on missiles." He turned to Leslie. "See, Danny here, he's one of the greatest. He's my pupil. In all realms. Metaphysics, sports, jazz, picking up ass, whatever. But he's just not very not good at being free. He's still at the stage where he needs corporate sponsorship." He did a few steps of a little soft-shoe in his old black Keds basketball sneakers on the sidewalk. Then he stopped, and said to Leslie, "If you want someone who's been around, why don't you come with me down to the Village tonight? I'll show you around the real scene, while Danny can stay home and study for his exams."

I could hardly believe what Herbie was saying, because although he was still speaking in a light, joshing tone, I knew he meant it.

Leslie just leaned back a little and smiled coolly, as if Herbie were an amusing court page. "Come on, whattaya say?" Herbie said. Then he turned back to me again and threw a couple of playful punches, which I blocked easily.

"Hey, why don't you come upstairs with me right now? We'll leave old Danny to fend for himself, and we can pitch some woo."

"Herbie...." I said, imploring him not to continue on this path.

"My mother's not home. She's out at her nine-to-five with the other squares. Danny here, he'd understand that. He's so fucking RESPONSIBLE, he's in danger of becoming elected to office or something." He turned back to Leslie. "But you ... I can tell, you're a hip chick. Come on upstairs with me. We can take off our clothes and play Garden of Eden."

"Hey, man," I said. "This isn't funny. We're getting married tomorrow."

"Not if I can have one night with this lovely morsel." He turned to Leslie. "Look, I'm going back to the Big Easy tomorrow. Why don't you come along? You're really more my type of chick than Danny's...."

"Hey, man, cut this shit out. You're going too far. Don't you see?" I stepped between him and Leslie, my anger rising, but also my hurt.

"It's OK." Leslie tapped me lightly on the shoulder. "We'd better get back. Your Mom's probably waiting for us." She took a step toward my house. "Nice meeting you, Herbie," she said.

"Yeah, have a good trip, man," I said, without conviction.

We walked up the street. Leslie was looking at the people watching us from the windows of the apartment houses, shining happily as if she were in the most fascinating zoo. Not noticing that all the women rocking their baby carriages on the sidewalk were staring at her bare feet in stunned disbelief. And that my mother was at our window, trying to hide a greenish terror that threatened to take over her face.

We waited up for my father to come home from work at midnight, preceded up the street by his three-pack-a-day smoker's cough. He came puffing in the door, short of breath, wearing a loose clip-on bowtie and a white shirt. I introduced him to Leslie. He gave her his most charming smile, which revealed his gold teeth and the side of himself—his basic generosity and hidden sweetness—that led most people to like him in spite of his rages and rampages. He shook her hand and told her he was glad to meet her, and then he turned to me and his face hardened, and he said, "Leslie is new here, and she doesn't know our ways, but you ..."

"What?" I was trying to read his face, which I was practiced at, since my survival had depended on this ability for my entire childhood. I saw the anger there, but I couldn't quite decipher its source. Then I understood what had happened. The sound of the tom-toms had reached all the way to Harlem.

"I want you to know something. You may be getting married, but if you live under my roof, you live according to my rules. What you do in Philadelphia or in Seattle is one thing, but as long as you live here, don't you ever, I mean, ever, let your wife run around in the street with no shoes on."

My jaw slackened. I turned toward my mother. She appeared to want to melt into the floor. "Everyone's talking," she said, apologetically. "Is it too much to ask?"

"This isn't the goddamn Lower East Side!" my father said. "If she can't afford a pair of shoes, I'll buy them for her."

"She can afford shoes. I don't see what's the big deal."

"To me, it's a big deal."

"I'll wear my shoes," Leslie said, quietly.

"Of course you will, dear," my mother said, moving toward her and giving her arm a sympathetic squeeze. She turned to my father. "It's just a little misunderstanding. The girl's come all the way across country." She turned back toward Leslie. "Would you like a piece of cake, dear? Chocolate swirl, fresh baked at Zaro's down the street."

"No thanks."

"Some pie?"

"Ceil, leave the girl alone," my father said, taking Leslie's elbow and leading her in a courtly fashion to a seat in the dinette. "If you want anything to eat, Leslie, you just take it yourself from the fridge. This house is your house too now, so you just make yourself at home and treat us like your own family."

Chapter Thirty-eight

Leslie Schmidt and I were married the following morning at the Bronx Borough Hall on Tremont Avenue. The taking of the vows was administered by a woman who had been making entries into some large books. It was not clear whether she was a Justice of the Peace or a clerk.

My parents took us to lunch at a delicatessen-style storefront restaurant near Yankee Stadium. Back at the apartment, my father laid ten one-hundred-dollar bills out on my bed, a very generous wedding gift. He returned to work, and we joined him at his store that evening.

We drove the few blocks to the Catholic church in Harlem in my father's huge white Oldsmobile. I could see that he was proud of the tolerance and understanding he had shown in setting up the Church wedding. I was proud of him as well.

Leslie wore her best white dress, the one she had on at the Inn in Seattle when Bob Maytall's wife had fallen into the fireplace. I sported one of my two suits. Leslie carried a bouquet from a Harlem florist, a gift from my father. She had set a white gossamer veil on her hair.

When the Priest shook hands with my father, I could see that something was wrong.

"You seem," he said uneasily, "to be dressed for a wedding."

"Isn't that ... what we're here for, Father Joseph?" my father said. I had never heard him call anyone "Father" before.

Leslie and I stood there, ready to be joined again in holy matrimony. "But ... but ... gee, I hate to say this," Father Joseph said, "but I'm afraid there's been some misunderstanding."

"Misunderstanding?"

"Well, yes.... You see, and you've been awfully good about all this," he said to my father, turning to Leslie and me to acknowledge my father's beneficence, "but you see, tonight is just to post the banns . . . to announce the wedding, so to speak. . . . It's next week that's the actual ceremony. . . ."

My father's face fell.

"It's really just a technicality," Father Joseph said.

"Well, is there any way we could somehow marry them tonight anyhow?" my father said. "I mean, the kids'll be awfully disappointed. . . ."

"Well, gee, Mr. Schwartz, I'm sorry, but I really can't. I mean, this is a rule that I just can't break. . . . But we can do the actual marriage next week, and I promise you there'll be no problem. . . ."

My father was crestfallen. He had taken such pride in all the arrangements he had made. But we resigned ourselves to doing what was required. We took some instruction and left the church in our wedding finery, with Father Joseph apologizing profusely.

We sat in the car at the curb, in Harlem. Leslie was holding her bridal bouquet in her lap, looking as if she were about to fold up and break into tears that would be difficult to stop.

"Boy," my father said. He turned towards Leslie. "I have to apologize."

"He really did his best, dear," my mother said. "You should see all the people he had to talk to set this up."

"I know," I said. "I appreciate it. It could happen to anybody."

"Well, you're already legally married," my father said. "So I guess there's no problem with you two living together for the week and then coming back to the city and we'll do this again."

"But what about my mother?" Leslie said, trying to keep herself from crying. "She doesn't know about the civil ceremony. Only the Catholic one. I'm not supposed to be living with Danny until I'm married. She's at home with my father right now, waiting for my call to tell her that I'm married. And then she'll expect the Polaroids of the wedding in a few days. I promised to send them to her special delivery."

"Gee," my father said, "I hate to upset your mother."

"I just can't bring myself to tell her that I came all this way and I'm not married," Leslie said.

"But you ARE married," I said.

"And we did see the priest and go to Church," my mother said, her spirit picking up.

"There's really no reason to hurt her," my father said.

I said, "Why don't you just call her and tell her we went to church tonight, and my father bought you flowers and we saw the priest, Father Joseph, and everything's fine and you're married? That way you won't really be lying, and we won't have to upset her unnecessarily."

Leslie sat there helplessly. Then she said, "Well . . . OK, I guess," in a timid, uncertain voice.

"Sure, dear," my mother said. "It'll all work out for the best." She met Leslie's eyes, and Leslie did seem somewhat reassured.

As my father parked the car in front of our house, Leslie exclaimed, "Oh, my God. I forgot. The pictures! My mother's expecting Polaroids. What are we going to do?"

"We can't go back to Harlem," my mother said.

"The church'll probably be closed now," my father said. "I think Father Joseph came in specially for us."

We sat there thinking. Then I said, "Hey! I've got it. You know Sacred Heart? Over by the Library?" I turned to Leslie. "They have this statue there, outside, a Virgin Mary and Baby Jesus, and they light it up with spotlights at night. It looks really nice. It's colored and everything. Why don't we drive over, and if it's lit up, we can take pictures in front of it. . . ."

Leslie looked like a person who, after being told she is doomed, has found out that there is more bad news to come.

"It looks real nice," I repeated, weakly.

Leslie nodded, and we drove to the church. Spotlights illuminated the colored sculpture, which was set on a low wall. My father led us out of the car, carrying the Polaroid camera. He gritted his teeth and smiled, and we all took pictures of each other. Leslie struggled to appear light-hearted and gay in her white bridal gown and her white veil, carrying her wedding bouquet from Harlem, standing in front of the Baby Jesus and the Virgin Mary, out on Shakespeare Avenue, in the darkness of a warm spring night, beside the Sacred Heart Church, where my basketball team had played a game

215

once and some of the people in the stands had spit on us because we were Jewish.

Two hours later we were driving toward Philadelphia, through the waste flats of Northern New Jersey. I was at the wheel, Leslie slouched at my side, in her jeans and sweatshirt now. She had withdrawn into herself, as if sucked in by some vacuum at her center. I managed to increase Leslie's distress by talking all the way to Philadelphia in a vain attempt to reassure her that things were actually going to turn out well. She said virtually nothing during the entire trip, not even so much as asking me to be quiet, as if my compulsive talking were part of the evidence she needed to confirm her depression.

Back at our little apartment, Leslie collapsed into a soft chair and stretched her legs out, allowing her shoes to slip halfway off her feet.

"It's going to work out," I said.

"I know," Leslie responded sharply, surprising me. Her eyes had lit up like burning stop signs on a dark night. "You've been telling me that all day."

"But I...."

"Damn it! Just shut up!"

"But...."

"Shut *up*! I'm sick of your 'It's going to be all right' bull. That's all you've been saying since I got here."

She rose suddenly, kicking her shoes off. One of them flew through the air across the room, almost hitting an old lamp.

"Take it easy, would you? The landlady's right downstairs."

"I don't give a shit about the fucking landlady." She faced away from me, furiously pulling off her jeans and almost falling onto the floor when one of her legs became stuck. She toppled onto the bed, and lay there on her side, struggling to untangle herself and becoming more frustrated. Finally she freed herself and she looked over at me with a furious expression on her face, as if I had been responsible for entangling her.

I kept silent, attempting to give her the space she needed to vent her rage, but her anger seemed to be growing. "Be careful of the landlady," she said, mimicking me.

"Will you come on. . . ." My own anger was rising.

"No I won't come on! Damn it!" She picked up her jeans and threw them into the corner of the room, almost hitting another lamp.

"Hey. . . ."

"The *landlady!*" she snorted with disgust. "God, I don't even know why I came here in the first place, if you want to know the fucking truth. Why? Why did I come? What the fuck am I doing here?"

She jerked her sweatshirt over her head violently, and heaved it into the corner. This time she hit the lamp, and the shirt stuck to the top of the shade.

"Come on, damn it. Cut the shit. You're gonna break something." I walked over to the lamp and removed the sweatshirt.

"I don't give a shit," she said. "Can't you understand that? Can't you hear what I'm saying?"

"I hear what you're saying!"

"I don't give a SHIT if I break something. Don't you understand? I've fucked up my whole LIFE."

Her voice was modulating between anger and regret, like two radio stations overlapping each other.

"Why the HELL did I come here? What am I doing here, for shit's sake? This is 3000 miles from my fucking home. I don't belong here. I don't belong here at all."

"Whatta you mean, you. . . ."

"Look, just shut up, will you! Will you just shut the fuck up for once in your life! You've been talking nonstop for twenty fucking hours. Give someone else a chance."

She pulled off her bra and flung it against the wall in the corner. She sat on the bed, her skin bright with rage, her eyes moonless and glum.

Then she turned to me, her jaw jutting forward. "It's no use. Don't you see? This was all wrong. Look at your parents."

"They're doing their best. They'll come to love you."

"Love me? Don't you see? How many people did they ask to our wedding? Tell me," she glared. "How goddamned many?"

I didn't answer.

"And *my* parents, sitting in Idaho, trying to make the best of this,

217

after I lied to them on the phone. Thinking I've been married in the Church like I promised them."

"We will get married in the Church. Next Friday."

"Damn it, don't you see? Everything's going wrong. Every single goddamned thing has gone wrong since I arrived here." She moved her head woefully from side to side. "How did I think I could ever be accepted by a Jewish family?" Then she began to get excited again, her fervor fueled by her words. "How did I ever get the idea that my parents would welcome a son-in-law who wasn't Catholic?" She stood up and began to pace wildly about. Her emotion was feeding on itself, and growing cancerous. "How did I ever let you talk me into this?"

She was staring at me as if she would have liked to kill me.

"WHAT THE FUCK AM I DOING HERE?" she shouted. Then, suddenly, she panicked. She lost control and began to rush about the room in a complete frenzy, turning over the furniture, tossing clothing against the walls, throwing her shoes up to the ceiling, screaming, "HOW DID I GET INTO THIS? WHY DID I COME HERE? WHY DID I GET MARRIED? I'VE RUINED MY FUCKING LIFE! I'VE RUINED MY WHOLE GODDAMNED FUCKING LIFE!"

"Take it easy, goddamn it."

"NO, I WON'T TAKE IT EASY!"

"The landlady...."

"SCREW THE LANDLADY!" She shouted. There was a kind of crazed glee in her eyes as she shouted as loud as she could so the landlady couldn't avoid hearing her, "SCREW THE FUCKING LAND-LADY!"

"Shut up!" I hissed back at her, trying to shout and whisper at the same time. "Will you just shut the fuck up!"

She moved toward me, her eyes burning like highway flares. "AND SCREW YOU, TOO! You talked me into this. *FUCK* YOU!" She reached toward me and gave me a short, hard shove with the flat of her hands against my shoulders.

"Take it EASY, goddamn it!" I spit out the words at her.

She moved toward me. Raised her hands as if she were going to shove me again, but I caught them at the wrists.

"Let me go!" She attempted to free her arms, but I hung on. "Let me GO!!!" she screamed. She twisted her arms this way and that until she finally succeeded in pulling out of my grasp. She paced swiftly around again, like a wild thing in a cage, all the time glaring into my eyes, and shouted, "Let me out of here, let me the hell OUT OF HERE!" Her fury building quickly, she turned toward a lamp and attempted to swipe it off the table with the side of her hand. I was able to catch it as it fell so it didn't break, but something cracked deep inside of Leslie instead, some last limit of her control, and she cried, "FUCK YOU! DO YOU HEAR ME? FUCK YOU!!" and she let out a wild shriek and ran into the bathroom, and slammed the door and locked it, and gave out a terrible howl of rage and frustration, as if she were sticking her tongue out in some grotesque manner while screaming this ghastly AGGGGGGGGGGGHHHHHHHH!, and there was a huge CRASH and the whole wall shook, and then a final hurt whimper as the din reverberated down into an awful silence.

I ran to the door. Tried to force it open.

"Leslie?"

She didn't answer.

"Leslie, speak to me! Are you OK?"

She still didn't answer.

"Leslie, please. Say something. I'm worried about you. Leslie?"

The door opened. She shuffled past me, downtrodden and ashamed, not meeting my eyes. She walked to the bed in just her little gray panties, and sat on it. She bent over and stared down at the rug.

I entered the bathroom. Chunks of plaster were strewn over the floor. Opposite the tub, a gaping hole loomed where Leslie had punched her fist through the wall. I could see into the guts of the wall, the wooden slats underneath where the plaster had been. I thought of the landlady downstairs, who had, no doubt, heard every word of our fight. And now I was going to have to explain this hole in the wall.

I returned to the bedroom. Leslie was still sitting on the bed, not meeting my eyes. "Well," I said, "you sure did a job on that wall...."

She looked up at me sheepishly, and flowered into a small, tentative, apologetic smile. I was so relieved that I smiled as well, and soon we were both grinning with fatalistic, "Oh, God, what have we done now?" expressions on our faces.

I moved next to her on the bed. I placed my arm around her bare, thin shoulders. She turned to me and I kissed her, gently.

"Your hand OK?"

She held her fist out, turning it over in front of me. The knuckles were bruised, but she flexed her fingers and everything seemed to be working. She began to cry, but this only made her look more lovely, sitting there so vulnerable, in her little gray panties on the edge of the bed, a thin girl with long legs, sobbing and yet smiling at the same time, both of us nodding our heads slightly as if we were listening to the same inaudible music.

After a while I rose and turned out the lights. I slipped out of my clothes and returned to the bed, where I took her in my arms as she pulled her panties down over her thighs.

Chapter Thirty-nine

The following Friday we were married in Harlem. Since we required two witnesses besides my parents, Father Joseph enlisted the services of a man fixing a pew and a woman who was mopping the floor.

In May, I signed up in the Army for three years, requesting Fort Devens, Massachusetts, while Leslie made arrangements to attend the nearby Fitchburg State College.

After my graduation, we drove up to The Bronx. We planned to stay with my family for two weeks while I showed Leslie New York, but I knew something was amiss after just two days. We had returned from visiting my cousin Louie the Mook. (Louie had taken to Leslie immediately, and she to him, liking his bashful, clumsy, blunt mook ways.) My mother met us at the door and guiltily informed me that my father wanted to speak to me when he came home at midnight.

When my father appeared, coughing his way down the deserted street, Leslie and I joined him at the table in the little dinette off the small kitchen in which my mother was scrambling my father's nightly eggs and onions. I noticed how my father had aged. On his head stretched a few strands of thin hair, which he combed across the crown. He had the beginnings of a potbelly which seemed out of place on a slim man, and his rough, pallid face reminded me of the moon.

"Listen, Danny" he said, lighting up a Chesterfield, "I'll tell you why I wanted to speak to you." He looked directly at me, ignoring Leslie who was sitting opposite him, her expression indecipherable but with an ashen cast. "Not to beat around the bush, I want you to go tomorrow and take some job interviews for yourself with I.B.M. and places like that."

I was completely astounded.

"Interviews?"

He nodded. "I want you to go downtown and begin to get yourself settled into a job."

"But ... but ... Dad! I can't go to any INTERVIEWS."

"Why not?"

"Because I'm in the Army."

"Whaddya mean, the Army?"

"The Army. The American Army. Like I've been telling you for the last couple months. I'm a soldier. I signed up for three years. I'm going to be an officer in the Medical Service Corps. I'm going to Texas for training. I told you all this."

"Do you have your uniforms?"

"I'll get them in Texas. That's why I'm going there. For orientation and all that."

"Do you have your orders?"

"That's what I'm waiting for. As soon as they find out exactly what day the class begins, they'll cut the orders. The papers'll be arriving here any day."

"Look, Danny, I'll be frank with you. You're not really in the Army yet. Anything can happen."

"But Dad, I SIGNED the papers. I passed my physical. I've been accepted into this program. They WANT me."

"Look, let me tell you so you'll understand. You're a married man now. This is your wife here at the table. You can't just loaf around and sponge off your parents now. You're not in school any more. A married man has got to have a job."

"But I HAVE a job. That's what I'm trying to tell you. I'm in the ARMY! I begin training at Fort Sam Houston with the other new officers in July."

"I don't think you're listening to me," he insisted, with a grim determination. "Do you hear what I'm saying to you in simple English? I want you to go down to I.B.M. tomorrow and apply for a job."

"I'm sure they'll be glad to have you," my mother called out from over by the stove. "You're one in a million. You're smarter than any other boy who'll apply."

Oddly, a strange and somehow sad desire to laugh came over

me at that moment. A sudden impulse to laugh crazily, which I had
to struggle to resist. "But, Dad ... don't you see? I can't just go into
I.B.M. and ask for a job. That isn't the way it's done. I don't even
know if I.B.M. has offices in New York. I think their headquarters
are in Poughkeepsie or something."

"Well, however it's done, I want you to come back here with a
job tomorrow."

"But ... But ... Dad, don't you see? Even if I could get an interview with I.B.M. or ... or some other big company, first of all, I
would have to write to them, and send them a resume and all that,
and set up an appointment. ... It would take weeks. But anyhow,
all this is besides the point, because what's the FIRST thing they're
going to ask if I apply for a job?"

He glared at me, sipping his coffee.

"OK, I'll tell you," I said. "The first thing they're going to want
to know is what is my draft status. And what am I going to tell them?
That I'm in no danger of being drafted because I'M ALREADY IN
THE ARMY?" I laid out these last words with a flourish, having
finally made my point. "You see, if I did that, I'd make a complete
laughingstock of myself."

"Look, I don't want to say it a thousand times, OK? Just get your
suit on tomorrow, and go downtown and get a job at I.B.M. And
listen, smart guy, I'm no fool. I don't necessarily mean you have to
actually BEGIN the job tomorrow. Just do the interview tomorrow,
so you can begin in a few days."

"God! Can't I make you understand?" I was half-shouting now.
"If I go for a job and I'm already signed up in the Army, they'll
think I'm goddamned CRAZY!"

"With your credentials, it'll be a snap," my mother said.

"Ceil, give me chance to talk," my father said. Then he turned
back to me. "I'll put it to you in plain English, Danny. Either you
get a job in the next couple days, or you have to leave."

"Leave?"

He nodded.

"What do you mean, leave?"

"Either you get a job, or you and Leslie have got to get out of
the house."

I looked deeply into his face. I found it almost impossible to believe this was happening.

"But . . . but where will we go?"

My father shrugged.

"We were planning on staying here for a couple weeks waiting for my orders. I thought you'd like to get to know Leslie a little, and to see me one last time before I go into the Army. Then we're going to Leslie's parents for a couple weeks. They haven't said anything about it. They WANT to have us there."

My father nodded indifferently.

"I can't believe this," I said.

"Just go tomorrow and get a job," my father said, "and everything'll be all right."

My mother served his eggs. He began to eat them along with his bagel, which she had toasted in the oven.

I looked toward Leslie. She was sitting gloomily, watching her finger make circles in the mist on her cold glass of apple juice.

"Let's just eat," my mother said. "Let's think it over for a while." My father gave her a dirty look, but she continued, "Danny, you want some chocolate pudding?"

I shook my head no. We sat there in silence, my mother looking guilty and miserable. After a while, I said disconsolately, "Maybe it would help if I told you what plans I'm making for my life."

"For your life?" my mother said hopefully.

"For your career? Your job?" my father said.

"Well, in a way. I mean down the road. See, first of all, like I told you a few weeks ago, I'm going to go into the Army. That'll be for three years. But after that, well . . . both Leslie and I have decided to teach."

"To teach?" my father said. "What're you talking about, to teach?"

"Well, Leslie's gonna get her degree in English, and then, I plan to go back to school. . . ."

"To go back to school?" He could not believe what he was hearing. What little color there had been in his face disappeared.

"Don't worry," I said quickly. "You won't have to pay for it. We'll . . ."

"Pay for it? You're goddamn right I won't have to pay for it!" He shoveled a spoonful of eggs into his mouth. "Back to school? What the hell are you talking about, back to school?"

"Now, Sid, don't get excited," my mother said.

"But he's just been to school," he shouted at her. "For six goddamn years!" Then he turned to me. "You've got a profession already. That's why I sent you to those goddamn out-of-town colleges. So you could make something of yourself. So you wouldn't HAVE to teach school or something like that." He turned to my mother. "What the hell is he talking about?"

"It's just talk," my mother said. "Don't get into an uproar over it."

"I'm going to be a professor," I said softly.

"No," my father said. "No. I don't believe this. I send this kid to an out-of-town college, to two goddamn out-of-town colleges, and it costs me thousands of dollars I had to work and slave for, and now he says all of a sudden he wants to teach." He still looked like this had to be some form of joke.

"Here, let me explain...." I said.

"No, there's nothing to explain. There's nothing at all to explain.... Just go tomorrow to I.B.M. and ..."

"Just give me a chance. See, I've really changed my mind about things, and I've found something I've always been looking for."

"Listen, don't give me that kind of crazy talk. I won't hear it."

"Sid, I told you, don't get into an uproar," my mother said, placing a dish of potato salad in front of him and taking the fourth seat at the table.

"But what's this nonsense he's talking? If he wanted to teach, I could've saved a fortune. He could've gone to City College like his cousins, for free."

I glanced at Leslie. She looked like she wanted to disappear. "You want a beer?" I asked her.

"Maybe a little more apple juice," she said, trying to seem like a "good girl."

I started to rise, but my mother hopped up first.

"Listen to me, so you'll understand," my father said, his mouth full of scrambled eggs, "Don't you get it? You have a degree in engineering, and a degree from the Wharton School. Those two degrees

225

together, don't you know what they're worth?"

"Anyone would give their right arm for those degrees," my mother said from over by the refrigerator.

"You can write your own ticket," my father said, sipping at his coffee. "So don't give me that nonsense about teaching. What does a teacher make? You know what a teacher makes?"

"But don't you see, Dad? That's what I've just begun to find out. Money isn't everything. There are so many other things of value in life."

My father began to choke on his eggs. He coughed and gagged, and couldn't catch his breath. My mother ran over to him, setting the glass of apple juice quickly on the table and patting him on the back while saying frantically, "Sid! Sid! Are you OK?"

He nodded while choking, and managed to gargle out, "Down the wrong pipe," while coughing up fragments of food.

Slowly he settled back down to regular breathing. My mother, after watching him carefully to make certain he was all right, resumed her seat.

"Take your juice, Darling," she said to Leslie. "It's good. Mott's." Leslie glumly reached for her glass of juice.

"Anyhow," I continued, "like I was saying, I've found out that money and winning, they aren't everything. I want to help people. I want to continue to learn. I want to get a job where I can work toward the enlightenment of mankind."

A shudder of silence gripped the room. My father looked at me with such despair on his face it seemed almost a smile. He knew he had lost. He had been completely defeated. He had sent me to the heart of American Business, the Wharton School, the High Church of Commerce, where we sang each day from the hymnal of dollars and cents, and I had taken everything that the wise men there had taught me and had turned it completely around to shore up my stubbornness and folly.

For my entire life he had been trying to teach me what was what, and now he saw that he had failed.

"You're gonna help humanity?" he said, in a tone that was surprisingly weak all of a sudden. But then, his voice annealed by his growing rage and disbelief, he said to my mother, "He's gonna help humanity!" He turned to me. "Don't you know what humanity is? Humanity is your Uncle Murray. Up on the fifth floor. I *gave* him an apartment. The best four-room apartment in the building."

"That's the God's honest truth," my mother said.

"And why did I give it to him? Because I like him?" He shook his head no. "Because he's married to my sister. That's why I *gave* him a rent-controlled four-room apartment that people would have paid a thousand bucks for under the table. But I gave it to him for nothing. Just because he's family. So what does he do in return? Does he thank me? Does he show a little gratitude?"

He shook his head no repeatedly as he finished his eggs, and my mother said, "He sues your father."

"He turns me into the rent commission every month."

"But why?" I said.

"Because he's jealous," my mother said. "Because he's only a civil servant and your father's worked himself down to the bone to build himself up and get these buildings."

"Any little thing," my father said. "The elevator breaks. A piece of plaster falls in the hall. . . ."

"And Murray always loses," my mother said.

"They throw out all the complaints. I run the best building on the block. But he just reports me again."

He was nodding his head as if he were signaling to God that he, Sid Schwartz, would remember all this. He turned to my mother. "So that's Danny's 'humanity,'" he said, despondently. "That's who he's gonna help. . . . Murray. . . ."

He finished his coffee and stood up.

"Listen, Dad," I said, "can't we both be reasonable? Can't I stay here for just, say, ten more days? A week? We've really got no place to go. And then I promise I'll go to Idaho, and I'll pay you back for any food we eat in the meantime. . . ."

My father looked at me with tired eyes and shook his head no. He turned and slumped off to his bedroom.

Leslie quietly excused herself and walked into our room. I sat at the table dazed, next to my mother, sipping my beer slowly. I felt drained of my vitality. In a zone somewhere East of Energy.

My mother said sadly, "The men in the street. The relatives.

They've probably been kidding him...."

I didn't answer. I felt like something had dropped on my head. A bag of mail I didn't want to read.

"I can't go for an interview," I said.

My mother didn't answer. She sipped at her coffee.

"Don't you see?" I said. I didn't feel like laughing anymore. Now I was struggling to keep myself from crying. "I wanted to show Leslie the City before I go into the Army. To give her a chance to meet the family.... I can't believe this is happening.... Don't you see how much you've both embarrassed me in front of my new wife?" I took a sip of my beer. "I told her so many good things about you.... I'm going into the Army. Who knows, I might not even come back if there's a war or something.... I'm here for two days, and you're throwing me out...."

"You're father's not throwing you out, Danny," my mother said in a pained voice. Family disharmony was always a torture for her. She took another sip from her coffee. "Look, just go downtown tomorrow. Who knows? Maybe it'll all work out for the best. With your grades! I'm sure they'll give you a job at I.B.M."

Chapter Forty

On the following morning Leslie and I packed up my old Dodge and headed for Idaho.

A gravity of sadness kept us grounded until we transfered to a Greyhound in St. Louis and headed for the vast, open territory of the American West.

Aldous Huxley said one of the great charms of America is the high ratio of geography to history, and in this regard, the West served as a kind of ocean in which our personal sorrows were soon drowned as we gave ourselves to the adventure of traveling across the vast country together for the first time. Man and wife, on our own, in the rugged, spacious terrain.

Jefferson was one of the most isolated towns of its size in America. Set in a valley at the foot of the mammoth Jefferson Hill, which one surmounted by driving up a series of switchbacks for seven miles, the town held no college or university to diversify its population, and no large highway passed through it.

Leslie's father farmed barley on the land he sharecropped on the hill. Her mother worked in the office of the town's single major employer, the President Lumber Mill.

Because the mill was the sole large source of income for the town, nothing was done about the fact that the gaseous effluent it spewed into the air caused the entire valley to stink of rotten cabbage and, according to the locals, even ate into the paint of their cars. The factory itself, with its belts and saws, created a noisy, nineteenth-century industrial environment in which workers were forever being chewed up and sometimes almost sawed in half, all of this taking place on the banks of a gorgeous, slow-moving river on which the logs were still floated down to the plant.

Leslie's father wore ancient overalls, discolored and clearly meant for real work. He was tall and slim, with a small head on which he swept his dark, thin hair back with his comb. He was called "Daddy" by the family, her mother was "Mommy," and Leslie herself was "Sissy." Her brother was a Naval Officer at Annapolis, working on his book on space navigation with a professor there. Photos of him, tall, slim and handsome, along with his framed math awards and his rifle-team medals from the University of Idaho, shone on all the walls of their small, simple, six-room house situated on the eastern edge of Jefferson.

Jefferson sloped off to pretty sections near the rivers, and gave way to wooded areas out in the country, but generally the town was somewhat bare, a kind of cattle town, as I imagined such a place, but without the cattle. With its two parallel main streets, it provided a circle for bikers and hot rodders to carouse around day and night, but it was also the central market town for several American Indian villages nearby, and this provided much of its interest for me.

When we arrived, Leslie's parents gave us five hundred dollars, an extremely generous gift as far as I was concerned. Immediately after meeting me, Leslie's father said, "I understand you're a Jewish fella."

I nodded. "Mostly my parents. I don't really follow it anymore."

"Well we've got a Jewish fella right here in our town. Helluva nice guy.... Looks like Jeff Chandler."

Leslie winked at me, and I had to hold back a smile.

"Oh, Daddy," Leslie's mother said, trying to keep him from playing his role as the professional unsophisticate, and yet enjoying it along with the rest of us.

"Sissy tells us you're from back East," he said.

"New York City."

He shook his head. "Helluva a big town. Listen, one thing I been meanin' to ask someone. We got ourselves TV here now. Got our own station. Can't get no others 'counta we're so far away out here. But I wanted to ask you, what's goin' on with all them colored people out there? I mean back East and down South. Rioting and all that ruckus. Heck, we got a colored family here in our town. Don't cause nobody no trouble at all. Never have. Nicest folks you wanna meet."

The strange thing about this statement was that it did not have an old-boy racist edge. In all innocence, he simply wanted to know. And he listened when I explained the situation to him as best as I could, nodding his head and saying once in a while, "If that don't beat all." And then, after he had checked me out for a couple of days, he took me aside and asked me if I wanted to become a Moose.

"A what?""

"A Moose."

"Oh," I said casually, trying to hide the fact that I didn't have the slightest idea of what he was talking about. "I see. A Moose."

He nodded proudly. I didn't want to hurt his feelings. I sensed this was his gift to me. Leslie's dowry, so to speak. But what the hell was a "Moose"?

Then I recalled something about "Elks" clubs. That must be it, I thought. Becoming a Moose must be like becoming some kind of Elk. After all, they both were big and had horns, and they both ran around in the mountains or somewhere like that, didn't they?

He kept nodding happily. "Anywhere you go," he explained, "you can eat at The Moose. You'll always find good people there. And good vittles."

I was nodding as well. "Well, gee, I really appreciate this. And maybe I'll take you up on it. It'll depend on where I get stationed in the Army. I don't think we have a Moose in the Bronx."

He kept smiling, and I was touched by his offer, even though I didn't feel I was ready to become a Moose yet.

On the other hand, he kept saying to Leslie, virtually every day, "Your room is still here, Sissy. We kept it just like you left it. You can move back into it any time."

"But Daddy, I'm MARRIED now. I have a husband. I can't just move back into my room."

"I know. But just you remember, Sissy, your room's always here, and it's always ready for you. Why don't you move back into it? I'll even get you a little car to drive around, and Mommy can maybe get you a job out at the mill."

"Daddy!" Leslie's mom would say, embarrassed, but he would just nod pleasantly with his big, simple smile and say, "I know, I know, I was just telling her."

And then the next day he would tell her again.

I enjoyed exploring the valley with Leslie and her family. We went to a Moose picnic, met many country musicians, and heard her parents play music together, he on the accordion and she on the piano, which he had taught her. Leslie's mother was quite talented in many ways. Judging from her photos, she had been an attractive young woman, and she now dressed in a small-town, middle-class, restrained manner that was an important part of her stretch to join the respectable class of people in the valley. She played piano, designed houses occasionally which her husband built, worked full-time at the mill and kept house as well, but in that regard she saw it as necessary to run a tight ship, and this was where Leslie and I got into trouble.

We were not encouraged to see the painter Sam Dawn and his mother, Bobbie. Sam was the town beatnik, a jolly, heavy-set, bearded, somewhat dangerous-looking but actually unbelievably innocent man with a shock of blond hair over his eyes, a round face and big belly. He had a babyish look to him somehow, when you looked closely, although he was a few years older than Leslie. He treated her with affection and respect, like a little sister, but had a crush on her, I suspected. His mother, Bobbie, had been like an accepting parent to Leslie during her teen-age troubles. Of course, Leslie took me to see them on the sly on the first day we were free.

Their house was little more than a shack, the walls covered with Sam's paintings. Sam played records of Japanese koto and flute duets, and we drank beer as Sam swung his arms about in broad, nervous gestures, and told us stories about the number of times he had been arrested for jaywalking in Jefferson, his reputation and position as "outsider" in the town being so firmly established that he could barely set foot on Main Street without getting locked up. His mother sat there quietly, sipping at a beer, her love for both Sam and Leslie shining in her eyes.

After about a week in the town, Daddy had still not succeeded in convincing Leslie to forget about me and move back into her old room. One day, Leslie and I took a tour of the mill, where I was struck by the large number of messenger men carrying envelopes around in the stumps of limbs that had been cut off by the saws in the midst of all the noise and confusion of the factory. ("They take care of their employees," Mommy said.) One man actually fell onto the moving tread along with the logs right in front of us. He journeyed quite a way toward the spinning circular saw before the screams of the tourists alerted an employee who pressed the emergency button and shut down the mill until the fallen worker could right himself and climb off the belt.

"After that, I need a beer," I said, as we stood outside the mill and put out our thumbs. The second car to pass was the old junker owned by Sam Dawn. He took us on a wild ride through the deserted small roads around the town. Although Sam was twenty-six, he was virtually howling with adolescent excitement as his car flew over the bumps and swerved around the curves. It was hard not to like Sam, but it was also difficult not to feel somewhat sorry for him, a gentle, big boy at heart, stuck in a town he couldn't leave because he had worked so long to create an identity for himself there, albeit a negative one.

After a while, we picked up a six-pack and stopped back at Leslie's parents' house.

"I'd better not come in," Sam said.

"Oh, Daddy's probably up at the farm," Leslie said. "Come on inside. We'll just have one beer in the kitchen. You'll be gone before anyone gets back."

Sam followed us tentatively into the house. We opened one bottle of beer apiece and nursed it while Sam, delighted to have someone in town he could really talk to, spilled out his feelings about Zen Buddhism, which he had been studying on his own. At one point, I noticed the head of Daddy pop up from the basement, but he quickly disappeared and we enjoyed our time with Sam, a colorful, likeable guy of a kind you didn't meet in The Bronx, or in many other places at that time.

After he left, Leslie and I were sharing a pot of coffee, still seated at the kitchen table, when Mommy came home. Daddy emerged from the basement. "Mommy?"

"Yes, Daddy."

"You missed the big party."

"Party?"

"Yeah. Sissy and Sam Dawn. Beerin' it up. Right here in your own kitchen!"

"NO!" she said, aghast. She turned to Leslie, her eyes sparking like the rim of a blown tire scraping the road. "You DIDN'T!"

"What are you talking about?" Leslie said to her father. He continued to ignore her. "Just as clear as the nose on your face. Her and Sam Dawn. Beerin' it up right here in your own kitchen. Just as sure as I'm standin' here."

"Sissy! How could you? You know this is my house. And I don't allow people like that in here. How COULD you do this?"

"I didn't do anything," Leslie pleaded.

"Home for one week and she's already goin' back to her old ways," Daddy said.

"I won't have this. I won't have trash like that in my house. And if you won't respect my home then you have no business here, Miss." Her face was aflame with anger.

"Gee, Mrs. Schmidt, we weren't beerin' or partying or anything," I said. "Sam just happened to pick us up hitchhiking at the mill and Leslie, to be polite, invited him in, and we just had one beer apiece. It's a hot day and all...."

"I won't have this beerin' in my house," Mommy said, still to Leslie.

Her father kept nodding his head. He seemed awfully glad to have found a way to please Mommy so. "Beerin' it up," he said. "Beerin' it up with Sam Dawn," like some Greek chorus telling Oedipus that this time he had really gone too far.

"I wasn't BEERIN!" Leslie suddenly stood up and shouted.

"I WON'T HAVE SHOUTING IN MY HOUSE!" Mommy shouted.

"I'M NOT SHOUTING!" Leslie shouted. "DAMN IT. I'M NOT SHOUTING. I DIDN'T DO ANY..."

"AND CURSING!" her mother shouted. "IF YOU WANT TO CURSE, YOU CAN GET OUT, YOUNG LADY. YOU CAN GO OVER TO BOBBIE DAWN'S HOUSE AND CURSE ALL YOU WANT."

"THAT'S WHERE I WISH I WAS! AT LEAST SHE UNDERSTANDS ME AND LOOKS AT ME WITH SOME LOVE AND CHARITY INSTEAD OF ALWAYS PUTTING ME DOWN."

"YOU PUT YOURSELF DOWN BY YOUR OUTLANDISH BEHAVIOR. CAN'T YOU SEE THIS IS OUR HOUSE AND WE HAVE TO LIVE HERE WHEN YOU'RE GONE? CAN'T YOU HAVE ANY RESPECT FOR ANYONE ELSE?..."

"Please," I said, "this is getting all out of proportion. Can't we all be reasonable?"

Daddy smiled a strange, satisfied smile, over by the stairs to the basement.

As a peace offering Daddy took us out to dinner at a place that offered twenty-eight different kinds of pancakes. Everyone in the town was proud of this restaurant. They believed there weren't many restaurants even in the big cities like Spokane or New York that offered more varieties of pancakes. Leslie's parents returned to their usual demeanor, and we didn't fight any more, but some easy, spring-training quality of our initial days in the West was lost, and a few days later, when my Army orders arrived, we decided to move on.

Once again, a sadness settled on us as we left. The trip back on the bus was long and uncomfortable, especially as we hadn't slept well the last few days in Idaho, with Leslie being quietly upset much of the time, the anger and sorrow of old wounds rising to the surface of her mind like scars.

In St. Louis, we checked into a flea-bag hotel in a dark, eerie warehouse district not far from the Mississippi. We stayed over for a day, looking at the sights. There was no need to rush. We had left both of our families earlier than we had planned.

St. Louis marked a transition for me. Probably for both of us. Despite the infernal heat and humidity, I found my spirit revivifying. I loved being with Leslie, on our own, drinking draft beer in some fetid dive in the dying, almost deserted downtown, with all our authority figures and their old familiar lines of demarcation thousands of miles away. The hot, decaying city was like a huge steam bath, the perfect place in which to sweat out the poisons of the past in a kind of fever that would leave us purified and ready to begin our lives anew.

The next morning, despite the incipient murderous heat, we

both felt ready to move on. We packed up the car and headed South. We hardly spoke a word. Every once in a while we would turn toward each other at the same time and share a quiet smile.

We were riding a wave of hope, traveling on our own again, proceeding according to the plan we had concocted to save our desperate lives.

We left the highway in the late afternoon in search of a cheap motel for the night. Driving through rural Arkansas, we re-encountered the sad ballast of history. The South.

I simply could not believe the conditions in which the Negroes of Arkansas were forced to live. The sight jolted and shook me, like whiplash in an auto accident.

The rows of sorry one-room shacks across a drainage ditch from the little state road. None of them painted. The gray wood rotting and warped. No telephones. Little electricity. No indoor plumbing. A kind of ghostland. A shadow nation.

Entire large families were jammed into the dilapidated one-room cabins. Many of the people were dressed virtually in rags. "Oh my God," I kept saying, shaking my head. "You read about this, but ... to see it.... It isn't the same.... I can't believe this is America .... It's heartbreaking...."

We came upon a little hamlet with a complex at the end of the two-block main street which included a service station, a run-down four-unit motel, and a small diner-like cafe with an old, peeling sign on the roof: "TOM AND JERRY'S."

We skipped supper and went to bed. Neither of us felt much like eating. I tried to cheer Leslie up by referring to the place as "Tom and Jerry's Gas and Lunch," but it didn't work. Suddenly our own lives had come to seem unpainted and splintered and warped.

In the morning, we filled up the car with gas. For the first time in my life, I saw segregated restrooms: "MEN" and "WOMEN" and "COLORED." As if "COLORED" were a third gender. And the two water fountains. One sleek stainless steel: WHITES. The other chipped and filthy: COLORED.

The white man who gassed up our car looked at our New York license plate and said, "I heah they're gonna try to get a nigger into Ole Miss in the fall." He wore a sly smile as he spoke. I was too shocked to even try to think of an answer, and there probably wasn't one anyway.

Leslie looked at me with cornered eyes.

We ventured into the little diner for breakfast, passing a pickup parked outside with a shotgun in the cab. After we sat down at one of the two tables, I noticed a Confederate flag pinned to the wall over the door. I wondered whether this was legal. Since there was a Negro man mopping the floor, I was shocked they would display the flag like that.

Besides the waitress, there were only men present. About five at the counter and two at the other table. All were wearing overalls. Most were heavyset. Farmers, I thought. In their fifties or sixties. Two of them looked to me like mean versions of the comedian Jonathan Winters.

The waitress was friendly to us. I could see the men glancing over at us from time to time. No doubt Tom or Jerry, or whoever the big, balding man at the grill was, had told them we were from New York.

We ordered ham and eggs. Though no one spoke directly to us, we knew we were the center of attention. They spoke instead to the slim, perhaps seventy-year-old Negro man with the short gray hair and mop.

"Hey, Lightning, you heah they're gonna try to get a nigger into Ole Miss in the fall?"

The Negro man kept mopping. Didn't look up.

"Lightning?" the man said, insistently now.

A friendly-looking guy, about five years younger than me, came in and sat at the end of the counter drinking a Coke. A white car pulled up outside. It said "SHERIFF" on the door. The man in it approached the diner. From a distance, he looked like a mean version of Jonathan Winters, too. Maybe several of them were related. After all, this was a very small, isolated town. I was getting paranoid feelings in my belly.

The officer in the white car entered the room and took a seat at the counter. Everyone greeted him with little nods of their heads and grunts of "Sherf." The waitress set a cup of coffee on the counter in front of him without asking. Then she brought us our ham and eggs.

The sheriff put three spoons of sugar into his black coffee. A man turned to him and said, "Orville was just tellin' Lightnin' that some old boys from the North think they're gonna come on down here and shove a nigger into Ole Miss in the Fall. We was wond'rin' what he thought about it."

The sheriff turned toward the Negro man, who pulled in his shoulders without looking up. He looked like he wanted to disappear. The young guy at the counter with the Coke caught my eye. I could tell that he wanted me to know that he wasn't a part of this.

"What you think about it, boy?" the Sheriff said.

"Sah?" the Negro man said, cautiously.

I felt like I wanted to disappear as well. They didn't care what the man they called "Lightning" thought about Ole Miss. They were just using my presence to vent some of their anger at the Kennedys and Northerners in general.

I looked at the big .38 revolver on the sheriff's hip. I wondered if the other pickups parked behind the diner had shotguns in their cabs. No one knew where Leslie and I were. No one would miss us for a couple weeks, and then they wouldn't know where to begin to look. With the bombings and the beatings and killings of Negro reformers and freedom riders, it wasn't really out of the question that they might decide to move their verbal toying with us into more dangerous arenas.

"Well, what you think, boy?" the sheriff said. He seemed demented somehow, when you looked into his eyes.

"Ah don' rightly know, sah." He looked up for a second as he spoke. Then tried to appear involved in his mopping.

A short guy at the other table taunted him, "You mean you don' rightly know what you think about some rich Papist Yankee up there in Washington tryin' a shove some goddamn nigger down our throats?"

They all looked at us. We ate our eggs quickly, not meeting their eyes.

"I went ta the colored school myself," the Negro man said. "Til the fourth grade. I din't try to get into no white boy school."

"You're damn right you didn't," Tom or Jerry said, scraping the grease off the grill with a spatula.

The sheriff said, looking directly at Leslie and me, "All I can say is, if any Yankees come down here ta Arkansas and try to give the niggers any ideas, there's gonna be blood on the floor, and it ain't gonna be Southern blood, I'll promise ya that."

All the other men nodded and looked over at us while they grunted a kind of Amen chorus of "That's for damn sure."

The Negro man picked up his mop and bucket and slid out the door while the men's attention was focused on Leslie and myself. I looked down at my plate and scooped up some eggs with my fork.

"You hear about it," I said to Leslie as I drove south towards Texarkana, "you read about it, but until you actually *experience* it...."

Leslie didn't answer. I knew she wanted to put it behind us. One more slap in the face you had to live with and pray to Jesus to forgive as you walked the gauntlet of your life in the fallen world.

But I couldn't get it out of my mind. "Could you believe that sheriff?"

"Maybe we should let it go...."

"But this is America!"

Leslie closed her window and lit up a Salem. As she opened her window again, she said quietly, "If what they said about Ole Miss is true, there's sure gonna be some trouble in the fall."

"Yeah. Kennedy'll have to send the fucking Army down." I turned to Leslie, and almost surprised myself when I said vehemently, "And you know something? I hope to hell he does. Who the fuck do they think they are?" Leslie drew on her cigarette. She blew the smoke toward the open window. I was becoming angrier. My words were like gasoline on the fire of my imagination.

"I hope he brings the whole fucking Army down here. And you know something else? I'll fucking volunteer! I'm glad I'm going into the goddamn Army. I mean it. I'm ready to kick some fucking ass. I'll fucking volunteer and go down there and shoot some of those morons...."

We drove along in silence for a while through the hot, humid afternoon. The wind rushed in the open windows, rippling the plastic wrappers on the clothing laid out behind us on the back seat. It wasn't clear whether the hot air streaming by actually made us cooler or merely served to heat us up like a blow-dryer.

We had sweated completely through the backs of our shirts, and were sticking to the plastic car seats. I was stewing in my anger, which had turned sour. But I knew Leslie had heard enough of my outpourings.

And then suddenly, as when you look at an optical illusion, I saw the entire situation at Tom and Jerry's in a different light. "Oh, my God!" I turned to Leslie. "Damn! I suddenly see it!"

"*What?*"

"Martin Luther King! ... *This* is what he's trying to respond to with love and nonviolence." I kept shaking my head from side to side. "I never really *saw* it before. I mean just one incident, and I'm ready to go out and shoot somebody.... But to try to *work* with it ... to try push back against all this racist bullshit and injustice without giving in to your anger...."

"Hey!" Leslie said sharply, nodding toward the windshield. We had gained rapidly on a big semi in front of us. I hit the brakes, slowed down and allowed a couple of cars behind us to pass, leaving us alone for a stretch. I glanced at Leslie. "Do you see what a great idea that is? I mean, it's ... *unbelievable!*" I inhaled slowly and deeply to try to calm myself. "I mean, it's not only a question of the anger of the racists. It's our anger, too. That's what I never really saw before. All of us. Vic Feuer ... Herbie ... Virgil's uncle Bill.... I mean, my God, to think about trying to deal with all that resentment and all those guns by walking down a street, armed with only ... with only a philosophy...."

I hit the brakes as we gained on a car in front of us. "And, God! VIRGIL! I suddenly SEE it!" I threw my head back in amazement. "It was VIRGIL who told me the secret! Peace is the Way! Jesus! Do you SEE it? Peace is the Way! The way you protest IS your fucking message. Everything you do is your fucking message. Shit, it's ... the means and the ends...."

I shook my head from side to side, overwhelmed by this rush of ideas. I turned to Leslie, afraid I had gone too far in my babbling and my crazy epiphanies, but immediately I had another thought that knocked me out and started me going again. "And the jazz musicians! My God! Charlie Parker and Miles Davis and Sarah

Vaughn and Dinah Washington. All of them. FILLED with fucking anger, like my father. But they turn it into beauty, for God's sakes! They turn it into angry beauty."

Leslie didn't say anything. She was sitting back, watching me follow my thoughts wherever they might lead.

I let a car pass. Then I said, "You know, whenever I've been really down, I've always turned to the Negroes. However depressed or lost I feel, I always know they have it worse than I do, and yet so many of them don't give into their anger or to despair...."

She nodded.

"We're gonna win," I said, suddenly. "I know it now. Virgil was right. Peace is the way!"

Leslie had an amused but affectionate expression on her face.

"Is something the matter?" I said.

"Nothing really."

"No ... Tell me...."

"Well ... It's just that ... to tell you the truth, I can't really picture you like Mahatma Gandhi or something, walking up the street to accept a beating...." There was no anger in her voice. "I mean, really, wouldn't you go and get something to throw back?...."

I felt my mood deflate.

"I ... I hope I haven't hurt your feelings," Leslie said. "I just meant that ... that you're still a Bronx guy at heart.... But I *like* that about you.... That you're a Bronx guy ...."

"No, it's OK.... It's true...."

I knew that she was right. A new insight wasn't a life. I was still a Bronx guy at heart. But as I drove along and thought about it for a while, I found that I didn't mind being a Bronx guy. After all, you had to start from somewhere.

I stepped on the gas and passed a slow car in front of us. When I pulled back into lane, I said, "But ideals have power, too. Even impossible ideals."

"I know," she said affectionately. She shifted over towards me on the seat. Put her arm around my shoulders. I leaned my head over and rubbed my hair against hers. She opened up into her big smile, and I felt that everything was OK again. That everything had always been OK, somehow.

In Texarkana, as I finished a burger, Leslie, her spirits rising, suddenly took a notion to call her roommate, Sue, still living in the flat in Seattle. She came back from the phone booth shining, a happy, almost crazy expression on her face.

"Oh, Danny, Danny. . . ." She swung into her seat opposite me in the booth. She had begun to weep a bit, yet I could see she wasn't sad, but rather overcome by a kind of helpless gratitude.

"What happened? What's going on?"

"It's Hal. He's alive. He tried to call me. He spoke to Sue."

"Hal? He's alive?"

"Yes. He's in Alaska."

"Alaska? What's he doing in Alaska?"

"Oh, Danny," she said, her voice saturated with feeling, "he's been there all the time. He was going kill himself, but somehow, he didn't."

"Did Sue say why?"

She shook her head no.

"I wonder what happened to him?" I said.

Not looking at me, she said, almost to herself, "Somewhere at the bottom, he must've found some light." Then she looked up again. "He's coming back. He's going to go back to Brannan and get married to Valerie. . . ."

"Hal's alive," I said, "He's alive!" and my head nodded up and down in little movements that seemed to be saying yes, yes, yes, as Leslie sat there opposite me, her hands folded in her lap, quietly crying.

It was twilight when we drove through the flat, rose-and-gray, dusty light of North Texas. The air was still hot. We had the windows of the Dodge wide open. The wind scooped in and spread out and floated Leslie's rich brown hair. The sky turned dark as we continued south and southwest. I was wearing a fresh white tee-shirt, which I could already feel wet on my back against the seat. Leslie was lost in her thoughts as she had been for hours. Nursing a bottle of Lone Star Beer with one hand and holding my Lone Star in the other.

"What're you thinking?"

"Oh, I don't know." Her voice seemed more Western in its twang since she had been home. "Our families, I guess."

"Kinda rough, wasn't it?"

She nodded. "I guess we made it pretty rough for them."

She took a sip from her beer. I could see little beads of sweat above her mouth, and a sweat mark under her arm on her white short-sleeve blouse. "They'll come around, I guess."

I nodded. "It'll just take some time."

I reached over, and she handed me my beer. I took a swig and passed it back to her. "Sure is hot, isn't it?"

She nodded. "And Herbie," she said. I looked over at her and saw she was smiling. It filled me with joy to see her taking it all this way. "I mean, my LORD!' she said, grinning widely now, "what a way to greet your cousin's wife!"

"And he didn't even go to New Orleans. The next day, for some reason, he went to Montreal."

We both laughed, and I continued, "And your old man. Hiding in the basement! I mean, this was after he asked me to become a Moose, for God's sake."

"They'll all come around," she said. We sat there in the hot wind, rocking slightly in a kind of unconscious harmony with each other.

"It's funny," I said, "but I was just thinking that right now, the whole U.S., it's like a big triangle, you know what I mean? Your folks up at one end, my folks up at the other, and the two of us heading down for the bottom point, thousands of miles away from anyone we know."

"I'm ready for it," she said.

"Yeah. I'm ready for it, too."

"I'm ready for a change," she said.

"I know one thing. I'm sure glad we're together."

She smiled, her eyes alight with love. She passed me my beer again, and I finished off what was left of it and tossed the bottle onto the floor at her feet. Way up ahead of us in the distance on the right, I could see lights.

"What's that?" Leslie said.

"Hey, I'll bet it's Dallas. Yeah! It's Dallas. It's gotta be. God damn! Dallas, Texas! I can't believe this. You don't know what this means to me. Danny Schwartz of Nelson Avenue in The Bronx, heading toward Dallas, Texas." I shook my head from side to side at the wonder of it.

I glanced at her. She was looking at me with tender amusement.

"I mean it, Leslie. Dallas, to me, it's ... the end of cattle drives, and cowboys, and big oil millionaires walking down the main street in ten-gallon hats...." She was watching me carry on with the sweetest look on her face, enjoying my mythologizing of America, my crazy hopes and dreams, my continual chatter, always trying to shape and bend words into some form of optimism that would enable me to go on with my life. I felt so lucky to be there with her at that moment, my wife, in my car, in OUR car now, heading toward the greatest adventure of all—the beginnings of a new life.

"Hey, let's stop right in town for the night," I said. "OK? I want to explore downtown Dallas."

She nodded, pleased.

"I want to see the Cotton Bowl. And Southern Methodist University. You know, when I was a kid in The Bronx, that was who I rooted for. S.M.U. Can you believe it? The 'Mustangs.' God, they had great players. Doak Walker. Kyle Rote. I loved those guys. They seemed so ... so *American*...."

I drove along, easily now. I was still finding it hard to believe this was happening to me. That this pretty girl had chosen to be *my* wife, that *I* was married, that I was somehow an Army officer—that I was going to leave my engineering and business degrees behind and become a teacher.

Yet, when I looked at Leslie, I knew that she was the closest friend I had in the world. And this made everything seem all right. I was traveling South into uncharted territory, but I was buoyed by my hopes, and I was no longer traveling alone.

Leslie finished her beer and placed it on the floor next to mine. She moved over next to me and set her head on my shoulder. I reached over and put my right arm around her. She cuddled up closer to me.

"You know," she said, quietly, looking away, up toward the sky over on her right, "I have this feeling, this really strong feeling, that everything's gonna work out all right."

We approached the rear of a big, old, gray truck groaning along the highway, showing perhaps a dozen license plates. I swung around it and passed it easily.

Then Leslie said softly, almost shyly, in the hot night air, "You know, I still believe in love." She pressed her head against my shoulder. I could feel her soft, damp hair through the flimsy cotton of my white tee-shirt. "In spite of everything, I believe that God is love. And that love is at the center of the universe . . . not death. . . ." She paused for a moment and then added, in a quiet voice, "No matter what comes into your path, if you go forward with love in your heart, I think you're doing the right thing, and somewhere, maybe not right here, maybe not even on Earth, but somewhere, it'll work out OK." She took a deep breath and then said, almost in a whisper, "It's in the stars."

I felt a great contentment fill me. My body was ringing with vibrant life. "I sure hope so. . . ."

"I know so," she said. "I know it in my heart."

I drove quietly for a while, smelling the rich, tangy North Texas air. It felt so good to be with Leslie. To be on the Earth.

And then, almost without thinking, I found myself saying, "You know what Dante wrote. Right at the end of *The Paradisio.*" I turned toward her. "'Love moves the sun and the stars.'"

We pressed our lips together. I turned back towards the road. Stepped down on the gas.

"God, it feels so good to be alive," I said. I kept my arm around her as we drove South, two star-guided lovers with most of our meager possessions stuffed into our old Dodge. In the distance up ahead of us, I could see the lights of the skyscrapers of Dallas, winking like diamonds in the huge, dark Texas night.